SURVIVORS
WILL BE
SHOT AGAIN

▼

Also by Bill Crider

SURVIVORS WILL BE SHOT AGAIN

A SHERIFF DAN RHODES NOVEL

BILL CRIDER

MINOTAUR BOOKS

A THOMAS DUNNE BOOK

NEW YORK

A THOMAS DUNNE BOOKS FOR MINOTAUR BOOKS.
An imprint of St. Martin's Publishing Group.

www.thomasdunnebooks.com
www.minotaurbooks.com

Library of Congress Cataloging-in-Publication Data

Names: Crider, Bill, 1941– author.
Title: Survivors will be shot again : a Dan Rhodes mystery / Bill Crider.
Description: First edition. | New York : Minotaur Books, 2016. | Series:
    Sheriff Dan Rhodes mysteries ; book 23 | "A Thomas Dunne Book."
Identifiers: LCCN 2016003503| ISBN 9781250078520 (hardcover) | ISBN
    9781466890824 (e-book)
Subjects: LCSH: Rhodes, Dan (Fictitious character)—Fiction. |
    Sheriffs—Texas—Fiction. | Murder—Investigation—Fiction. | BISAC:
    FICTION / Mystery & Detective / Police Procedural. | GSAFD: Mystery
    fiction.
Classification: LCC PS3553.R497 S87 2016 | DDC 813/.54—dc23
LC record available at http://lccn.loc.gov/2016003503

Our books may be purchased in bulk for promotional, educational, or business use. Please contact your local bookseller or the Macmillan Corporate and Premium Sales Department at 1-800-221-7945, extension 5442, or by e-mail at MacmillanSpecial Markets@macmillan.com.

First Edition: August 2016

10 9 8 7 6 5 4 3 2 1

This book is dedicated to the memory of Judy Crider.
She was always the one.

SURVIVORS
WILL BE
SHOT AGAIN

▼

Chapter 1

▼

Sheriff Dan Rhodes was standing at the back of the Pak-a-Sak looking at the Dr Peppers in the big cooler when the man with the gun came inside. Rhodes hadn't had a Dr Pepper in years, and he'd missed the taste a lot. He was thinking that maybe it was time to give up his boycott of the company that had begun when they'd fixed it so he couldn't order Dr Pepper with real sugar over the Internet. The boycott didn't appear to have hurt their business one bit, after all, and nobody even knew about it except Rhodes and his wife. A Dr Pepper sure would taste good.

Besides that, Rhodes had read an article about a 104-year-old woman in Fort Worth who attributed her longevity to drinking three Dr Peppers a day. She'd told the reporter that her doctors told her that drinking Dr Pepper in that quantity would kill her, but the doctors kept dying and she kept right on living. That sounded good to Rhodes, but it looked as if he wasn't going to get a Dr Pepper today.

"Gimme all your cash," the man with the gun said to the clerk.

His voice was muffled because he had his black sweatshirt pulled up over the lower half of his face. He wore a black knitted cap pulled down low on his forehead.

The man hadn't noticed Rhodes. He was short and jittery, full of nervous energy, hopping from foot to foot and waving his pistol in front of Chris Ferris, the clerk on duty.

Rhodes wasn't in any mood to deal with an armed robber. He supposed he'd have to, however, since he was the sheriff.

"Are you nuts?" Ferris asked the robber. Ferris had been robbed before, several times, and he was more calm than a first-timer would've been. "You can't rob me. The county sheriff is right here in the store."

"Yeah, right," the robber said, "and so is Taylor Swift. Gimme the money."

"How about lottery tickets instead?" Ferris asked. "Maybe some jerky."

"First the sheriff and now jerky? You think this is a joke? Just shut up and gimme the money before I start shooting."

"He wasn't joking about the sheriff," Rhodes said from the back of the store as he started to walk toward the front. "I'm right here."

The robber turned around. The gun he held in his right hand was a snub-nosed revolver like something from an old black-and-white gangster movie, the kind they didn't make anymore.

"You don't look like a sheriff," the robber said.

"Sheriffs don't wear uniforms," Ferris said. "That's him, all right."

"I didn't see no sheriff's car outside."

"My wife sent me for a loaf of bread," Rhodes said. He pulled a loaf of bread off the shelf as he passed. "I'm not on duty. That old pickup out there's mine."

"You just stop right there," the robber said, half turning so that he could see both Rhodes and Ferris. He had the gun pointed at Rhodes, more or less, but he was still moving it around.

"You can't shoot both of us," Ferris said.

The robber looked at him. "I can shoot you one at a time, dumbass. Now get the money."

Rhodes continued to walk forward.

The robber turned his head toward him. "I'll shoot you first, Sheriff, if you really are the sheriff. I told you to stop."

Rhodes was only about eight feet from the robber now, so he stopped.

"My wife's going to be disappointed if I don't bring this bread home," he said.

The robber ignored Rhodes and said to Ferris, "Get that money. Now!"

"I think you should go for the jerky," Rhodes said. "More nutrition. Less jail time."

The robber turned toward him again, and Rhodes tossed the bread underhanded at the robber's head, spinning it like a football.

"Catch!" he yelled.

Rhodes knew he was taking a chance. If the robber pulled the trigger, there was no telling where the bullet would go, but Rhodes thought the odds were in his favor. He was likely to get shot anyway if the robber's nervousness got any worse.

The robber didn't catch the bread. He didn't even try. He jerked his head to the side, and the loaf hit him in the chest. Rhodes jumped forward. Taking two giant steps, he clamped one hand on the robber's wrist and the other on the cylinder of the gun as he forced the robber's hand down. The robber grunted and tried to pull his hand loose, but Rhodes held tight, making sure he had a good grip on the cylinder so the revolver wouldn't fire.

The robber squirmed and kicked. Rhodes held on and dragged him toward the counter. The robber dug in his heels, but Rhodes was considerably bigger. The robber didn't stand a chance.

"Call the sheriff's office," Rhodes told Ferris, who was watching the action as if he were at a movie.

"Oh," Ferris said. "Sure."

He picked up a cell phone from behind the counter and made the call while the robber continued to struggle with Rhodes. The struggles caused the sweatshirt to slip down, revealing the robber's face, which was red with the effort he was making to escape Rhodes's grip.

"Dang, is that you, Rayford?" Ferris said, putting down the phone after completing his call.

"Shut up!" the robber yelled.

Rhodes wrenched the gun from his hand, and the robber broke away. He started toward the door, but Rhodes put out a foot and tripped him. The robber fell and skidded a foot or two toward the door. When he started to get up, Rhodes said, "Just lie there for a while. I have the pistol now, and I'd hate to have to shoot you."

The robber turned his head to look. Rhodes made sure he could see the gun.

"Put your hands on your head," Rhodes told him. "Lie still."

The robber did as he was told.

"That's Rayford Loomis," Ferris said. "We went to Clearview Middle School together. Had history and English class together, too, and maybe PE."

"Is that right?" Rhodes asked. "Is your name Rayford?"

The robber didn't say anything.

"It's him, all right," Ferris said. "I haven't seen him in a few years, but that's him. I never thought he'd rob a store where I was working."

"I didn't know you worked here," Loomis said. He paused. "Wouldn't have made any difference if I'd known, I guess."

Rhodes knelt down on one knee beside Loomis. "Rayford Loomis, I'm putting you under arrest for attempted armed robbery. That's for starters. I might think of some other charges later, like illegal possession of a firearm, but right now I'm going to tell you what your rights are. Is that clear?"

"I got it," Loomis said.

Rhodes quoted the standard Miranda rights. "Do you understand what I told you?"

"I'm not stupid," Loomis said.

That was debatable, considering the circumstances, but Rhodes didn't feel like arguing the point.

"All right," Rhodes said. "You can stand up. Slowly."

"I can't stand up with my hands behind my head," Loomis said.

Rhodes stood and moved away from him. "All right. You can give yourself a little help. Just be careful."

Loomis used his arms to push the upper half of his body off the floor, got to his hands and knees, and then stood up.

"Hands back on your head," Rhodes said.

Loomis complied, and Rhodes heard the distant sound of a siren.

"Here comes your backup," Ferris said. "I need to find me another job. I'm tired of getting robbed."

"It's been a while since the last time," Rhodes said.

"Not long enough," Ferris said. He looked at Loomis. "I can't believe you'd stick me up, Rayford. Where've you been since middle school, anyway?"

"Daddy moved us to Dallas so he could look for work," Loomis said. "I didn't much like it up there. Dropped out of school, got a job, got laid off, ran out of money." He shrugged. "I thought

I'd try Houston, see if there was any work there, but I needed some cash. Passed by here and thought there might be some in the cash drawer."

Rhodes had a feeling it wasn't the first time that Loomis had needed a little money and used the gun to get it.

A county car squealed to a stop in the parking lot, and a uniformed deputy got out as the noise of the siren trailed off. He came into the store with his big .357 Magnum drawn.

"Hey, Buddy," Ferris said.

"Hey, yourself. What we got here, Sheriff?"

Buddy was thin but wiry. He thought of himself as a tough guy, like his idol, Dirty Harry, which was why he carried a revolver nearly as big as he was.

"Got a disarmed robber," Rhodes said. "You can cuff him."

Buddy holstered the .357 and cuffed Loomis, pulling down one arm at a time.

"Get an evidence bag," Rhodes said, showing Buddy the gun he'd taken from Loomis. "I need to secure this."

When Buddy went out to get the bag, Ferris said, "I sure am glad you were here, Sheriff. Rayford might've shot me if you hadn't stopped him."

"I wouldn't have done any such of a thing," Loomis said. "I never shot anybody in my life. Never even thought about it."

"Looked like you were thinking about it to me," Ferris said.

Buddy came back with the evidence bag, and Rhodes put Loomis's revolver in it and sealed it.

"Take him in and book him," Rhodes told Buddy. "I'll follow you and put the gun in the evidence room."

"Let's go," Buddy said, taking Loomis by the arm and leading him out of the store.

"I don't really think he'd have shot me," Ferris said as he

watched Buddy assist Loomis in getting into the backseat of the county car. "I shouldn't have said that. He just needed some money and a break. I could tell his heart wasn't in it."

"You can be a character witness for him at his trial," Rhodes said.

Ferris shook his head. "Nope. He pulled the gun. Nobody made him do it."

"That's right. It was all his idea."

"How come you don't have a gun?" Ferris asked. "Aren't officers supposed to carry one even when they're not on duty?"

"Not the sheriff," Rhodes said, not that he wasn't armed. He had a pistol, a little Kel-Tec PF-9, in an ankle holster. He liked the concealment that the ankle holster provided, but the pistol wasn't easy to get to in an emergency. Luckily, he hadn't needed it. The bread had worked just as well.

Rhodes looked around. "Where's my loaf of bread?"

Ferris pointed. "Over there on the floor. You want to get a fresh one?"

Rhodes walked over and picked up the bread with his free hand. "I wasn't really here for bread." He tossed the loaf to Ferris, who caught it easily. "I was here for a Dr Pepper."

"Have one on the house," Ferris said.

"No, thanks," Rhodes said. "I'm not thirsty anymore."

Chapter 2

▼

Rhodes hadn't had any time off in months, but as there hadn't been any major criminal activity going on in the county that day, he'd decided he could afford to take a break beginning at noon. He'd enjoyed not having to deal with the criminal element in Blacklin County for a couple of hours and had hoped to spend the entire afternoon without thinking about crime and criminals. It was just his luck that he'd be in the Pak-a-Sak when somebody showed up to rob it. Except that it wasn't luck. It was his own fault. He'd let the thought of a Dr Pepper tempt him. Anyway, it had turned out to be good luck in a way. He'd prevented the robbery, and the robbery had helped him resist the urge to buy the Dr Pepper.

Rhodes was in no hurry to get to the jail, so he drove around for a while in his rattletrap pickup. Nobody recognized him. He didn't get out in the truck often enough for anybody to identify it with him, so he was happily anonymous as he checked out Clearview's downtown area, or what was left of it. Many of the buildings that had been there when he was growing up were gone now. Some had fallen down, and others had been demolished. Of the ones that were left, a few were being restored and there were a couple of new ones, including a senior center that stood next to an antiques store owned by Lonnie Wallace, who also owned the Beauty Shack down the street. And of course there was Randy Lawless's office complex, the Lawj Mahal, as Rhodes thought of it. It occupied most of a half-block area that had once held six or seven businesses.

Everything was quiet. Only four or five cars were parked on the streets, with a couple in the parking lot of the Lawj Mahal. Rhodes didn't see a single pedestrian. The downtown would never be what it once was, no matter how many buildings were restored or how many new ones were built. All the action was out on the highway around the Walmart, and if Clearview was growing at all, that's where the growth was and would be.

Rhodes decided he'd given Buddy long enough to book Rayford Loomis, so he went on to the jail. He was a block away when Buddy passed in the county car, going in the opposite direction, light bar flashing, siren wailing. Rhodes wondered what that was about. It could be anything. People fighting at an RV park, a mother who'd called about a son who'd taken money from her purse, somebody stealing a propane tank, harassing phone calls from a blocked number, a stolen cell phone, or a lost one, or a dozen other things. A hundred. Even in a small county on a slow day there was always something going on.

Rhodes parked his pickup outside the jail and went inside. As soon as he walked in the door, Hack Jensen, the dispatcher, started talking, just like he always did.

"Hail the conquering hero," Hack said.

That was something Hack had never said before.

Rhodes looked around the room. "Where's the hero?"

"You know where," Hack said. "He's standing in your shoes. Caught a robber, took away his gun, and whipped him with a loaf of bread."

"I didn't whip anybody," Rhodes said.

"That ain't the way I heer'd it," Hack said. He'd taken to listening to old radio shows on the computer, which is where Rhodes thought he'd picked up the line. "The way I heer'd it—"

"Where do you get all your information?" Rhodes asked.

Hack looked sly. "I got my sources."

That was the truth. Even Buddy didn't know about the bread.

"The prisoner talked, didn't he," Rhodes said.

Hack grinned and touched a finger to his pencil-thin mustache. "Yep. Sure did. Seemed like he was kinda embarrassed by the whole thing. You want to know what else?"

Rhodes did have a bit of curiosity about what else, but he knew that Hack wasn't going to tell him, not right away. Hack and Lawton, the jailer, always had plenty of information that they wanted to share with Rhodes, but they made him drag it out of them. It was their way of entertaining themselves. Either that, or they were on a mission to drive Rhodes crazy. So far they hadn't succeeded in doing that, but there were times when Rhodes thought they'd driven him close to the edge.

"I need to enter something into evidence," Rhodes said. "Then you can tell me."

"If you want to wait, that's just fine with me," Hack said.

Rhodes took care of the paperwork on the revolver and put it in the evidence room, finishing up as Lawton came in from the cellblock.

"I got our new customer all settled down and tucked in,"

Lawton said. He noticed Rhodes. "Well, well, look who's back from his so-called day off."

Lawton was Hack's opposite in appearance, being clean-shaven and rounder, but he was the dispatcher's full partner in trying to annoy Rhodes.

"Caught yourself a gunslinging crook without even havin' to pull your own pistol," Lawton said. "Ain't just anybody who could do that."

"He don't know the rest of the story," Hack said.

"You didn't tell him?"

"Nope."

"You want me to tell him?"

Rhodes tried not to smile. If there was anything that could start a fight between Hack and Lawton, it was Lawton trying to tell one of Hack's stories before Hack had had the chance to draw it out for a while.

"I was the one started tellin' it," Hack said. "I'll be the one to finish it."

"I was just askin'," Lawton said.

"You oughta know better than to have to ask."

"Well, it's as much my story as it is yours anyway. I was right here when—"

"You better watch out," Hack said.

Lawton bristled. "You can't tell me what to do."

"Yes, I can. I got seniority."

Hack was right about that. Rhodes knew that the dispatcher had been hired at least a year before Lawton. Both men were past what some people considered retirement age, but they'd never shown any desire to leave their jobs, maybe because they enjoyed aggravating Rhodes whenever they could.

"I'll tell you what," Rhodes said. "I'll flip a coin and we can decide that way who gets to give me the bad news."

Hack looked at him. "I never said it was bad news."

"Me neither," Lawton said.

"It's never good news with you two," Rhodes said.

"That ain't so," Hack told him. "Anyway, this ain't bad news."

"Depends on how you look at it," Lawton said. "Some might take it one way, some might take it another way."

Rhodes sighed. "Why don't you just tell me?"

"I was gettin' to it," Hack said. "You're too grouchy, you know that? I think it's 'cause you got the low T."

"Don't start that again," Rhodes said. "My testosterone's just fine."

"Sure is," Lawton said. "I'll vouch for that. Nobody with the low T's gonna face down a crazy gunman with nothin' but a loaf of bread."

"I'm glad somebody's on my side," Rhodes said. He hardened his tone. "Now tell me what's going on."

"Just the usual," Hack said. "Local hero sheriff is gonna be the star of the Internet again."

"Jennifer Loam," Rhodes said.

Loam, who'd been a reporter for the local newspaper, had been a victim of downsizing. Since reporters weren't exactly in high demand, she'd started her own news Web site, *A Clear View of Clearview,* and she had enough advertising to keep it going almost immediately. The way she managed that, in Rhodes's opinion, was by sensationalizing local news, especially news that involved law enforcement. Any of Rhodes's accomplishments, no matter how small, were inflated so as to become something on the order of Batman's exploits in Gotham City.

Hack and Lawton laughed, and Hack said, "I guess we don't

have to tell you, then. You bein' an ace lawman and all, you fig-
gered it out yourself."

"What was she doing here?" Rhodes said.

"Came in to ask about the fella we arrested for exercisin'," Hack
said.

Rhodes shook his head. *Here we go again.*

"That's not against the law," he said. "What was he doing?"

"Jumpin' jacks."

Rhodes didn't say anything.

"In his underwear," Lawton said. Hack gave him a look, but
Lawton didn't notice. "Tighty-whities. I'm a boxers man myself."

"Too much information," Hack said. "Point is, the fella wasn't
exercisin' in the privacy of his own home but out in the middle of
the street. Can't have that. Might've got hit by a car."

"It was Henry Horton," Lawton said, as if that explained everything, which it did. Horton had some form of dementia, and lately
he'd taken to leaving his house and wandering off, though not in
his tighty-whities.

"Ruth took care of it," Hack said, meaning Ruth Grady, one of
the deputies. "Went over to get him inside while I called his wife
and had her come home from the high school."

Lucille Horton was the school nurse, and Rhodes knew she was
having problems dealing with her husband's condition.

"She's going to have to find somebody to stay with him,"
Rhodes said, "or get him into a nursing home."

"She knows it," Hack said. "She told Ruth she's workin' on it."

"You still haven't told me where Buddy was going."

"Oh, that," Hack said.

"Yes," Rhodes said. "That."

"That's nothin' much. Just somebody's found a 'mysterious
package' on the front porch. Tom Gatlin. You know how he is."

Rhodes nodded. He'd dealt with the mysterious Gatlin himself a time or two. He sometimes ordered things, forgot he'd ordered them, and then been surprised when a package showed up on his front porch. He'd call the sheriff to come out and make sure there wasn't a bomb or a box of anthrax on his property.

"What we need is a bomb squad," Lawton said. "Then we could let the professionals handle it."

"It'll be a book or a new shirt," Hack said. "Last time it was a new flashlight. It ain't like we got a mad bomber on the loose around here. Buddy'll take care of it."

Hack might have said more on the topic, but the telephone rang. Hack answered it and talked for a couple of minutes. When he hung up, he turned to Rhodes and said, "Since your day off is over with, you might's well take a run down to Billy Bacon's place."

"What's the problem?"

"Thieves got a bunch of his stuff."

"Again?" Lawton asked.

"That's right," Hack said. "Again."

Chapter 3

▼

Rhodes stopped in the turn-in for the gate to the B-Bar-B ranch and waited until the gray dust from the county road settled before getting out of the big black and white Chevy Tahoe. Blacklin County had had a lot of rain earlier in the year, much more than average, in fact, but there had been none for the last couple of weeks.

The Chevy Tahoe was practically new, only a couple of weeks old. Mikey Burns, one of the county commissioners, had convinced the other members of the commission to buy two of them for the sheriff's department, although Burns had made it clear to Rhodes that he'd rather have gotten a couple of Mine Resistant Ambush Protected vehicles free from the United States Army. Lots of other small counties had them, Burns said, but Rhodes was happy with the Tahoes. He didn't think anybody would be planting mines in Blacklin County.

Rhodes looked past the closed gate and saw Billy Bacon standing next to a weathered tin barn with rust streaks running down its sides and roof. The barn formed part of one side of a small corral. Billy's dark green and dusty Dodge Ram pickup was parked by an old hand-dug well nearby. Bricks had fallen away from the well's wall and lay on the thin grass around it, along with thin gray pieces of concrete that had covered the bricks. The bricks might have once been red, but now they were a faded pink.

Billy saw the Tahoe and waved. Rhodes opened the door and got out. He was still getting used to being so high off the ground when he drove. He didn't have to use the assist step, but anyone shorter than him would have needed it.

A chain was looped around a post and around the end of the gate frame. The heavy padlock that had held the ends of the chain together lay on the ground where it had fallen after it had been cut away with a bolt cutter. Rhodes put on a pair of nitrile rubber gloves and got an evidence bag. He didn't think there would be any fingerprints on the lock, but you never knew. He put the lock in the bag, sealed it, and put it in the Tahoe. He tossed the gloves in, too, and pulled the gate open. It was well balanced and squealed only a little bit. It was painted silver, and the B-Bar-B brand was welded to it in two-foot-high red letters. The hinges of the gate were to Rhodes's right and attached to a tall post that looked like a telephone pole cut in half. Rhodes noticed four nails in it that had white cardboard behind them as if something rectangular had been ripped down from the post.

Billy had been watching all this. He called out to Rhodes, "You might want to drive on in, Sheriff, and get your vehicle away from the road. People come around that corner too fast sometimes, and you don't want that thing to get hit."

Billy was right about that. Rhodes was in enough trouble with the commissioners about damages to county vehicles already. He didn't mind walking, but he didn't want the Tahoe to get a scratch on it.

Billy gave an impatient wave. He was a loan officer in the Clearview First Bank, but about twenty years ago he'd been a star running back on the Clearview Catamounts football team. They'd called him "Shakin' Bacon." His powerful legs had eaten up the field in huge gains, and the town had loved him. As had the college recruiters. He'd been good enough to get a full scholarship to Texas A&M, but a car accident during the summer before he was to begin college had shattered his right kneecap and put an end to his football career. Walking wasn't easy for him even now, but loan officers didn't have to do much walking.

Rhodes got back into the Tahoe and drove through the gate. He stopped just inside the fenced area and started to get out.

"No need to close the gate," Billy called. "All the cattle are down in the back pasture. I just closed it out of habit."

Rhodes got back in the Tahoe again. He was getting plenty of exercise with the new vehicles if getting in and out and stepping up and down counted as exercise, which they certainly did in Rhodes's book. He drove the fifty or so yards to where Billy was waiting for him. Billy still looked a little bit like a running back, but one who'd put on a few pounds. His wide shoulders stretched the white cotton shirt he wore, and his stomach lapped over the buckle of the belt that held up his faded blue jeans. Rhodes could identify, though he wasn't as hefty as Billy. Billy couldn't exercise much because of his knee. Rhodes, however, didn't have that excuse. Maybe climbing into the Tahoe was helping.

When he stopped the Tahoe by Billy, Rhodes didn't get out. He just pushed the button that let down the window so Billy could talk to him. Rhodes could smell hay and the musky manure scent of the corral, a mixture that wasn't unpleasant to anybody who'd grown up around cattle.

"I tell you what, Sheriff," Billy said, sounding a little nervous as if he thought the criminals might still be around, "these thieves are gonna run me out of the ranching business. This is the third time they've hit me in the last few months. And I'm not the only one down here they're stealing from, as you well know. It's about time you came to have a look around instead of sending one of your deputies."

"Down here" was the southeastern part of Blacklin County, a few miles farther east than Able Terrell's compound. Rhodes had dealt with Terrell before, but so far Terrell hadn't made any complaints about theft from his place. There were some who thought they knew why.

Others who owned property or homes closer to Bacon's place were the ones who were being hit. Some of them, like Melvin Hunt, had lost high-ticket items. Hunt's welding rig, which cost around ten thousand dollars, had been stolen not long after the thefts had begun. It could easily have been driven a few miles to the interstate and then straight south to Houston or straight north to Dallas in a couple of hours, never to be seen in Blacklin County again.

"Looks like with all the evidence you have, videos and all, you'd have caught 'em by now," Billy said.

Rhodes didn't know what Billy meant by the "and all." Aside from the video, there wasn't much of anything else. Billy himself had supplied the video evidence of the thefts from his place. His security camera had recorded it and stored it in something called "the cloud." Rhodes didn't know for sure what that was, but he knew it didn't have any connection to actual clouds.

One man showed up in the video, but he was smart. He was

covered from top to bottom in loose-fitting camo gear, a hood pulled over his head and drawn tight around his face. He stayed away from the outside camera most of the time, and he stuck to the heavy shade of a metal canopy. When he came within range of the inside camera, he never looked directly at it. Rhodes wasn't sure that there was only one thief, but if there was another person involved, he was keeping out of camera range.

"The videos haven't been much help," Rhodes said. "It's impossible to tell anything about the man in them except maybe his size."

Billy took off his Clearview Catamounts cap and wiped his forehead. It was the first week of September, still summer in Texas. The late afternoon sun was warm, and some days it was downright hot. Billy looked at Rhodes. "On the TV shows, they can enhance those videos to where you can practically see somebody's fingerprints."

Rhodes suppressed a sigh. "Sometimes those TV shows exaggerate the abilities of their technicians and their computers."

Billy returned his cap to his head, covering his thinning gray hair. Rhodes remembered that when Bacon had been Shakin' Bacon, he'd had long hair that hung out from beneath his helmet and bounced when he ran free down the field. Those days were gone, however. Rhodes could remember when his own hair had been thicker and longer, too, and now he had a thin spot of his own on the back of his head. Maybe he needed a cap like Billy's.

"Well," Billy said, "you won't be getting any video this time. You know why."

Rhodes knew. On their last visit the thief or thieves had stolen Billy's video camera, the final indignity. Billy hadn't replaced the camera.

"I haven't looked to see what they got this time," Billy said.

His mouth had a bitter twist. "Since the thieves come in the afternoon when I'm at the bank, I thought I'd sneak down here early, maybe catch them in the act, but I was too late. My wife thought I was crazy. She told me I'd get hurt if the thieves saw me, but I'm not scared of them. When I got here and saw the lock was cut on the gate, I figured I'd better call you before I looked things over. Wasn't that much left here for them to take, so I don't know why they bothered to come back."

"There must've been something," Rhodes said.

"Not enough to make them happy. See my well?"

Rhodes nodded.

"They did that," Billy said. "Just out of meanness. Tried to knock down the whole wall. Lot of the bricks fell down in the well. Just meanness."

Rhodes didn't know what to say to that, so he nodded again.

"Get on out of the truck and come look in the barn," Billy said.

Rhodes got out. The tin door cut in the wall of the barn was a full step up off the ground. It hung open, but Rhodes couldn't see very far inside.

Billy stepped up into the barn with some difficulty and disappeared into the dark interior. Rhodes followed him. The only light came from the doorway and some nail holes in the tin roof and sides. It took Rhodes's eyes a couple of seconds to get adjusted. When they did, he looked around. All he saw was a few bales of musty hay that might have been there for years and the bare tin walls.

"You ever haul hay?" Billy asked him.

"One summer when I was in high school," Rhodes said.

He remembered how it had been, tossing the heavy bales up onto a trailer where another boy, Robert Haskins, had stacked them. When the trailer was loaded, they'd drive to the barn, unload it, and then go back for another load. The bales were heavy and dusty. By the end of the day Rhodes had been so tired he could hardly move. He'd itched all over, and his eyes and nose had been red and runny.

"Don't haul much of it on wagons anymore," Billy said. "I just have it rolled up instead and leave it out in the field instead of bailing it. That's what everybody does now. Been that way for years. Can't hardly find a regular bale anymore."

"I wouldn't want to have to load a hay wagon now," Rhodes said.

"It wasn't so bad," Billy said. "Tell you the truth, I kinda liked it. It was good for me. Kept me in shape for the football season. You played a little ball, too, back in your day, didn't you?"

Billy was talking fast. He seemed jittery. Rhodes couldn't figure out why.

"I didn't play much," Rhodes said, thinking that his day hadn't been so long before Billy's.

"I remember hearing about you. Will o' the Wisp Rhodes, they called you."

Rhodes had gotten lucky in the first game of the season, returned a kickoff for a touchdown, and gotten a nickname. He'd been injured in the next game and spent the rest of the season on the bench. That had been his whole football career.

"That nickname was mostly a joke," Rhodes said.

"Maybe so, but you were a hero for a little while there." Billy paused. "Folks still blame you a little bit for what happened with the team a while back, I guess."

Rhodes knew what he meant, but it hadn't been Rhodes's fault that a football coach had been murdered. Rhodes had just followed the investigation to its logical end.

"I think they're getting over it," he said, but he knew better.

The Clearview Catamounts hadn't gone to the championship as everyone had thought they would, and that was a terrible thing to people who took their high school football seriously, which meant just about everybody in the state of Texas. Nobody in the town of Clearview would ever get over it. They'd pass along the story to their kids and grandkids, and long after Rhodes was gone people would be talking about the time the sheriff cost them the state championship. They might not remember Rhodes's name, but they'd all know the story. Not that it would matter to Rhodes.

It was hot and close in the barn because of the sun shining on the tin roof and sides all day, and dust motes floated through the little shafts of light from the nail holes. Rhodes sneezed.

"Dusty in here," Billy said, waving his hand in front of his face as if to ward off any germs that Rhodes might have expelled. "Nothing left but hay, straw, and dust."

"What about mice?" Rhodes asked. He wasn't fond of mice.

"Might be some mice, but they don't come out during the day. Nothing much for them to eat anymore, so maybe they're all gone. Look over there."

Rhodes looked. He didn't see anything except a spot where the floor might have been a little less dusty.

"That's where I had my daddy's saddle," Billy said. "They took the saddle, the saddle stand, the tack, everything. It wasn't worth a whole lot, but it was my daddy's. He's been dead ten years now. It was about the only thing of his I had left. You know who I think is doing this?"

Rhodes wanted to say that he wasn't a mind reader, but in this case he was. Or at least he knew just about what Billy was going to say. Others had expressed opinions about the thefts, and Rhodes expected that Billy shared them.

"It's Able Terrell," Billy said when Rhodes didn't answer

quickly enough. "Him and that bunch in his compound. They're the ones behind it."

"You have any evidence to support that claim?" Rhodes asked.

"They live there all to themselves, act like they don't have to depend on anybody else. They have to get money some way or another. Thieving is one way to do it. That or making meth. You oughta arrest the whole lot of 'em."

Rhodes didn't believe that Terrell was guilty of either of those things, although his son had been involved in some thefts once before. Nothing like that was going on now, however. Or Rhodes hoped it wasn't.

"We need evidence to make an arrest," Rhodes said.

"You could at least search his place."

"For that we'd need a warrant. We don't have any cause to justify one."

"They don't need any warrants on the TV. Did you ever see that show about a guy called Castle?"

Rhodes shook his head. "Can't say that I have."

"Well, when the cops on that show go after somebody, they don't worry about any warrant. They just bust down the door and go on in with their guns out and ready to blast away."

"Like I said, TV shows exaggerate sometimes."

"Maybe so, but that's the way it oughta be. We're too soft on crime around here. You need to get you a SWAT team together and go in that compound like you did the last time."

Rhodes and his deputies had been forced to go after a killer in the Terrell compound. It wasn't something Rhodes wanted to do again.

"That wasn't exactly a SWAT team," he said.

"Whatever. The Terrells are the ones behind all this. You need to stop 'em."

"Get me the evidence, and I'll do it," Rhodes said.

Billy didn't respond other than to walk over and kick a clump of dirt on the floor. Dust flew into the air.

"Did the thieves take anything besides the saddle and tack?" Rhodes asked.

"I don't know," Billy said. "I haven't been down to the new barn yet. When I saw the door open here, I checked inside and then called your office. I didn't go any further. I didn't want to mess with the evidence if there was any."

"All right. We'd better have a look, then."

"Can't you go by yourself? I'd just get in the way."

"Who'll tell me if something is missing if you're not there?"

"Oh," Billy said, looking unhappy. "Yeah. I guess I need to come."

"You go first," Rhodes said. "I'll come along in the Tahoe."

"We can walk," Billy said. "It's not that far."

Rhodes wondered about Billy's knee but said, "That's fine. I can use the exercise."

"So can I," Billy said. "My dang knee's killing me, but I can make it."

He went out of the barn, stepping down gingerly from the door, and Rhodes followed. Billy led him to another gate, this one mostly hog wire with a wooden frame, and opened it.

"You go on through," he told Rhodes. "I have to keep this one closed. I don't see any cows, but they might come wandering up anytime. They get down there in the creek bottoms, and I sometimes don't see them for a week. I don't go there. Nothing but thick woods and tall weeds. Might be a chupacabra down there, or a bigfoot for all I know."

Rhodes knew about the bottoms. He'd been born not more than a mile from where they were now, and before his family had moved to town when he was about ten, he'd spent a lot of time roaming around in the woods, fishing in Crockett's Creek, and looking for deer and bobcats and armadillos. He'd seen plenty of deer and armadillos, but only a couple of bobcats.

Rhodes walked on through the gate, and Billy closed it behind them. A worn track off to Rhodes's right showed where Billy drove his pickup to the rest of his pasture, or the parts of it that he could get to. A bit farther along there was a copse of oak trees, and the shaded ground under them was as ragged as if it had been turned up by a walking plow pulled by a halfhearted mule. It would've been hard to walk there.

"It's the damn wild hogs," Billy said, catching up with Rhodes and seeing where he was looking.

Billy seemed twitchy to Rhodes, who supposed that the thought of losing more of his things was getting to him.

"The hogs get under the trees and go after the acorns," Billy continued. "I've got dozens of those hogs on this property. Hundreds, maybe. They've rooted up half my acreage. I have hunters that come out here on the weekends, but they can't kill them all. They're ruining the place. If the thieves don't run me off from here, the wild hogs will."

Rhodes knew all about the hogs. There hadn't been any when he'd wandered in the bottoms, or if there had been, he hadn't seen them. Now, however, they were all over Blacklin County, the state, and the country. Not all of it, but in thirty-nine states at last count. They'd be in more before long. They hadn't gotten into the towns of Blacklin County yet, not more than a couple of times, but Rhodes thought before long they'd be bolder. He'd read recently that they were invading a new housing addition in Fort Worth and tearing up the newly sodded lawns. They were like an unstoppable army. The state's latest eradication effort, which Rhodes thought would be about as effective as the others that had been tried, was Hog Out Month. It was coming right up, but Rhodes wasn't sure that Blacklin County was participating.

"Hogs, thieves, world's going to hell," Billy said, shaking his head. "Barn's over there."

It would've been hard to miss. It was a white metal building almost the size of an airplane hangar, probably not more than ten years old. The canopy Rhodes had seen in the video extended out from the near side. A couple of tables sat under the canopy. Aluminum lawn chairs with frayed or missing webbing sat beside them. Some rusty tools in wooden boxes were on the tables, along with some plastic buckets. Rhodes couldn't see what was inside the buckets. An old power mower missing its engine lay turned on one side. The wide double doors at the end of the building stood open.

"I put a case-hardened steel padlock on those doors," Billy said. "Had one on the gate, too. Bolt cutters go right through 'em like they were rat cheese."

"The thieves didn't take the tools," Rhodes said.

"Old and rusted. They've taken everything worth a dime."

Rhodes walked up to the barn and looked around under the canopy. Most of the plastic buckets were empty. Some held crushed aluminum cans.

"I should take those into town and sell 'em," Billy said. "I could get maybe fifty cents. Wasn't worth the thieves' time, though."

Rhodes left the tables and went to the open doors. He looked inside the building, which was dark and full of shadows.

"I have electricity in this one," Billy said, reaching inside the doorway and flipping a switch. Fluorescent lights came on all along the ceiling, and it was easy to see that the place had been pretty much cleaned out except for some stacks of cardboard boxes along the walls and the big green tractor with yellow wheels and an enclosed cab that sat in the center of the building.

"They haven't taken your tractor yet," Rhodes said.

"I keep the battery in my pickup," Billy said. "I'm surprised they haven't brought one of their own and used it to start up the tractor so they could steal it."

"What's in the boxes?"

"Nothing. They're empty. You never know when you might need a good box."

Rhodes walked into the barn. He had gone only a step or two before he saw what looked like a pair of camo-clad legs sticking out from between a couple of stacks of boxes. The legs were attached to the body of a camo-clad man.

"Who's that?" Billy said. He was standing a couple of feet behind Rhodes.

"Let's have a closer look," Rhodes said.

"Maybe he's all right," Billy said. He didn't move any closer. His voice quavered. "Maybe he's just sick or something."

Rhodes knew better than that. He had a feeling that Billy did, too. The smell should have been a clue. The body had been there long enough for the process of decay to begin.

Rhodes pushed a stack of boxes aside, careful not to move them too far. The boxes hardly weighed anything. Billy hadn't been kidding about that.

Rhodes knelt down. The man on the floor was dressed entirely in camouflage clothing. Even his boots were camo-colored. A hood was over his head, which was turned to the side. Two blood-stained holes were in the front of his jacket. A couple of blow-flies buzzed around the holes. A trail of ants crawled under the wall and up onto the man's head. Another trail led back under the wall to the outside. Rhodes didn't want to think about what they might be taking out with them.

The flies buzzed away when Rhodes reached to move the hood aside. Rhodes didn't move it, however. He didn't need to move it. He recognized the man's profile.

"He's not sick," Rhodes said. "He's dead."

"Dead?" Billy didn't sound surprised. "Who is it?"

"Melvin Hunt."

"Who?"

"Melvin Hunt. You know him."

"Melvin? That doesn't make any sense. What was he doing here? He couldn't be the thief. He had things stolen from his place."

There were a number of things Rhodes could have said in reply to that statement, as he could think of several reasons why Hunt might have been there, but he said nothing at all. He moved the hood aside and felt for a pulse in Hunt's neck, though he knew it was a wasted gesture. He felt only the cold flesh. Hunt had been dead for a while, all right.

"Are you sure he's dead?" Billy asked.

"I'm sure." Rhodes stood up. "I have to make some calls. You can come on out of here with me."

Billy didn't hesitate. He was out of the barn well ahead of Rhodes and walking fast back toward his pickup.

"Did you come down here yesterday?" Rhodes asked, catching up with him.

"No. Why would you ask that?"

"Just wondering."

Billy opened the gate, and Rhodes went on through. He walked to the Tahoe and got Hack on the radio.

"Send the JP and the paramedics to the B-Bar-B," Rhodes said.

The justice of the peace would declare Hunt dead. The paramedics would take the body away.

"What's happened?" Hack asked. "Is Billy okay?"

"He's fine," Rhodes said. "It's somebody else who's dead."

"Who?"

"Later," Rhodes said, knowing it would get Hack's goat. "I don't want the word to get out yet. You never know who might be listening in."

Rhodes was thinking of Jennifer Loam. If she found out, the news would be on the Internet before the paramedics could even get to the body.

"Is it the thief?" Hack asked.

"I'm not sure," Rhodes told him. "Is Ruth through at the Hortons'?"

"Yeah. She says Lucille's going to try to get Henry into a home real soon."

"Good. Send Ruth down here to help me out with the crime scene."

"I need to tell her what's goin' on if I do that."

Rhodes knew that Hack was just angling for information for himself, so he said, "Just tell her it's a crime scene. That's all she needs to know."

He signed off, racked the mic before Hack could protest, and got some evidence bags and a pair of nitrile rubber gloves. Billy stood not far away, so Rhodes walked over to him.

"Hunt's been dead a while," Rhodes said. "He might've been killed yesterday."

"I wasn't here yesterday," Billy said, his voice shaky. "I told you that already."

Billy had been oddly nervous from the moment Rhodes had

arrived, and Rhodes was pretty sure he'd known that Hunt was in the barn and that he was dead.

"I remember," Rhodes said. "You also made it a point to tell me that you hadn't been in the barn yet."

Billy removed his cap and wiped his forehead. Rhodes didn't think the day was warm enough to warrant his doing that again.

"You think I knew Hunt was in there?" Billy asked. "Is that it?"

Rhodes was sure that Billy knew the answer to his own questions.

"Did you know?" Rhodes asked.

"No, I didn't know. And you can ask Nadine if I was here yesterday. She can tell you I came home right after work."

Billy's wife, Nadine, had been Nadine Cooley in high school, a cheerleader the same years that Billy had played on the football team. Rhodes had seen her at a few games, a bouncy blonde with plenty of team spirit and a loud alto voice that carried well in a football stadium. She'd supported the team a hundred percent, and Rhodes thought she'd support her husband the same way.

"I'll have to talk to her," Rhodes said. "Just to be sure you're in the clear. I don't doubt that you are."

"You'd better not doubt it," Billy said. "I never killed Melvin. I still can't believe it's him in there."

"Believe it," Rhodes said. "I'm going back to take a look around. The JP and the paramedics will show up in a little while, and one of my deputies will be here before they are. You can wait here and show them where to go."

Billy looked relieved that he wasn't going to be required to return to the barn. "All right. I'll do that."

Rhodes nodded and started back to the barn. As he did, he decided to take a short detour by Billy's pickup, just to have a look at it. You never could tell what you might see.

When Billy saw where Rhodes was headed, he came after him at a fast limp.

"Hold on, Sheriff," he said. "What're you doing?"

"Always did like these Dodge trucks," Rhodes said. "The department's been driving Dodge cars for a while now. Thought I might like one of these pickups for myself. Maybe replace that old rattletrap of mine."

"Yeah, the Dodge is a good pickup," Billy said, catching up with him, "but you don't need to be looking at mine right now. You should go see about Melvin."

Rhodes kept walking. "Not much I can do for him."

"You could . . . investigate or whatever it is you do."

"I have someone coming to help me with that."

Rhodes had reached the pickup. He stopped a few feet away and looked into the bed. It was empty except for a rectangular piece of plain white cardboard. It looked almost new. The four corners of the rectangle had been torn away as if the cardboard might have been pulled down off a wall. Or a post. Rhodes went over and stood beside the pickup bed.

"What's that?" he asked with a nod at the cardboard.

"Just some trash I was going to haul off," Billy said, not looking at it.

"You shouldn't leave trash in the bed of a pickup," Rhodes said. "It always blows out when you're driving down the highway. It's bad for the environment, and you might get a ticket for littering if an officer sees you."

"I was going to put it in the cab with me before I left," Billy said, staring off into the distance. "Come on, you need to go to the barn."

"I'm going in a minute. I'm curious about that piece of cardboard, though."

"I told you. It's just a piece of trash I picked up."

"Where did you pick it up?"

Billy looked flustered at the question. "I . . . I didn't pick it up, exactly."

"You mind if I look at it?"

Billy clearly didn't want Rhodes to look at the cardboard, but he said, "I guess not."

"Thanks," Rhodes said.

He reached into the pickup bed and flipped the cardboard over. There was text on the side that had been facing down, professionally printed black lettering in all caps, with two crossed rifles in the middle. Above the rifles were the words TRESPASSERS WILL BE SHOT. Below the rifles were the words SURVIVORS WILL BE SHOT AGAIN.

Chapter 4

▼

"That's not what it looks like," Billy said, staring at the sign.

"It looks like something that used to be nailed to a post by the gate," Rhodes said. "Is that what it is?"

"Well, yeah, that's where it was."

"But you took it down. Recently. Just before I came. Right?"

"Well, yeah, that's right."

"Why'd you do that?"

Billy started to take off his cap, caught himself, and dropped his hand to his side. "I just nailed it up there last week, and I got to thinking it wouldn't look very good to whoever came down here to see about this new thievery."

"You know that Melvin Hunt was shot twice, don't you?"

"Yeah, but . . . damn."

It usually took Rhodes a little longer to get someone to incriminate himself. Billy might have been a good football player, but his mental speed couldn't have been his strong suit.

"How'd you know?" Rhodes asked.

This time Billy did remove his cap and wipe his forehead. Rhodes waited.

"I . . . didn't know," Billy said after a while, putting the cap back on. "I was just guessing. I mean, the sign's just a sign. It doesn't mean anything."

"The fact that it was in your truck instead of on the post does," Rhodes said. "It means you knew Melvin was shot twice. It means you were in the barn before you called my office. It means you might even have been down here yesterday and shot him."

"Whoa, whoa, whoa, Sheriff," Billy said, holding up his hands with the palms outward as if to ward off an impending collision. "Hold on a minute. I was in the barn, okay? I went in there and saw Hunt, and I could tell he was dead, so I called your office. That's what any good citizen would do, okay? I should've told you about him, but I was afraid you'd suspect me, what with that damn sign. I should never have put it up. Anyway, I thought I'd just have you come down here and let you find Hunt. It's the same as if I found him, okay? You aren't saying I killed Melvin, are you? That I came down here yesterday and killed him?"

"I'm not saying you killed him. I'm just wondering about it. I think he's been dead for about a day, though. You could've been here then. You have a gun in this pickup?"

"No. No. I don't have a gun in there, okay? I don't even own a gun."

Rhodes didn't believe it. Just about everybody in Blacklin County had a gun.

"I'm going to check on that," Rhodes said, knowing it might not do any good. Billy could have bought a gun at a flea market or from somebody he knew, and there wouldn't be any record of it.

"Okay, I have a gun," Billy said. He really was too easy. "It's for home protection, and that's where it is, at home. It's not really mine, okay? I just bought it for Nadine because she's worried that somebody might break in some night. You read about those home invasions all the time."

Rhodes didn't read much about home invasions, because as far as he knew there hadn't been one in Blacklin County. All the ones Rhodes knew about had happened in places with large populations and affluent housing additions. Blacklin County lacked both those things.

"So it's Nadine's gun?" he asked.

"Well, no, it's my gun. I mean, I bought it in my name, but it was for Nadine. It's a .38 revolver. She knows how to use it."

Rhodes was a bit surprised to hear it. He knew that Nadine had been having some unspecified medical problems. In fact, according to the word around town, even the doctors couldn't put a name to what was plaguing her. She'd been to specialists in both Houston and Dallas but hadn't found much relief.

"Has Nadine practiced with the .38?" Rhodes asked.

"Sure. No use to have a gun if you don't know how to use it, is there? We come down here sometimes and shoot at targets at the stock tank. We use the dam as a backstop. It's safe."

"If Hunt was shot with a .38, I'm going to want to have a look at yours," Rhodes said. "We might need to run a ballistics test on it."

"Wouldn't you need a warrant for that?"

"I can get one if you don't want to cooperate."

Billy took a deep breath. "Look, Sheriff, we're getting off on the wrong foot here. I didn't shoot Melvin, and I wasn't here yesterday, okay? Nadine will tell you. I came straight home from the bank and we had supper at the house. You can ask her."

"I told you I might have to do that."

"Sure. I understand." Now that everything was out in the open, Billy spoke more confidently. "She'll tell you that it's just like I said."

Rhodes didn't doubt it.

"I'm going to have to take the sign," he said. "Evidence."

"It's just a sign, okay? That's all it is."

"Right," Rhodes said. He wondered if he could shoot Billy if he said *okay?* one more time. He was the sheriff, after all. The grand jury might not want to indict the sheriff. Then again, it might. Rhodes sighed and took the sign to the Tahoe, where he put it into the backseat.

As he closed the Tahoe's door, Ruth Grady came through the gate in the county's second Tahoe. She drove down and parked beside the one Rhodes had driven. When she got out, she had to use the assist step. She was shorter than Rhodes, barely tall enough, in fact, to meet the department's height requirement, but height didn't matter when it came to being a good officer. She was efficient, all business, and fully devoted to her job. She also looked good in a Western hat, something that Rhodes couldn't say about himself, which is why he never wore one, even though the thin spot on the back of his head could have used the cover.

Ruth's only flaw, as far as Rhodes was concerned, was that she was currently dating Dr. C. P. Benton, better known as Seepy, a math instructor at the local community college. Benton had somehow gotten the idea that he was an unofficial adjunct to the department and was always looking for some way to insinuate himself into an investigation. He'd never interfered with anything Ruth was working on, however. He confined himself to pestering Rhodes. Most recently he'd started a ghost-hunting business, but that had been only a passing summer fad. Now that the college was back in its regular session, Benton had given up on the ghost hunting. Permanently, Rhodes hoped.

"Hack told me you had a crime scene, Sheriff," Ruth said as she approached Rhodes and Billy. "More thefts, Mr. Bacon?"

Billy nodded, and Rhodes said, "It's worse than just thefts. Melvin Hunt's in the big new barn over there. He's dead, been shot a couple of times. We need to look at the scene before the body's moved."

Ruth didn't show any surprise. "Hunt's the one whose welding rig was stolen, isn't he?"

"He's the one," Rhodes said. "Let's go see what we can find."

He led the way, opened the gate, and shut it behind them. Ruth looked back at Billy.

"He have anything to do with it?" she asked in a low voice.

"Yet to be determined," Rhodes said. "He claims he didn't."

"That's what I'd claim, too, if I were in his shoes," Ruth said, "but is he telling the truth?"

"Also yet to be determined," Rhodes said. "He's already lied a few times. He called to report a theft, but not the body, which he didn't want to admit he'd seen. He had, though. It's been there a while, maybe as much as a day. I have a lot of questions about the whole situation."

They reached the barn and went inside. Rhodes put on the nitrile rubber gloves and led the way to the body. Before doing anything else, he took photos of it with his cell phone. He didn't much like the cell phone. Somehow it made him feel as if he were on a leash, but he had to admit that it took much better pictures than the old Polaroid the department had owned years before. Not only that, but he could e-mail the pictures right back to any computer at the jail, which is what he did as soon as he'd taken them.

When he'd e-mailed the photos, Rhodes searched the body, hoping to find something useful. Hunt had a cell phone in one pocket, but it was an old flip phone. It wasn't going to have any videos or photos that might help Rhodes determine who might have wanted to kill Hunt. There would be phone numbers in its memory, however, so those would need checking.

Hunt also had a wallet, but there was nothing of interest in it, only three twenties and two tens, Hunt's driver's license, a couple of credit cards, and an insurance card. No photos. His pockets held a quarter and a dime.

"He didn't have a weapon?" Ruth asked from about fifteen feet away, where she had been looking at the area around the tractor.

"I haven't seen one," Rhodes said. He put the phone and wallet into evidence bags. "That doesn't mean he didn't have one, though. Whoever killed him might have taken it."

Ruth left the tractor and came over to where Rhodes stood. "You think Hunt is the one who's been stealing from Billy?"

"Kind of looks that way. But—"

"But we have to keep an open mind," Ruth said. "I know, but it's good to speculate, just the same. Why did Billy lie to you?"

"He probably hoped I'd believe him."

Ruth grinned. "If he thought you would, he doesn't know you very well. Lying to you just makes him look more like a suspect than he would have if he'd told the truth."

"He called to report it," Rhodes said. "That's in his favor."

"I would've called it in, too, if I'd killed Hunt. I'd try to deflect suspicion. Not that it's working."

"It's okay to be suspicious," Rhodes said, "but let's not get carried away."

"I won't," Ruth said. "I have another question, though. How did Hunt get here? Where's his car?"

"I wondered about that," Rhodes said. "I think he came with someone else. There might've been two people stealing from Billy instead of just the one we saw on the video."

"Thieves fall out?"

"That's a possibility. There are some others. Maybe he was here hoping to catch the culprits. We'll have to see what we can turn up before we decide. Have you found anything here that would help us?"

"No," Ruth said. "Somebody was careful. Picked up his brass or used a revolver. I didn't look under the body, but the bullets might be there. Or they might not. As for anything else that might be here, this place doesn't look like it's ever been swept out, so there's no way to separate what the killer left behind from every-thing else—that is, if he left anything at all. I don't see any holes in the wall, so I guess the slugs are still in the body."

Rhodes wasn't discouraged by the seeming lack of evidence. He'd always had a lot more luck with talking to people than he'd had with finding clues. He and Ruth continued to search through-out the barn but still found nothing that appeared likely to be help-ful. They stopped when the ambulance drove up and parked just outside the big barn door.

Ruth went out to tell the paramedics to wait until the justice of the peace got there. They didn't have long to wait, as the JP wasn't far behind the ambulance. He got out of his car and entered the barn. It was his job to make the declaration of death, and he took it seriously.

The JP was named Franklin. He was a big man with a grim look, which Rhodes thought was appropriate to the situation.

"Seems like you never call me unless somebody's died, Sher-iff," Franklin said. "I do weddings, too, you know. Call me for a happy occasion, why don't you."

"I'll try to do that next time," Rhodes said. "We don't get a lot of calls about weddings, but I'll keep you in mind. Meanwhile, come on in and have a look at Melvin Hunt."

"Melvin Hunt?" Franklin looked up at the roof of the barn, then looked back at Rhodes. "I know him. Well, I don't really know him. I've heard of him. What's he doing here in this barn?"

"That's what I'd like to know," Rhodes said.

Franklin nodded and followed Rhodes to where the body lay.

"Looks dead to me," Franklin said. He squatted and felt for a pulse in Hunt's neck. "Dead, all right. Looks like he was shot twice. One high up on the shoulder, another one right about where the heart would be. Looks like the first didn't get him, but the second one finished the job."

"Survivors will be shot again," Rhodes said.

"What's that?"

"Nothing," Rhodes said. "Just talking to myself."

"Sure. Anyway, his color's bad, too. How long's he been here?"

"Don't know for certain," Rhodes said. "A while, though."

Franklin stood up. "Thought so. You know who did it?"

"Not yet," Rhodes said.

"But you will."

"That's right," Rhodes said.

"You and Sage Barton," Franklin said. "You always get your man."

"You're thinking of the Mounties," Rhodes said.

He wished people wouldn't bring up Sage Barton. Barton was the two-gun hero of a series of wild adventure-romance novels by a couple of writers who'd attended a writing conference in Blacklin County a few years before. To Rhodes's surprise, the novels had sold very well and might even be filmed, or digitized or whatever they did now. It seemed as if everyone in the county had read the books and reached the conclusion that Rhodes was the model for the main character. Rhodes didn't know how they could think that, since he shared none of Barton's heroic abilities. Recently Seepy Benton had suggested that Barton was modeled on him because their initials were S. B. Rhodes had done all he could to encourage this idea, but apparently the only person who believed it was Seepy Benton himself.

"The Mounties, Sage Barton, and you," Franklin said. "Always get your man. You will this time, too."

"Thanks for the vote of confidence," Rhodes said, thinking about how a vote of confidence for someone usually came just before that someone got fired.

"You know it's the truth," Franklin said. "Well, I'd better get back to town to do the paperwork and let you get started on catching whoever did this."

Rhodes wasn't sorry to see Franklin go. As soon as he got outside, Ruth brought in the paramedics to remove Hunt's body. The wheels of the gurney wobbled a bit on the concrete floor, sounding like the wonky grocery carts that Rhodes always got when he used one.

When the paramedics were ready to pick up the body, Rhodes turned it over to check for exit wounds. There were none, so as Ruth had surmised, the slugs were still in the body. They'd show up in the autopsy.

As the paramedics were putting the body on the gurney, Rhodes took Ruth aside.

"I'm going to leave you to finish working the scene," he said. "Maybe you'll turn up something. I need to go tell Hunt's wife what's happened."

"Funny that she hasn't called the department about him," Ruth said.

"Not so funny," Rhodes said. "He has a little drinking problem. He's gone missing before. The difference is that this time he won't be coming home."

"I'm glad you're the one who has to deliver that news instead of me," Ruth said.

"I'm not," Rhodes said.

Chapter 5

▼

Rhodes didn't often think about his boyhood. He was usually too involved in the present to think about the past or the future, but driving the winding dirt roads that would take him to the Hunt home brought back things that he hadn't thought of in years, like the house where he'd lived the early part of his life. It was gone now, but part of an old barn still remained on the property, or at least it had been there the last time Rhodes had driven by. The roof had collapsed, and by now there might not be much of it left. Rhodes had gathered eggs in that barn and learned to milk a cow. He hadn't milked a cow in many years, but he could still remember his father putting a bucket under the cow's udders, positioning Rhodes on a three-legged stool, and letting him lean into the cow's warm side. Rhodes's hands had been too small to do a very good job of squeezing the teats, but he'd been able to get some milk to stream into the bucket before his father finished the job. He'd even been allowed to drink some of the warm milk, something that would now no doubt be considered quite unsanitary and possibly dangerous.

Rhodes grinned at the memory. His family had moved to town before he'd become an expert milker, but he thought he could still milk a cow if called upon.

He rounded a curve, crossed the wooden bridge over Crockett's Creek, and saw that the old barn where his house had been was almost gone, fallen completely down and almost hidden by vines and bushes that had grown up over and around what was left of it. That was why it was better not to think about the past. What was left of it never lived up to the memories.

Rhodes drove past and around another curve, turned left onto another road, and drove a half mile to where the Hunts lived. He pulled off to the side of the road, stopping the Tahoe in front of the house. It had been new when Rhodes was a boy, but it hadn't been fancy even then. It hadn't been kept up, and now showed its age. The paint was flaked and peeling, and a few loose shingles lay on the roof. A pane in one of the windows had been replaced by cardboard. The yard was mostly weeds, and it hadn't been mowed in a while. The house sat up on concrete blocks, and the space between the house and the ground was covered with tin that had been painted white like the house, though some of it had been bent away and not straightened. It was streaked with rust. The satellite dish on the roof looked like new, however.

Rhodes couldn't remember exactly when the Hunts had moved into the house, but it had been a good many years earlier. The original owners, an old couple named Phelps, had moved somewhere to be closer to their children. Houston, Rhodes thought, or Dallas. They were probably dead by now.

Melvin's wife, Joyce, had worked in town for a while at the Walmart, but she'd quit a few years ago and hadn't had another job as far as Rhodes knew. Melvin made a little money doing odd jobs around Clearview, and he'd done welding for people who needed it until his rig had been stolen. Hunt might've been the one who cut out the B-Bar-B brand and welded it to Billy's gate for him. Rhodes would have to remember to ask Billy about that.

The welding rig had been kept in the barn in back of the house. The barn was in no better condition than the house, but at least it hadn't fallen down. Yet. Rhodes didn't think it was going to last much longer if something wasn't done.

Rhodes looked through the windshield of the Tahoe at the trees in back of the barn. They grew thickly all the way down to Crockett's Creek, and Rhodes wondered if the Hunts had experienced any problems with feral hogs. It seemed likely, but something like that would be the last of Joyce Hunt's concerns now.

Rhodes got out of the Tahoe and shut the door. As soon as he did two black-and-brown short-haired dogs of indeterminate breed charged out from under the little porch in front of the house and headed straight for him, barking loudly, teeth bared. There was some leopard hound in their background somewhere.

Carelessness. That was what came of thinking about the past. You forgot about the present and what might get you in trouble. Rhodes should have thought about the dogs. There were almost always dogs at houses this far out in the country, and the people who had them didn't usually keep them around as companions. They wanted real watchdogs who could protect their property from other animals and unwanted guests, and this pair didn't appear to be in a friendly mood. They appeared to be in the mood to rip somebody's arms off, and the nearest somebody with arms was Rhodes.

Moving with an alacrity he hadn't experienced since the long-gone Will o' the Wisp days, Rhodes opened the Tahoe door, jumped inside, and slammed the door. He was just in time. The dog that had been two steps ahead of the other, unable to stop his forward momentum, slammed into the door with enough force to shake the vehicle. Or maybe Rhodes was just imagining that. The Tahoe weighed nearly six thousand pounds, after all.

The dog wasn't hurt. He and his partner stood outside the Tahoe, jumping up and trying to bite Rhodes through the window, their claws scratching the paint as they slid back down. The Blacklin County Sheriff's Department decal was going to be a mess. The county commissioners wouldn't be happy about that.

Rhodes could have unlocked the shotgun and given the dogs a bit of a surprise, but he didn't want to do that. He saw an old GMC pickup sitting beside the house, so he figured someone, probably Joyce Hunt, was home. Eventually she'd come out to see what was happening and call off the dogs. Or Rhodes hoped she'd call off the dogs. If she didn't, he could always use his handy cell phone to call her and ask her to do it. He was prepared to wait a while before trying that option, however.

He didn't have to wait long. Up at the house a screen door opened and a woman stepped out on the porch. It was Joyce Hunt. She wore a pair of jeans, low-heeled work boots, and a sweater. Her gray hair hung down almost to her shoulders. She stood for a second looking at the dogs and then called out to them.

"Gus-Gus! Jackie! You get back here right now!"

Gus-Gus and Jackie didn't pay her any mind. They kept jumping against the side of the Tahoe and biting at the window.

"Did you two hear me?" Joyce yelled. "Get away from that car and come back here right this minute!"

The two dogs dropped to the ground, and Rhodes leaned over to look out the window. They were still right beside the Tahoe, but they were looking back toward the house.

"I mean it," Joyce said. "Get up here right now."

The dogs hesitated for another couple of seconds, then trotted toward the house. When they got to the porch, Joyce bent over and patted them. Rhodes thought she was probably telling them what good dogs they were. She straightened up and called out to Rhodes. "You can get out now. They won't bother you."

Rhodes hoped he could believe her. He considered taking the shotgun, but that would be cowardly. He opened the door. Gus-Gus and Jackie turned to look at him at the sound. Their looks weren't friendly in the least, but Rhodes got out of the Tahoe. The dogs growled low in their throats.

"You can come on up, Sheriff," Joyce said. "You don't have to worry about the boys. I won't let them hurt you."

Rhodes thought that was neighborly of her. She might have changed her mind if she knew what he was there for.

"You boys go lie down," Joyce told the dogs.

The dogs paid her no attention. They kept their eyes on Rhodes and continued to make low growling noises.

"Just go on into the house," Joyce said when Rhodes got almost to the porch. "I'll stay out here with the boys until you get in and close the door. They'll be fine."

Rhodes wasn't worried about the condition of the dogs. He was more worried about his own. He stepped up on the porch, staying as far from the dogs as he could, which wasn't far, considering how small the porch was. The dogs stayed still, but they both stared balefully at him as he went by them and into the house, pulling the screen door shut behind him. It was a flimsy door and wouldn't last long if the dogs threw themselves against it, but they didn't bother. As soon as he was inside, they jumped off the porch and disappeared as if they'd forgotten all about him.

Rhodes looked around the room he found himself in and saw

a sagging sofa, a battered coffee table, a cane-bottomed rocking chair, and a couple of end tables with lamps whose shades had accumulated a good bit of dust. The flat-screen TV facing the sofa was on but muted. Rhodes saw Alex Trebek mouthing a question that some gray-haired professorial type wearing a bow tie appeared to answer.

The screen door opened, and Joyce Hunt came inside.

"The boys aren't as mean as they sound," she said. "They don't like strangers, though, so they're good watchdogs."

Rhodes nodded. "I'm sure they are."

"I guess this isn't a social call," Joyce said.

"No," Rhodes said. "It's not."

"I'm going to sit down," Joyce said. "You have a seat, too."

She sat in the rocking chair, leaving the sofa to Rhodes. He sat on it, and the cushions sagged down even more.

"Is it about Melvin?" Joyce asked. She pushed her hair back. Her face was browned and wrinkled. "I haven't see him since yesterday."

"Yes, it's about Melvin," Rhodes said. He'd never found a good way to tell someone about the death of a family member or a loved one, so he just did it the best way he knew how, which was straight out. "I hate to have to give you this news. Melvin's dead."

Rhodes never knew what to expect when he said those words. Sometimes people started to cry. Sometimes they said nothing. Sometimes they tried to hit him. And sometimes they denied it. That's what Joyce did.

"That can't be," she said. "He was just fine yesterday. Healthy as a horse. He's not dead. Not Melvin. You must be wrong about that."

"I wish I was," Rhodes said, "but I'm not. Melvin's dead. Somebody shot him."

"Melvin? Shot?" Joyce started to rock back and forth, slowly, her hands gripping the low arms of the chair. "Who'd shoot Melvin, Sheriff?"

"I don't know who shot him. He was in Billy Bacon's barn. Do you know what he was doing there?"

"He doesn't always tell me where he's going. Sometimes he's gone a day or two, but he always comes back." Joyce's hands tightened on the arms of the chair, and her knuckles whitened. She started to rock faster. "He'll be back tonight or tomorrow. He always comes back."

"Not this time. Do you have another vehicle besides the one parked outside?"

"No. That's the only one. What difference does that make?"

"Melvin had to get to the barn somehow or the other. Did he walk?"

"He never tells me where he's going or how he's going to get there. Sometimes somebody picks him up and they go drinking. Sometimes they pick him up here and sometimes they don't. He might walk to Walter Barnes's house. Maybe he's with Walter right now."

"He's not with Walter. Do you have somebody you can stay with tonight?"

"My sister. She lives in Clearview. Ellen Smalls. Why?"

Rhodes knew the Smalls family. Will and Ellen lived not too far from the Dairy Queen.

"You get some things together, and I'll take you to your sister's," he said. "You should pack a bag. You might want to stay a couple of days."

"Melvin might come back and wonder where I am."

"Melvin won't be back. You get out a suit for him, or whatever you'd like to have him dressed in. You can see him tomorrow."

Joyce stood up. So did Rhodes. She looked a little shaky, so he took her elbow to steady her.

"I'm fine," she said. "It's just that Melvin . . . he's always come back before."

"Where does he go?" Rhodes asked, dropping his hand.

"I told you. Off with friends. He doesn't tell me much. I need to get his suit. He hasn't worn it in years. I don't know if it'll fit."

"I'm sure it will fit," Rhodes said, not adding that if it didn't, it could be adjusted so it would look as if it did.

"I'll be right back," Joyce said.

She went out of the room, and Rhodes sat back down. A couple of magazines lay on the coffee table, but they were as dusty as the lampshades. The TV remote was beside them, and it wasn't dusty. Rhodes left it where it was and watched *Jeopardy!* in silence. The professorial type in the bow tie won the final round just as Joyce came back into the room. She had a man's black suit draped over her left arm and an old-fashioned hard-bodied suitcase in her right hand.

Rhodes stood and took the suitcase. Joyce picked up the remote and turned off the TV set. Setting the remote back on the coffee table, she said, "I called my sister. I can stay with her, but I'm worried about the boys. I can shut them up in the barn for a day or so, I guess, but they need to be let out every day."

"I'll check on them for you," Rhodes said. "I can give them some food and water if it's safe."

Joyce laid the coat across the back of the couch. "That would be kind of you. The boys won't bother you. Come on outside and I'll introduce you."

Rhodes wasn't so sure that was a good idea, but he knew he had to pay another visit to the house. He set the suitcase down and followed Joyce outside. The dogs came out from under the porch in a hurry, but Joyce calmed them.

"You boys sit where you are and behave yourselves. This is the sheriff, and he's going to look after you for me."

The dogs stood in front of the porch giving Rhodes the stink eye. They didn't appear ready to be friends, but at least they weren't growling. Rhodes figured it was up to him to give them a chance to get to know him. He squatted down on the porch, not facing the dogs and not looking at them. Joyce stepped off the porch and patted the dogs on the head.

"Which one is which?" Rhodes asked, still not looking at the dogs.

"Gus-Gus has the big black spot on his head," Joyce said. "Jackie's a little bigger, and there's no spot there. They're good boys, aren't you good boys, yes, you are."

When she'd patted the dogs and rubbed their sides, one of them moved over to the porch for a better look at Rhodes. The other followed. They moved around a little, looking at him from different angles. Gus-Gus approached him and sniffed at his leg. Jackie followed and sniffed as well. Rhodes thought they might have caught the scent of his own dogs, Speedo and Yancey. He'd played with them that morning, and their scents would linger, at least for dogs. Dogs could smell things no human could detect.

After the dogs had sniffed for a few seconds, they seemed satisfied that Rhodes wasn't an enemy. He risked extending his hand, palm down, and Gus-Gus licked it. Rhodes gave him a light pat. Gus-Gus didn't mind, and then Jackie moved him out of the way so he could get a pat, too. Before long, Rhodes was sitting on the porch, and the two dogs were treating him as an old friend.

While they got acquainted, Joyce went back inside the house.

In a minute or so, Rhodes heard the back door slam, and Joyce walked across the backyard to the barn. She was carrying a sack of Old Roy dog food, and Gus-Gus and Jackie deserted Rhodes to follow her. They went off at a run and beat her to the barn. Rhodes went along after them, passing a well on the way. A frame over the well held a rope and pulley for drawing water, but there was also a pump. Rhodes figured the pump carried water to the house. The well reminded Rhodes of the one at Billy Bacon's place, the one that had been kicked almost to pieces. Someone didn't like Bacon, all right.

The big barn door was closed, but there was a regular-sized door next to it. That one was open, and Joyce went through it, the dogs at her heels. Rhodes was only a short way behind them. The inside of the barn wasn't entirely dark, thanks to a few holes in the roof. It was much bigger and airier than Billy's older one. The dogs would be comfortable enough there for a day or so. Joyce poured some dog food into a big pan that sat near another empty pan and a galvanized bucket. Rhodes picked up the bucket and said he'd get the water.

It had been a long time since Rhodes had drawn water from a well. He pitched the bucket into the well and the rope followed it down. When he heard a splash, Rhodes waited a while for the bucket to fill, then hauled it back up, the pulley squeaking a little. It could've used some oil. The bucket reached the top, and Rhodes swung it over the side of the well so he could pour the water into the bucket he'd brought from the barn.

Off to the left the roof of a storm cellar stood about a foot off the ground. Not many people in the county had a storm cellar, but Rhodes knew of four or five others. A tornado had passed through a corner of the county about thirty years ago, and the cellars had all been dug about that time.

Gus-Gus and Jackie were still waiting when he returned to the barn. He poured the water from the bucket into the pan, and both dogs turned to drink.

"Was Melvin afraid of storms?" Rhodes asked Joyce.

"No, he wasn't afraid of much of anything. The cellar was here when we moved in. I've never even been down in it. It has water in the bottom, Melvin says, about six inches, and there are spiders down there. I don't like spiders. Melvin says you never know if a snake might be down there, too. I'd rather face a tornado than a snake."

Rhodes hoped he'd never have to make that choice, but he was pretty sure he'd pick the snake.

"Will the dogs mind being shut in the barn?" he asked, setting the bucket down.

"We put them in here all the time," Joyce said. "They sleep on those raggedy old blankets over there. They don't mind it as long as they get outside once or twice a day."

"Is this where Melvin kept his welding rig?"

"Yes, but it got stolen. We should've gotten a lock for the doors, but we thought people were honest."

Rhodes wasn't sure anybody really thought that anymore.

"We have locks now," Joyce said. "Melvin said we had to get them."

"A good idea," Rhodes said.

"I'll take the food to the house," Joyce said. "I'll put it inside the back door. I'll have to give you a key if you come back to feed the boys. I can come back myself if it's too much trouble for you."

"I don't mind doing it," Rhodes said. "I'd like your permission to look through the house, too. Maybe it would help in the investigation."

"All right, if it will help. I still can't believe Melvin's . . . dead."

"It takes some getting used to."

"I'm not going to get used to it. You'll find out who did it, won't you?"

"I'll do my best," Rhodes said.

Chapter 6

▼

On their ride to town, Rhodes asked Joyce a few questions about Melvin, hoping to get some useful information. He didn't get much, but he did find out that Melvin's best friend was Riley Farmer and that when Melvin went off on a binge, it was Riley he usually went with. Joyce insisted that Melvin hadn't been on a bender in a long time.

"He's been feeling better about things," she said. "Even when the welding rig was stolen, he didn't go off and get drunk."

She didn't have any explanation for why Melvin's bad habit had improved, but she was happy that it had. Rhodes also learned that Melvin had no enemies, at least as far as Joyce knew. No surprise there. Murder victims were always beloved by everyone, to hear their family and friends tell it.

"No enemies at all?" Rhodes said.

"Not a one," Joyce said. "Unless you count Billy Bacon. He wasn't an enemy or anything like that, but those two just didn't get along."

Billy hadn't mentioned that little tidbit.

"What was their trouble?" Rhodes asked.

"Melvin got turned down for a loan. He really needed the money at the time. We were gonna fix up the house, get the place looking better. Billy said no, said that Melvin didn't have any collateral. Or a job except what he could get fixing things up or welding a little now and then."

Rhodes could see how Billy would think that way. As a loan officer, he had to be sure about the risk he was taking.

"Did Melvin ever try to get back at Billy?" Rhodes asked.

"If you're thinking that Melvin would steal, you'd be wrong. Melvin was as honest as the day is long."

"I'm sure he was," Rhodes said, though he didn't necessarily believe it. Whoever had kicked down the well at Billy's place could have done it because of a grudge rather than from just pure meanness.

"Anyway," Joyce said with a catch in her voice, "things were getting a little better. We got the insurance from the welding rig, and that helped some. Money wasn't so tight. Maybe that's why Melvin wasn't drinking."

The fact that their finances had improved wouldn't matter if Melvin was the type to hold a grudge. "And Billy was the only one he had a problem with?"

"Well, there's Gene Gunnison."

Gunnison lived just off another of the county roads not far away. Rhodes knew of him but had never met him. His house was back in the woods, and he was considered by some to be a kind of outlaw who hunted and fished on the property of others without bothering to ask permission. There had been a few calls to the department about him, and Rhodes had sent a deputy to check things out each time, but no solid evidence of his trespassing had ever turned up. Supposedly his grandfather had been a bootlegger who'd sold illegal whiskey and avoided capture for years before winding up in prison.

"What was Melvin's problem with Gunnison?" Rhodes asked.

"Melvin thought Gene was sneaking around the property. He thought he might've been the one that stole the welding rig."

Rhodes had been wondering about that theft. Something wasn't right about it.

"How could anybody get by the dogs?" he asked.

"The boys knew Gene. He used to visit now and then, back when we first got them. He'd bring treats for them. Melvin says he was probably just getting friendly with them instead of us, just waiting for his chance to steal something."

"Do you think he stole the rig?"

"I don't know. Anyway, he and Melvin patched it up, I guess. They get along all right now. I hear it's the Terrells that are stealing things. That's what Melvin told me."

"Everybody's heard that," Rhodes said. "That doesn't mean it's true."

"It doesn't mean it's not true, either."

Rhodes had to give her that point. "So Melvin had a problem with Able Terrell, too."

"I wouldn't call it a problem. He just didn't hardly ever see him. Nobody does 'less he wants 'em to, and he doesn't want 'em to. He knew Able before he moved into that compound of his. Didn't like him much then, and never changed his mind."

It was true that nobody ever saw Able Terrell unless he wanted them to, which would make it hard for Rhodes to talk to him. It had to be done, though. Later.

"What about a gun?" Rhodes asked. "Did Melvin have one?"

"He had a deer rifle and a shotgun," Joyce said. "They're in a rifle cabinet in our bedroom. I saw them when I was packing."

"What about a pistol?"

"He had one. It's in the bottom of the rifle cabinet."

"Did you see it when you were in the bedroom?"

"No. It's in the bottom. There are doors on that part."

Rhodes wondered if Melvin had left it there or if he'd had it with him. He'd check when he went back to the house. For now, that was all the questions he had.

Rhodes dropped Joyce off at her sister's house. By that time the fact of Melvin's death had begun to sink in, and she was sobbing quietly. Rhodes told the Smallses a little about the situation and left them to give Joyce what comfort they could. It wouldn't be much, not in her position.

Rhodes drove to the jail. It was late afternoon, and his day off hadn't gone at all the way he'd planned. Instead of relaxing, he'd averted a robbery and started a murder investigation. Now he just wanted to write up his report and get something to eat. It wasn't going to be that easy, however. As he walked in the door, Hack started in on him.

"You been gone awhile," Hack said.

"Trouble at the Billy Bacon place," Rhodes said.

"Trouble is right, but nobody told me about it. Nobody ever tells me anything." Hack paused and shook his head. "That's all right, though. I'm just the dispatcher. I'm like the furniture. Don't matter if I know what's going on or not."

"I tell you everything," Rhodes said. "Eventually."

He didn't add that *eventually* was how Hack and Lawton told him things. Hack was no doubt well aware of that. Rhodes had the sign from the post and other things that he'd taken from Billy Bacon's ranch. He took them into the evidence locker and filled out the forms. He came out and sat at his computer.

"No, sir, you don't tell me everything," Hack said, picking up as if there had been no interruption. "You still haven't told me what happened out there at Billy Bacon's place. That's all right, though. You don't have to tell me. I got ways of findin' out what's goin' on. I got my sources."

Rhodes ignored him, put on his reading glasses, and started working on the report.

"See, you don't give a rip about me and whether I'm in the loop or not. Me and Lawton do all the work around here, but we don't get any respect. It's a shame, is what it is."

Rhodes turned in his chair. "You get a lot of respect, and you already know what happened. So I don't really need to tell you, do I?"

"You don't even care who my sources are."

"I'm just guessing here, but I'd say that Deputy Grady finished up at the crime scene and came by here a little while ago. Did she have anything for you to tell me?"

"Not a thing except she didn't find any clues."

Rhodes hadn't expected her to. It had been his experience that clues didn't turn up as often in Blacklin County as they did on TV.

"Then she went to check on Oscar Campbell," Hack said.

Oscar was a regular caller to the department. "Naked people coming through his windows again?"

"Third time this year. They like this warm weather."

"How many this time?"

"He said three, same as usual."

"What did he want Ruth to do about it?"

"Chase 'em out of the house. You know that."

Oscar Campbell was in most respects a normal guy, friendly to his neighbors, able to function quite well in what passed for society in Clearview. He just had one little quirk. He didn't see dead people; he saw naked people, and they were coming through his windows. He'd call the sheriff's department about the problem now and then, and once the deputy who responded to the call had checked the house and assured him that the naked people were gone, he'd be just fine until the next time.

"I'm sure Deputy Grady will do a good job of clearing out the house," Rhodes said. "Now I need to finish this report."

"Ruth has herself a new idea for those naked people," Hack said. "Just been waitin' for Oscar to call."

Rhodes did a bit of the report, waiting for Hack to continue and knowing he wouldn't. Rhodes kept on working until he was about half through before he gave in.

"What new idea?" he asked.

"Made it up herself," Hack said. "More or less. She told me Seepy helped out."

If Seepy Benton was in on the new idea, Rhodes wasn't sure he wanted to hear about it.

"Is it legal?"

"Bound to be. I figger it'll work, too. Seepy's a professional."

"A professional what?"

"Ghost hunter. You know that."

Rhodes took off his glasses, closed his eyes, and squeezed the bridge of his nose between his thumb and forefinger. "What do imaginary naked people have to do with ghosts?"

"Not a thing," Hack said.

Rhodes put his glasses back on and leaned back in his chair. "Hack, just tell the story."

"You're mighty impatient lately."

"I have a murder investigation to work on. That makes me impatient. Tell the story."

"All right, if you're gonna be that way about it. See, Seepy got the idea from an ad he saw for some ghost repellent. He thought it might be something he could offer his customers."

"He's not working the ghost-hunting job right now," Rhodes said.

"Nope, but he's always thinking. You know how he is. That mind of his is workin' all the time."

Rhodes knew. "Does ghost repellent work?"

"Don't matter if it does or not, according to Seepy. As long as somebody believes in it, that's as good as if it works."

Rhodes was beginning to catch on. Seepy had solved a similar problem once before. "So Seepy made some kind of repellent?"

"Nudist repellent," Hack said. "Got him a big spray bottle at Walmart's and printed up a label. Ruth showed it to me. Looks real professional, like it's the real thing. She's gonna spray some of the stuff around all the windows at Oscar's house and leave the bottle with him. She figgers that'll solve the problem."

"What's in the bottle? Water?"

"Water that Seepy fixed up with some colorin' and odor. Smells pretty good."

Rhodes thought it might work. It would depend on Oscar. He turned his chair back to the computer and said, "I need to get this report done."

"You do that," Hack said. "Don't mind me. It's not like I'm doin' anything important. I'm just takin' up space around here."

When Rhodes was finished with the report, he called Ivy and asked if she wanted to go out to dinner. She said yes, and he told her that he'd pick her up when he was done with interviewing someone.

"Who?" Ivy asked.

"Billy Bacon and his wife. I'll tell you about it later. Where do you want to eat?"

Ivy preferred healthy food at home, and Rhodes had even been persuaded to try turkey bologna. It wasn't his favorite thing. The good news was that when they ate out, Ivy was happy to eat things that she didn't often serve at home.

"We haven't been to the Jolly Tamale for a while," she said. "Does that sound good?"

It sounded great, but Rhodes tried not to be let his enthusiasm show too much, even though visions of chiles rellenos danced in his head.

"It'll do," he said.

After he'd hung up, he asked Hack if he wanted some Mexican food.

"You gonna bring it to me?"

"Sure."

"It'll still be hot when you get here with it?"

"Absolutely."

"Guess that'd be nice, but I don't want it. Lawton's gonna bring me a cheeseburger. I like a good cheeseburger 'bout as well as anything."

"Don't say I didn't offer."

"Be better if you'd keep me in the loop."

"I'll try to remember that," Rhodes said. "Call Mika and have her come in tomorrow. She can check the cell phone to see if she can find anything useful."

Mika Blackfield did the forensics work for the department. She'd come to Clearview with her husband, who was a pharmacist at Walmart. When she'd applied for a job with the sheriff's department and told Rhodes that she had a degree in criminal justice, he pushed the commissioners to hire her. They'd complained about the salary and allowed her to work only part-time, but she'd been very good at the job. Rhodes was happy with the hire, and so was everybody else.

"I'll call her," Hack said. "Anything else you want me to tell her?"

"She knows what to do," Rhodes said. "When Ruth comes in, tell her to go back to Billy Bacon's place and see if she can turn up any clues in the daylight."

"I bet she'll keep me in the loop about it if she does," Hack said.

Rhodes decided to leave without getting into that argument again.

The Bacons lived in an old home built during Clearview's boom days, a time when a seemingly endless supply of oil had been pumped up from beneath the ground and the town's population had doubled and tripled and quadrupled within months. That had been almost a century ago, and the people back then had thought the oil would last forever. It hadn't, of course, and in only a few years Clearview was a small town again. A few people had made a great deal of money, however, and several of them had built their homes on the edge of town along the same street. The homes had outlasted the oil.

All the homes were large and showy, and most of them had been bought and sold several times over the years. One of them now belonged to Billy Bacon. It was just down the street from the home of Clearview's mayor, Clifford Clement, and Rhodes hoped he wouldn't have to deal with Clement in this investigation. The mayor had been mixed up in a couple of other recent problems, and he didn't much care for Rhodes. Rhodes had to put up with him, however, since the city of Clearview contracted with the sheriff's department for its police services.

Rhodes parked in the driveway of Billy's house behind Billy's pickup. He got out of the Tahoe and admired the grass of the lawn, which was as green as the grass in a picture of Ireland, before he went to the door and rang the bell.

Billy came to the door. Seeing Rhodes, he said, "I didn't expect you so soon."

Rhodes thought it might already be too late. Billy would have had time to tell Nadine the situation and make sure she said what he wanted her to say.

"Better to get it over with," Rhodes said.

Billy stepped back from the door, holding it open. "Come on in, then. We'll go in the den."

The den was down a hallway and through a door to the left. It was obviously Billy's room. Pictures of him in his high school glory days hung on the wall, along with a framed jersey. A football covered with signatures sat on a little table. A couch and recliner were both covered with soft-looking brown leather, and the desk on one side of the room even had a leather top.

"Have a seat," Billy said. "I'll go get Nadine. She's in the kitchen. Don't be too hard on her, okay? She's not feeling well."

Billy left the room, but Rhodes didn't sit. He walked over to the football and picked it up. He recognized a few of the signatures as belonging to Billy's teammates from back in the times when Bacon was shakin'. Billy must miss those days when he was the best-known and best-loved person in Clearview.

Rhodes set the ball back down as Nadine and Billy came into

the room. Nadine no longer looked like the cheerleader Rhodes remembered. She was still short, still compact, but she looked old, much older than Billy, though her hair wasn't thinning and graying like his. It was still blond and short, but Rhodes was sure the color wasn't natural. She looked tired, and her gait was more of a shuffle than a walk.

"Hello, Sheriff," she said. "Billy says you want to talk to me."

"Just a few questions if you don't mind," Rhodes said.

"I don't mind. Let's sit down. I can't stand up very long."

She and Billy sat on the couch. Billy had to help her. Rhodes took the chair. The leather was as soft as it looked.

"Go ahead, Sheriff," Nadine said, leaning forward so as not to sink into the depths of the couch. "Ask your questions."

"A couple of things to start with," Rhodes said. "Billy, you didn't tell me that you and Melvin had a little falling-out. It was about a loan, I believe."

Billy sighed. "I have to turn down a lot of loans. That was one of them. It was just business."

"Melvin didn't see it that way. He needed the money, and you were neighbors. You said he didn't have any collateral."

"I can't help how Melvin felt. The only collateral he had was that property of his. Do you know how long it's been since any of that property sold? I'll tell you how long. Years. Land isn't worth anything if you can't sell it. I couldn't see my way clear to making the loan."

"All right," Rhodes said. "What about the brand on your gate, the B-Bar-B. Did Melvin make that for you?"

"Yes. Made the gate, too, for that matter, but that was before the loan thing came up. I paid him good money to do it. Too bad he lost his rig. Maybe he could've made some more money."

"Maybe. Now I have a question for you, Mrs. Bacon."

"Call me Nadine."

"Sure," Rhodes said. "Billy tells me he was home with you last night."

Nadine nodded. "That's right. He was right here all the time."

It was what Rhodes had expected her to say. "He says he bought you a gun."

"Yes," Nadine said. "It's for home protection. You hear so much about home invasions on the news."

Following the party line, Rhodes thought, wondering just how much coaching Billy had given her.

"Guns can be dangerous if you don't know how to use them," he said. "I hope you've had some training."

"Billy taught me how to use it. I haven't had any classes or anything because I don't have a concealed-carry license. We just take the pistol out for target practice sometimes. Or we did. We haven't been out much since I got sick."

"I'd heard you'd been sick," Rhodes said. He looked at Billy, who was keeping quiet. "Have the doctors been able to help?"

"Ha," Nadine said.

Rhodes looked at Billy again.

"They've tried," Billy said. "They've done all kinds of tests, tried all kinds of medications. Nothing works."

"Just go ahead and tell him all of it," Nadine said. "If everybody in town doesn't know already, they'll find out. Tell him."

Billy looked down at the floor.

"You don't need to hang your head," Nadine said. "It happens to all kinds of people. It happened to Rush Limbaugh and Cindy McCain. It even happened to Elvis. It's nothing to be ashamed of."

Billy looked up, but he still didn't speak.

Nadine looked at Rhodes. "He can't handle it. People stealing his stuff, a dead man in his barn, and me. It's all gotten to be too much for him."

Rhodes thought he knew what she was talking about, but he wanted to make sure. "What about you?"

"I'm a prescription drug addict, Sheriff. Hooked, lined, and sinkered. It's all legal, so you don't have to arrest me."

Billy finally spoke up. "It's not her fault, Sheriff, okay? It's the damn doctors. They got her hooked, and now they can't get her off."

"Benzos," Nadine said. "That's what they call them on the street."

Rhodes knew the word. It meant Valium, Halcion, Librium, things like that. He didn't think Nadine had ever been on the street to hear the term. She must have heard it on TV. Maybe on some cop show.

"She'd had some problems," Billy said. "We went to a lot of doctors, all over the state. The best. They couldn't find anything really wrong with her, and it was making us both crazy. They said it was all imaginary."

"It's not," Nadine said. "It's Morgellons. It's real. Joni Mitchell has it, and now she's had an aneurysm, too, poor thing. I was tired all the time, and I had things growing out of my skin. It was driving me crazy."

"You can't believe the stress," Billy said. "It got to her. The doctors prescribed Valium for all the anxiety she was having over the testing and uncertainty. She got dependent. The doses they gave her were too large."

"It could happen to anybody," Nadine said. "Look at Elvis."

"The thing is, you can't just go cold turkey," Billy said. "If you want to get off the benzos, you have to taper off, okay? It can take forever."

"The worst part is, the drugs didn't work," Nadine said. "They didn't find what was wrong with me, and the benzos didn't help my anxiety except for a little while. Plus I still have the symptoms. Now I'm worse off than ever."

"You didn't come to hear this," Billy told Rhodes. "You came about the gun."

They'd strayed a bit from the topic of the gun, true, but Rhodes always listened to what people told him. You never knew when something helpful would come out.

"That's all right," Rhodes said. "I'll keep it confidential."

"Even if you do, it won't do any good," Nadine said. "People gossip about me already. I know they talk about me down at that Beauty Shack where I get my hair done."

The Beauty Shack was where a lot of women, including Rhodes's wife, had their hair done. Men, too. It was a hotbed of information exchange, which was what Ivy preferred to call gossip.

"Nobody will hear anything from me," Rhodes said.

Nadine looked skeptical. "If you say so. Anyway, you're wrong if you think Billy had something to do with killing Melvin Hunt. He was with me. You could look at the gun if you want to. Go get it, Billy."

Billy looked questioningly at Rhodes, who nodded.

Billy stood up. "I'll be right back."

When he left the room, Nadine said, "Like I said, it's been hard on him, having me like this, Sheriff. He's always been so healthy, and I used to be, too. We've both had a hard time dealing with my illness, especially with me being hooked on the benzos. They're terrible things. I'm better now, a little, and I have something to help me, but it's still hard."

"I know," Rhodes said.

"You think you do, but you don't, not unless it's happened to you or to somebody you care about. Billy's a good man, and he's taken care of me. He didn't kill Melvin Hunt. I know he didn't."

Rhodes didn't know what to say to that, but he was spared from coming up with an answer when Billy limped back into the room holding a revolver with the cylinder swung out. His thumb and forefinger encircled the cylinder.

"It hasn't been fired in a while," Billy said, handing the revolver to Rhodes. "See for yourself."

Rhodes took the revolver, checked to be sure the cylinder was unloaded, and sniffed the barrel. He smelled gun oil and solvent. All that told him was that Billy could have cleaned the gun after using it a day earlier.

"I'd like to take it with me," Rhodes said. "Just in case."

"What if the home invaders come tonight?" Nadine asked.

"It won't go anywhere if you leave it with us," Billy said. "You can come get it anytime you need it for testing."

Rhodes passed the gun back to him. "All right, but keep it handy."

"We always do," Billy said.

Chapter 7

▼

The Jolly Tamale wasn't crowded, so Rhodes and Ivy were able to get their favorite booth near the back. While Ivy looked over the menu, Rhodes told her a little about what he'd been doing that day.

"I've already heard about your heroic takedown of the robber," she said. "I read it on Jennifer Loam's news site. I'm surprised she hasn't put something on there about the murder."

"She's usually right on top of things like that," Rhodes said. He'd already decided on a chile relleno and didn't need to look at the menu. "I'm sure it'll be there tomorrow."

Ivy closed her menu. "Anyway, we know who did it."

Rhodes looked at her. "We do?"

"The wife," Ivy said. "When the husband is killed, it's always the wife."

"It is?"

"You need to watch some true crime shows on TV," Ivy said. "It's always the wife unless she's the one who's killed. Then it's the husband."

"Not always," Rhodes said.

Ivy just smiled at him as if she knew she was right. Rhodes didn't try to change her mind. That was always a losing proposition.

The server brought some chips, salsa, and water and asked if she could take their order. Ivy ordered veggie enchiladas, and Rhodes asked for a chile relleno. The waitress left. Rhodes took a chip and dipped some salsa, which turned out to be just right, not too hot and not too bland.

"If it's not the wife," Ivy said, "then who is it?"

Rhodes finished chewing and wiped his mouth with his napkin, a real cloth one, an amenity that a lot of places in Clearview no longer provided.

"I'll let you know when I find out," he said.

"When will that be?"

"Eventually," Rhodes said, thinking of Hack as he dipped another chip into the salsa.

"What about Billy Bacon?" Ivy asked. "Is he a suspect?"

Rhodes crunched the chip, chewed, wiped his mouth, and drank some water. "You know what I always say. Everybody's a suspect at first. Have you heard anything at the Beauty Shack that I should know about Melvin's wife?"

"No, not a thing," Ivy said. "Nobody's ever exchanged information about her."

"What about Nadine and Billy Bacon?"

"Everybody admires Billy for the way he's stuck by Nadine. Some people think her problems are psychological. Even the doctors, or so I've heard."

"What do you think?" Rhodes asked.

"The doctors haven't found anything, but that doesn't mean there's no problem."

Rhodes didn't ask about the prescription drug addiction. Ivy would have mentioned it if it had been discussed. Maybe Nadine's personal life wasn't the open secret she thought it was, and since Rhodes had promised not to say anything, he kept his mouth shut.

"Sometimes she looks a little out of it," Ivy said. "I think she's on some kind of medication."

Rhodes nodded and was glad to see their server arrive with their meals. She warned them about touching the hot plates. Rhodes looked at his chile relleno with eager anticipation, but he didn't dig in. It would have to cool off for a short while before he ate. If he burned his mouth, he couldn't enjoy the food.

Just as he thought the food had cooled to the correct temperature for eating, his cell phone rang.

"You'd better answer it," Ivy said. "It's probably an emergency."

"If it's Hack, it's an emergency," Rhodes said, digging the phone out of his pocket. "With him, it's always an emergency."

Sure enough, it was Hack, and it was an emergency.

"You need to get to the Lansen place right now," Hack said.

"I'm about to eat," Rhodes said.

"That's a shame. Kathy Lansen called. Somebody's broke into the house, and Rex's gone after 'em with his gun. I'd send Andy or Duke, but they're out on patrol in Milsby and Thurston. You're the one that's left. You can get out there quicker than they can."

"Buddy and Ruth are left."

"Yeah, but they're off the clock. The sheriff is the one who's never off the clock."

"All right, but you call Andy and tell him to get out there for backup. Milsby can patrol itself for a while."

"I'll do that, but you better get movin' before Rex kills somebody."

"I'm on the way," Rhodes said.

He ended the call and explained to Ivy what had happened.

"Do you think this is connected to the burglaries at Billy Bacon's place?" she asked.

"Bacon's place is a long way from here, and it sounds like a different kind of burglary," Rhodes said, "but you never know. Sometimes people change their methods. You go ahead and finish your enchiladas. I'll come back for you when I get this sorted out."

"That might take a while," Ivy said. "I'll get a ride home. I'll take your chile relleno and save it for you."

"Okay. I'll be home when I can get there."

"I know," Ivy said, and Rhodes left.

For a long time after they'd married, Ivy had worried too much about Rhodes, but she'd finally begun to understand that he had to do his job and that so far he'd always managed to get back home. Sometimes he hadn't been in the best condition, but he'd gotten there just the same.

The Lansens lived on a county road not far off the highway that led to Obert, a small town that Rhodes had visited many times in the course of investigations. In fact, the Lansens lived not far from Seepy Benton. Rhodes hoped Benton hadn't managed to get himself involved in the current situation.

Rhodes put the flashers and the siren on as he drove out of the parking lot. Hack had made the situation sound urgent, and if Rex Lansen was chasing burglars and waving a gun around, it was. Rhodes roared across the overpass, past the community college building, and up a low hill before turning off the highway. He turned off the siren and flashers. He wouldn't need them on the county road. It was likely to be deserted at that time of the evening, or just about anytime, for that matter, and Rhodes didn't want to alert Seepy that there was something going on.

As he neared Seepy's house, however, he saw that his precautions weren't necessary. Headlights came on in Seepy's driveway, and Seepy's car pulled out into the road and headed in the direction of the Lansens' place. Amateur interference. Just what Rhodes didn't need, but he was going to get it anyway.

Seepy pulled into the unpaved driveway at the Lansens' house, and Rhodes was right behind him. Seepy got out of his red Ford Escape that Rhodes knew he'd bought just recently, followed by a very large dog.

Rhodes knew the dog. It was a leopard dog, or at least partly, and its name was Bruce. Rhodes was the one who'd arranged for Bruce to live with Seepy, having more or less rescued Bruce from a couple of cousins who didn't treat the dog well. While Seepy sometimes complained about the cost of keeping Bruce fed, it was clear that he'd bonded with the dog.

Seepy, with Bruce at his heels looking more like a small calf than a dog, walked over to greet Rhodes as he got out of the car.

"What are you doing here?" Rhodes asked.

"That doesn't sound very friendly," Seepy said.

Bruce didn't say anything. He just sat back on his haunches and looked at Rhodes.

"There's been a burglary reported here," Rhodes said. "It could be dangerous. You shouldn't get involved."

"Rex called me and asked me to bring Bruce over," Seepy said. "He thought maybe Bruce could hunt down the burglars."

Rhodes thought that was a terrible idea, but before he could tell Seepy that, Rex Lansen came around from the back of his house. He had a flashlight in one hand and a pistol in the other. He was a short, squat man with broad shoulders and bowed legs, and he was clearly upset.

" 'Bout time you got here, Sheriff," he said. "I was just about to go after 'em myself, with the help of Dr. Benton and his dog."

"They might be more heavily armed than you are," Rhodes said.

"It's just some damn kids," Rex said. "Me and Kathy came back from the Walmart and saw them run out the back door. Little turds had kicked it in. Gonna have to buy a new door now, plus replace whatever they broke. No telling what all they took. Got Kathy's jewelry, for sure."

"How many were there?" Rhodes asked.

"Looked like four of 'em."

Rhodes looked around. He didn't see a car. "How did they get here?"

"I don't know. All I know is that they ran like racehorses when I drove up. Let's go get 'em."

"Not a good idea," Rhodes said. "I'll wait for my backup. When he gets here, we'll look for them."

"Backup? Are you afraid of 'em? I told you they were just kids."

"If a kid shoots you, you're just as dead as if an old person does it," Rhodes said. "Where did they go?"

"Off across my back pasture. Nothing back there but trees and weeds. They're probably hiding in the trees. We could get 'em easy." Rex looked up at the sky. "Nice full moon coming up, so we won't hardly even need a flashlight."

"Best you go back in the house and wait," Rhodes told him. "The deputy and I will handle it when he gets here."

Rex drew himself up to his full height, which still put the top of his head at about Rhodes's chin. "This is my property. You can't tell me what to do."

"Sure he can," Seepy said. "I took the course at the sheriff's academy for citizens of the county. If you mess with him, he can arrest you for interfering with an officer performing his duties. Right, Sheriff?"

Rhodes wished Seepy had kept his mouth shut, but he said, "That's right. Better go on in and let me take care of this."

Rex gave Seepy a venomous look. "What about *him*?"

"He's going home," Rhodes said. "And his little dog, too."

"You have me blocked in the driveway," Seepy said, "and you might need Bruce."

"Bruce?" Rex said.

"It's a good name for a dog," Rhodes said. He thought about mentioning that Rex was also a good name for a dog, but he was sure that wouldn't help matters. "You go on in the house and start making a list of what was stolen."

Rex turned and stomped away. He didn't get far before his wife came out into the yard. She was shorter than Rex and just about as wide. It sounded to Rhodes as if she were crying.

"What is it?" Rex said.

"They got Papa's ashes."

"Damn," Rex said. He turned to Rhodes. "We had Kathy's daddy's ashes in a little urn in the bedroom right by the jewelry box. It was a pretty little metal thing. They must've thought it was valuable."

"We'll get it back," Rhodes said.

"What about Papa's ashes?" Kathy said.

"Them, too."

"They might dump them out."

"Don't worry," Rhodes said. "We'll get them back safe and sound."

"You better," Rex said. He put his arms around his wife's shoulders. "Let's us go on in and see what all else they got."

Rhodes watched until they were inside, then asked Seepy,

"Have there been any other incidents around here lately, strangers around, anything like that?"

"Not that I know about," Benton said. "If any strangers come around my house, Bruce takes care of them. Right, Bruce?"

Bruce remained silent. He was a much better behaved dog than he had been when Rhodes first encountered him. As hard as it might be to believe, Seepy was a good influence on him.

"The Lansens need a dog," Seepy said. "Or two."

"They sure do," Rhodes said. "I'll suggest it. Meanwhile, you and Bruce can go on home. Rex won't mind if you drive on his yard."

Seepy started for his car. Bruce gave Rhodes another brief glance and went after him. Rhodes looked down the road and saw the light bar flashing on a county car. Andy was about to arrive. Seepy must have seen the lights, too. He got out of his car, leaving Bruce inside.

"I don't want to get run over," Seepy called to Rhodes.

Rhodes sighed. Andy turned into the drive and parked behind the Tahoe.

"What's going on, Sheriff?" Andy said when he got out of the car. "Hey, Seepy."

"Hey, Andy," Seep said.

"There's been a break-in," Rhodes said. "Teenagers, probably. Four of them. They ran off through the back pasture."

"You think this is connected to those burglaries in the southeast part of the county?"

"We didn't see any teenagers on the video."

"Copycats," Andy said. "They heard about those burglaries and decided to try one of their own."

"Maybe," Rhodes said.

"They still out there somewhere?"

"Unless they had a car they could get to, or maybe some ATVs. I haven't heard anything start up, though."

"We going after them?"

Andy was always ready for action, maybe a little too ready. He wasn't quite as eager as Buddy, though, and Buddy had been around for a while. Andy would be just fine.

"We'll take a look, see what we can see."

"Seepy going with us?"

"He's going home," Rhodes said. "Right, Seepy?"

"Right," Seepy said, not sounding any too happy about it.

He got in his car but didn't close the door. He turned and looked back at Rhodes. "You want to take Bruce? He might be able to sniff out the culprits."

"You take Bruce with you. I'm not sure he likes me enough to help out."

"I could go, too."

"Home is where you're going," Rhodes said.

"Right."

Seepy pulled the door closed, started the car, and backed out into the yard. He turned the car around and drove away, waving as he passed Rhodes.

"You didn't wave back," Andy said.

"I was preoccupied," Rhodes said. "Let's get our flashlights and take a walk down through the pasture to see what we can find."

"Wild hogs, most likely."

"I sure do hope not," Rhodes said.

Chapter 8

▼

The moon was rising higher, and it was bright enough to throw shadows on the pasture as Rhodes and Andy walked through the weeds that swished against their pants legs. They didn't need the flashlights.

"Hunter's moon," Andy said. "Or close to it. I don't think whoever named it that had hunting burglars in mind, though."

The night air was turning cool, and Rhodes wished he'd brought a jacket.

"Better burglars than hogs," he said.

"You think they'll be armed?"

"The hogs?"

Andy laughed. "The burglars."

Rhodes had mentioned the possibility to Rex, but he didn't think it was likely, not if the burglars really were kids, as Rex had said. It was always better not to take a chance, however. In Texas even the kids were sometimes armed.

"They might be," he said. "We'd better be ready for them in case they are."

Andy drew his service weapon, a .38 revolver. Rhodes stopped walking, bent down, and got his Kel-Tec from its ankle holster. He'd taken a lot of heat for the ankle holster, but as the sheriff he had a lot of contact with citizens who might be spooked if he carried a handgun openly. Even in Texas there were a few people like that around. Not many, but a few, and Rhodes didn't want to scare them when he was talking to them about a case. The little pistol held seven 9 mm bullets, which Rhodes considered adequate for any situation he was likely to encounter. The only problem was getting to the pistol. He wouldn't have had to throw a loaf of bread at Rayford Loomis if he'd had the pistol in a handier spot.

As they approached the trees that marked the end of the pasture, Rhodes put a finger to his lips, and Andy nodded. Rhodes didn't know if the burglars were somewhere in the trees or if they were still running, but the best approach was to assume that they might be lurking nearby.

It wasn't easy for Rhodes and Andy to walk quietly once they entered the trees. Sticks and leaves lay all around, and Rhodes worried that any minute some feral hogs would break from cover and trample him. He'd had too much experience with the hogs to doubt the possibility. It was much darker among the trees than it had been in the pasture, but Rhodes didn't want to turn on the flashlights and warn the burglars they were coming.

After about five minutes of walking, Rhodes heard something ahead. He stopped and held up a hand. Andy didn't ask why. Both stood quietly, listening. Rhodes could make out talking, and he moved forward as quietly as he could. He stopped again when the voices became clear, and Andy stopped beside him.

"It's drugs, that's what it is," someone said.

"Meth?" another voice asked.

"Maybe. Could be coke."

"I didn't know old people snorted that stuff," said a third voice.

Andy nudged Rhodes in the ribs with an elbow. Rhodes held up a hand and shook his head.

"Let's try it and see."

"What if they come after us?"

Someone laughed. "They're too old to come after us."

Someone didn't know Rex Lansen very well, Rhodes thought.

"I'll try it," the first voice said. "Hand it here."

Leaves rustled, and then Rhodes heard a couple of loud sniffs, followed immediately by a hacking and coughing fit.

"Come on," he said to Andy, and he walked toward the coughing. Within twenty yards he came upon four young men sitting near a big tree trunk. One of them was struggling to recover from the coughing fit while a second pounded him on the back. They didn't notice Rhodes, but the other two did. They jumped up and started to run, darting among the tree trunks as agilely as squirrels.

"Go, Andy," Rhodes said, and the deputy started after them while Rhodes watched the others.

"Having a problem?" Rhodes asked.

"Drugs got him," the one who wasn't coughing said. "Call an ambulance."

Rhodes saw a fancy metal urn lying on the ground beside what must have been Kathy Lansen's jewelry box.

"It's not drugs," Rhodes said, worrying about his promise to bring back the ashes. "He'll be all right."

"He's dying!"

"He's not dying." Rhodes gestured with his pistol. "You stand up and put your hands on your head."

The boy did as he was told, settling his hands on the fedora that sat squarely atop his head, but he wasn't happy about it. Maybe he was afraid he'd crush the hat. He was a skinny youngster who had a scraggly goatee and wore jeans and a T-shirt that said HATERS GONNA HATE on the front. The fedora reminded Rhodes of the one that Seepy Benton wore occasionally, but Benton had been wearing his for years, long before the current bunch of hipsters had appeared.

"Noah's gonna die and it's all your fault," the boy said.

"I'm not the one who snorted ashes," Rhodes said, looking at Noah, whose coughing had eased a bit. "You better stand up now, too, Noah. Hands on your head."

Noah stood up. He was a bit shorter and heavier than his friend, and he didn't have a fedora or a goatee. He did have on jeans and a black T-shirt, but his shirt was devoid of slogans.

"I need to wipe my nose," he said.

"Go ahead," Rhodes told him. "One hand only."

Noah wiped his nose. He didn't look more than fifteen, but that didn't mean much. As he got older, Rhodes had more and more trouble guessing people's ages.

Rhodes touched the badge holder on his belt with his left hand. "I'm Dan Rhodes, the sheriff of this county. What's your last name, Noah?"

Noah sneezed.

"It's Noah Newsome," the other boy said, helping him out. "I'm Todd Rankin. What did you mean about snorting ashes?"

Rhodes pointed with the pistol. "You see that urn there?"

"What's an urn?"

Rhodes wondered if English teachers still gave vocabulary tests. "It's a kind of vase, usually one used to keep ashes in."

"Why would anybody want to keep ashes?"

At least Todd was curious. Maybe that was a good sign.

"They're the ashes of a cremated relative," Rhodes said. "In this case the ashes of Mrs. Lansen's father."

Todd looked at Noah, who was sniffling, his eyes wide.

"Dude!" Todd said. "You sniffed some dead guy."

Noah started to cough again. After a couple of heaves, he turned aside, bent over, and vomited. Todd jumped away from him.

"Don't go anywhere," Rhodes said. "He'll be fine. Ashes aren't poison."

"Yeah, but a dead person up your nose . . ."

Andy came walking back through the trees, alone.

"What happened?" Rhodes asked.

"They got away," Andy said. "I got my feet tangled up in some kind of vine and tripped. By the time I got untangled, they were long gone."

Todd smirked.

"That's okay," Rhodes said. "Todd can tell us who they were."

"I'm not a snitch," Todd said, seemingly forgetting that he'd already told Rhodes Noah's last name.

"You will be when the sheriff gets you in the back room," Andy said. He looked at Noah. "What's his problem?"

"Snorted ashes," Rhodes said.

"Like Keith Richards?"

"Except these weren't Noah's own father's ashes," Rhodes said.

"Who's Keith Richards?" Todd asked. "What back room?"

"Maybe I should just shoot him," Andy said.

"Wouldn't be right," Rhodes said, "but don't tell him who Keith Richards is."

Noah straightened up again, wiping his mouth with the back of his hand. He didn't look well.

Todd looked at Andy, who smiled. It wasn't a pleasant smile.

"Names?" Andy asked.

"Bryan Stout and Nic Chambers," Todd said without hesitation.

"We can pick them up later," Rhodes said. "Right now we'll take these two to jail."

"Jail?" Todd said.

"Graybar Hotel," Andy said. "The Slammer. The Big House."

"What's he talking about?" Todd said, looking at Rhodes.

"Your education is sadly lacking," Andy said. "You'll have plenty of time to study in jail. Maybe you'll even find out who Keith Richards is. Put your hands behind your back."

"What? Why?"

"Handcuffs," Andy said.

"Handcuffs?"

"That's right. Handcuffs. Hands behind your back."

Todd complied, looking distraught. Andy stepped behind him, holstered his .38, and secured Todd's hands with zip-tie cuffs.

"Your turn," Andy told Noah.

Noah didn't speak. He just lowered his hands and put them behind his back.

When both boys had been cuffed, Rhodes said, "Better pat them down, Andy."

"Right. They might be carrying sidearms or switchblades."

They weren't carrying anything, however, and Andy looked a little disappointed when he reported it.

Rhodes pointed at the ground and said, "I see a jewelry box and an urn. What else did you two take from the house?"

"That's all we had time to grab," Todd said. "Those old people came back and we just ran."

"Good," Rhodes said.

Andy picked up the urn and looked inside.

"Any ashes left?" Rhodes asked.

"Looks like most of 'em," Andy said. "I doubt Ms. Lansen will know the difference." He picked up the lid and replaced it. Then he got the jewelry box. "Unless somebody squeals."

"We won't say anything," Todd said. "Right, Noah?"

Noah nodded.

"If you took anything else and those other two ran off with it, we'll find out," Rhodes said.

"I swear that's all we got," Todd said.

"I hope so," Rhodes said. "Let's go."

He and Andy marched Todd and Noah out of the trees and back to the Lansen house. Todd and Noah walked awkwardly because it was hard for them to balance with their hands behind them. Rhodes didn't feel too sorry for them, however.

Rex Lansen was waiting in the backyard when they arrived. He took the urn and the jewelry box from Rhodes and thanked him.

"Kathy'll be glad to get these ashes," Rex said. He stared at Todd and Noah, who looked away. "What about the others?"

"We'll get them," Rhodes said. "We know who they are."

"Good. I appreciate you getting these ashes back. Kathy would've grieved forever about 'em if you hadn't."

Rhodes didn't mention that not quite all the ashes were there. Nobody else said anything, either. Rex went back into the house, and Rhodes put his hand on Todd's upper arm.

"I'll take this one in my car," Rhodes told Andy. "You get the other one."

"He doesn't smell too good," Andy said.

"I know," Rhodes said. "That's why I'm taking this one."

Both boys looked quite unhappy, and Rhodes thought Todd might cry as he put him in the back of the Tahoe, first removing his hat. What the boys didn't know yet was that they wouldn't be spending any time in jail. Andy had been exaggerating for effect, hoping to give the boys a little scare. They'd be taken to the juvenile processing office, which was in the jail, all right, but which was really just a room for temporary detention. Not exactly a four-star hotel, but not nearly as bad as a cell.

Since they'd already admitted what they'd done and named their partners in crime, Rhodes didn't even have to interview them. They'd go to the jail and wait in the processing office until their parents showed up. Rhodes would release them into their parents' custody, and they might not even face charges if Rex felt lenient. Or even if he didn't. They were juveniles, and as far as Rhodes knew the burglary was a first offense. Still, going to the jail would be good for them. It wouldn't hurt them to be a little bit scared for a while.

Rhodes hadn't taken Todd in the Tahoe just because Noah smelled bad. Todd had been talkative, and Rhodes wanted to talk to him about the burglaries at Billy Bacon's place. It didn't seem likely that Todd and his friends were responsible. Neither Todd nor Noah was big enough to have been the person on the video. It could have been one of their friends, however, either Bryan Stout or Nic Chambers.

"What's your father's name, Todd?" Rhodes asked.

Todd was sunk back in the rear seat, his voice so weak that Rhodes could barely hear him.

"Ross," Todd said. "Ross Rankin."

Rhodes knew who Ross was. He had an air-conditioning business that was quite successful. It was hard not to make money with an air-conditioning business in Texas.

"What about Noah's father?" Rhodes asked.

"He's just Mr. Newsome. I don't know his name. He's a bookkeeper or something like that at the hospital. Are you going to call my parents?"

"Have to," Rhodes said. "It's the law."

"Damn," Todd said.

"No bad language," Rhodes told him.

Todd didn't respond.

"What about your friends? Bryan and Nic."

"They're not my friends. They're Noah's friends. I barely know them." Todd paused. "It was all their idea. Noah and I just went along with them. It's not fair that they got away."

Rhodes figured this was just a bit of passing the blame, which was only to be expected. Everybody did it.

"They got away from you," Todd said. "It's not fair."

Rhodes didn't feel like getting into a discussion about the fairness of life. He was more interested in transportation.

"Did they have a car?" he asked.

"Yeah. We parked it around the curve past the Lansens' house. We came in through the woods."

So they'd gotten back to the car. They'd be home by now, hoping that Todd and Noah wouldn't give them away but knowing better.

"They didn't get away," Rhodes said. "We'll round them up. Are they older than you?"

"Yeah. They're both sixteen."

More juveniles. Rhodes didn't think any of them would have been capable of stealing a welding rig, much less disposing of it.

"What else have they talked you into?" he asked.

"Nothing," Todd said.

Rhodes didn't believe him. "Seems like you're familiar with drugs."

"That was Noah who sniffed the ashes, not me. I don't know anything about drugs."

"Right. And you're not a thief, either."

"I'm not. I never did anything like this before, and neither did Noah. We should never have listened to Bryan. He's really the one who got us into it. He said it would be easy and we could get some money."

"To buy drugs with?"

Todd didn't say anything for a while, so Rhodes just waited.

"Marijuana's not a drug," Todd said after a while. "It's like a medicine."

"Your state legislature wouldn't agree."

"They're old. They don't know anything."

Todd and Noah hadn't had any drugs on them, so Rhodes didn't think they were too experienced with marijuana. They certainly weren't experienced with meth or cocaine. Or ashes.

At the jail Rhodes took Todd and Noah to the room that served as the juvenile processing center, which was just like the other two interview rooms. It held an old wooden table that had a scarred top and a couple of folding chairs. The walls were painted a bilious green and had gray and brown stains of undetermined origin on them. It wasn't a pleasant place, but then it wasn't supposed to be.

Rhodes got the name of the parents of Bryan and Nic, and Andy stayed with the boys while Rhodes called the parents of all four of them and told the parents of Nic and Bryan to bring in their sons.

It took more than an hour to get everything sorted out. The parents were unhappy; the boys were even more unhappy. Rhodes wasn't exactly Mr. Jolly himself. The parents raised their voices, made threats, withdrew the threats, and apologized. Finally everyone calmed down and matters were settled, at least for the time being, and Rhodes released the boys into the custody of their parents. When they'd gone, Rhodes told Hack that he was going home.

"Might make it in time to watch the news," Hack said. "If you rush."

"I'll rush," Rhodes said.

When he got home, Rhodes and Ivy sat at the kitchen table while he ate the warmed-up chile relleno and told her what had happened at the Lansen place. Yancey, a little puffball Pomeranian, bounced around his ankles, yipping. The cats, Sam and Jerry, lay in their usual spots by the refrigerator, not in the least bothered by Yancey, whom they were experienced at ignoring, especially when they were asleep, as they were now and most of the rest of the time as well.

"It's too late to go outside and play," Rhodes told Yancey. "Go to bed."

Yancey continued to yip halfheartedly for a few seconds, then gave up and slunk off to his doggy bed in the spare bedroom.

"It's about time for us to go to bed, too, I guess," Rhodes said when he'd finished telling Ivy about events of the evening and tossed the paper plate the chile relleno had been on.

"I still can't believe that boy snorted the ashes," Ivy said, pushing back her chair and standing up.

"He didn't know what he was doing," Rhodes said. "I'm sure he regrets it."

"Meanwhile you have a murder to solve."

"That's true, but I have to deal with a lot of other things at the same time. The county needs to raise my salary." He stood up. "I'm going to take a shower."

"I was planning to take one, too," Ivy said. "Should we try to conserve water?"

Rhodes grinned. "We'd be fools not to," he said.

Chapter 9

▼

The next morning Rhodes was up early and didn't even take time for his usual romp in the backyard with Yancey and Speedo, the border collie who lived out back in a Styrofoam igloo.

"They're going to be upset," Ivy said. "They expect you to play with them."

Yancey was already standing at the back door, waiting to go outside. He hadn't started yipping yet, but it was only a matter of time.

"You'll have to take my place today," Rhodes told Ivy. "I have other dogs to see to."

"I hope Yancey didn't hear that," Ivy said. "It's bad enough that you aren't going to play with him. You should eat something before you go. Breakfast is the most important meal of the day."

"I think they've proved that's a myth," Rhodes said.

A couple of pieces of toast popped up in the toaster on the kitchen counter. Rhodes grabbed them and buttered them with some kind of artificial butter that Ivy favored over the real thing.

It was supposed to be heart healthy, but Rhodes didn't trust it. It was, however, better than nothing.

"I'll take this toast with me," he said, and he left the kitchen munching on a slice. Behind him, Yancey started to yip.

"Don't forget to feed him and Speedo," Rhodes said as he made his escape.

Gus-Gus and Jackie acted quite excited when Rhodes showed up to feed them. As soon as he got out of the Tahoe, he heard them barking from inside the barn. He got the bag of dog food from the house and took it to the barn. The dogs were, if anything, noisier than before. They were scratching at the door and throwing themselves against it. If he hadn't seen them eat the previous afternoon, Rhodes would have thought they were starving. As it was, he just thought they were crazy.

He set the dog food down and thought about how he was going to go about opening the barn door. He didn't want to let the dogs outside because he was afraid he wouldn't be able to get them back into the barn, so he had to be careful, especially as they were growing more and more agitated. They jumped against the door, and their barking was continuous.

Rhodes opened the door so that only a sliver of space showed between the edge of it and the wall. It was enough. The dogs both hit the door at once, hard, jerking it out of Rhodes's hand. He stumbled backward, trying to catch his balance, but the dogs hit him at the run and knocked him down. He fell against the food bag, expecting them to maul him as they ripped it open, but they weren't interested in him or the food. They ran right over him as if they didn't even know he was there.

Rhodes pushed himself away from the food bag and stood up,

thinking of a line from a Sherlock Holmes movie he'd seen on television long ago, something about the footprints of a gigantic hound. Now Rhodes had one right in the middle of his chest.

The dogs turned the corner of the barn, and Rhodes went after them. They were headed for the woods in full cry, and if they got into the trees he might never catch them, not that there was much hope of catching them even if they didn't. Rhodes didn't think of himself as a runner, and even if he had been, he wouldn't have been able to catch up to the dogs if they didn't want him to. Dogs were just naturally faster than humans, and they didn't seem to have nearly as much trouble running over rough ground and through the weeds.

After about a hundred yards, Rhodes slowed down and began to walk. He thought he might as well go back to the house and see if there was anything there that would help him in finding out who killed Melvin. The dogs would come back by themselves when they got hungry, or he'd come back and see about finding them later.

He'd taken only a few steps back toward the house when something else occurred to him. The dogs knew him, so his presence wouldn't have stirred them up. They might have been hungry, but they ignored the food bag. Something else had gotten them excited. Or someone else, someone who might have been there when Rhodes arrived, someone who had come to look around the house, too. Rhodes had showed up, and whoever it was had left quickly and gone through the woods. That's what had upset the dogs. That's who they were after.

Or not. Maybe they were just having fun, but Rhodes didn't think so. He turned around again and started to run. The dogs were well into the woods when Rhodes got there, but he could hear them barking. They didn't seem to be moving, so he thought he could catch up to them.

When he did, he found them standing on the bank of Crockett's Creek, still barking, although there was nothing to bark at except for the trees along the bank, a stump sticking up out of the dark water, and a turtle sunning himself on the stump. A smell of mud and dampness came up from the creek.

Considering the rain they'd had earlier in the year, the creek was flowing up near the top of the bank. It hadn't been that full for a long time, and it was good to see it that way. Rhodes watched the turtle. He liked turtles and tortoises. The turtle was still as a stone for a minute. Then it slipped off the stump into the water with no sound at all and hardly a ripple. The dogs continued to bark.

"What's the problem?" Rhodes asked the dogs, who, while they didn't have an answer for him, at least stopped barking. They turned and gave him quizzical looks, as if he might tell them what or whom they'd been chasing because it had slipped their minds.

"I don't know who it was," Rhodes said, but he thought he knew what had stopped them in their pursuit. Whoever they'd been chasing had gone into the water, and they'd lost the scent.

"You two go on back home," Rhodes said. "I'll look around and see if I can figure out what's going on here."

That comment got pretty much the reaction Rhodes had expected. Gus-Gus and Jackie looked at him, panting a little, their tongues lolled out. They didn't make any move toward going home. Rhodes wondered if he could stare them down and intimidate them into bending to his will. He didn't think it was likely.

"All right," he said. "I'm going to take a look around. You can come with me."

He looked along the edge of the creek bank, and a little farther along he saw deep impressions in the mud leading to the water. He didn't want to get into the water himself to see if the person of interest to the dogs had come out on the other side, if he'd even crossed. The tracks could be a trick.

The creek was about twenty yards wide from bank to bank, so he couldn't jump it. Even if it had been twenty feet, he couldn't have jumped it. Twenty inches maybe would've been possible. As it was, Rhodes would have to look for a place to cross or forget it and hope the person had come back out on this side, or stayed on it.

Rhodes walked along, with the dogs trotting behind him, to the side of him, and occasionally out in front of him, snuffling and sniffing at every tree and mound of dirt. Soon Rhodes came to a place he recognized. It didn't have an official name, but when he'd been a kid everyone had called it the Deep Hole. It wasn't really very deep, but it was deeper than the rest of the creek, and it had been a good place to fish. Rhodes remembered that once when he was four or five, not long before the family had moved to town, his father and several other men had decided to seine the hole.

Rhodes hadn't been allowed in the water, but he'd been allowed to stand on the bank and watch. The men came up with some fine big bass and catfish in the seine, and there had been a fish fry that night for everybody within a radius of several miles. The men put mealed filets of fish into wire-mesh baskets, tossed in some hush puppies, and lowered the baskets into big black pots of boiling oil. They brought the filets and hush puppies out hot and crisp, and Rhodes could still remember the taste. He'd never eaten any better fish than that, or better hush puppies, either.

But what he remembered even more than the food was that one of the fish in the seine had been a grinnell, a long, odd-looking fish, almost prehistoric in appearance. Rhodes had never seen one before, and he'd never seen one since, but he sure remembered that one. The men tossed it back into the water. They said it wasn't an "eating fish."

Rhodes remembered something else, too, a water moccasin. Rhodes didn't like snakes any more than Indiana Jones did, and he especially didn't like water moccasins. He didn't like their thick black bodies, their flat, triangular heads, or the whiteness inside their mouths. This particular snake had become tangled in the seine, and nobody wanted to touch it to get it out. Rhodes didn't blame them, then or now.

Finally, after some discussion, Rhodes's father had said he'd take care of it, and he'd calmly grasped it behind the head and patiently unraveled it. When it was free of the seine, he'd grabbed its thrashing tail and swung it around his head like a bullwhip before giving it a final pop that separated its head from its body and sent the head flying toward a couple of the men, who scrambled and yelled and splashed to get out of the way. One of them fell face first into the creek, which gave everyone a good laugh. Rhodes still considered it one of the most amazing things he'd ever seen anyone do.

Gus-Gus and Jackie barked and brought Rhodes back to the present. He was reminiscing a lot more than usual lately and wondered whether it was the surroundings he found himself in or if he was getting old. He looked around for the dogs and found that they'd run ahead of him and were eating something they'd found at the base of a tree. It might have been better not to wonder what it was, but Rhodes was curious. However, by the time he got to the dogs, they'd consumed whatever it was and hadn't left a trace that he could see.

For all he knew they might have found the remains of a dead

squirrel or just some interesting dirt. You never could tell with dogs.

Rhodes looked around. A dead tree had fallen over across the creek, and while it would've been tricky for someone to walk across the creek on the trunk and onto the bank by hanging onto the dead branches, it would have been possible. It might even have been simple for someone with good coordination and balance. Rhodes wouldn't have wanted to try it himself, but he thought he could do it if he had to. Rhodes didn't see any tracks anywhere around, but that didn't mean a thing.

Rhodes called the dogs over. They no longer seemed interested in tracking anybody, and although they sniffed around the uprooted tree for a few seconds, they didn't strike a scent. Or if they did, they didn't care.

A squirrel chittered up in a tree, and some leaves drifted down, turning slowly as they fell. This distracted the dogs. They ran over to bark at the leaves and the squirrel, and Rhodes looked around for signs that someone had walked around the uprooted tree. Maybe if he'd been Kit Carson or Daniel Boone, he could have spotted something significant, a broken twig or a crushed leaf, but he wasn't a frontiersman or a tracker, and he didn't find a thing.

He walked along the bank staring at the ground. The dogs gave up on the squirrel and ranged well ahead of him, not caring where they went. Rhodes kept hoping that he'd find a sign of some kind. A considerate person would have left a clue or two, he thought, but the people Rhodes dealt with were rarely considerate. He was about to give up and turn back on his search when the dogs began to bark. He saw them turn away from the creek and run through the trees, so he followed them.

He walked up a slight incline, and before he reached the top he saw the back of a house among the trees. Behind the house and a little to the left of it was a big barn that looked newer than the house.

The dogs ran ahead of Rhodes and around to the front of the house. They didn't bark. Rhodes watched them disappear, then stopped and thought about where he was. The house must belong to Gene Gunnison, and Rhodes wondered if Gunnison had been the one who'd run away from the Hunt place. He figured he might as well see if Gunnison was home and ask him.

When he got to the back of the house, Rhodes gave it a quick inspection. It sat up on concrete blocks and hadn't been painted in years, but it looked solid. The grass and weeds could have used a good trim, but the tin roof had only a few rust spots and probably didn't leak.

Rhodes walked on around to the front of the house, intending to knock on the door, but he saw that he wouldn't need to. Someone, undoubtedly Gene Gunnison, sat on the front porch in an old wooden rocking chair. He was a big man, and he filled the chair with no room left over. His thick gray hair hung over his ears and down his neck. Rhodes suspected there wasn't a thin spot in back.

Gunnison's left foot was encased in a black fabric walking boot and rested on a overturned galvanized bucket. A black-lacquered walking cane hung from one arm of his chair. Gus-Gus and Jackie stood in front of the porch looking at him.

Rhodes remembered that like Billy Bacon, Gunnison had once played football for the Clearview Catamounts. In fact, he'd played about the same time Billy had, but Gunnison had been a lineman, offense or defense, Rhodes couldn't remember which. Maybe he'd played both ways. High schoolers still did that in those days.

"I know these dogs," Gunnison said in a bass rumble when Rhodes approached the porch. "They ain't yours."

"That's right," Rhodes said. "They belong to the Hunts. I'm looking after them today."

"You're a long way from the Hunts' place."

"Getting some exercise. You must be Gene Gunnison."

"That's me, all right. Who the hell are you?"

Rhodes touched the badge on its belt holder. "Sheriff Dan Rhodes."

"Huh. What're you sneaking around my property for, then, lawman?"

"I wouldn't say I was sneaking. These dogs chased somebody away from the Hunt place, and I followed them to see if I could find out who it was. This is where we wound up."

"Wasn't me they were chasing." Gunnison took the cane from the chair arm and gave the walking boot a light tap on the toe. "I got a pretty bad ankle sprain. Can't get around very well."

"I can see that. What happened?"

"Stepped in a hole. You gotta watch where you're going around here, and I didn't. Got distracted."

"Anybody else been around here today?"

"Not a soul. People don't come around here much. I ain't exactly what you'd call neighborly. What's Hunt done that he's got you looking after his dogs for him?"

"He's dead," Rhodes said.

"Dead?" Gunnison didn't sound surprised or regretful, just curious. "How'd that happen?"

"Somebody killed him."

Gunnison hung the cane back on the arm of the chair. "Too bad."

"I heard you and Hunt didn't get along," Rhodes said.

"We had a little bit of a disagreement once upon a time," Gunnison said. "Stuff happens. Don't mean I killed him."

"What did you fall out about?"

"I think that's my business, mine and Hunt's, and since he ain't going to be talking about it, neither am I. Wouldn't do any good now, and I don't like to speak bad of a dead man. I hope you ain't accusing me of killing him."

"I'm not accusing you of anything. We're just talking."

Gunnison snorted. "Ha. Just talking. That's a good one. A lawman doesn't ever just talk, and like I said, I'm not very neighborly. I don't have a lot of little talks with anybody. I didn't kill anybody, either. I'm laid up with this bum foot, so I ain't been away from the house for a while. I'm not up to walking very far, much less killing anybody."

"You know Billy Bacon?" Rhodes asked.

"Sure. Used to play football on the Catamounts, same as me, and has a place down here. I can't say as he drops around for little talks like you do, though."

"He's had some things stolen," Rhodes said. "So has Hunt. Lots of other people, too. Anything turned up missing around here?"

"Nothing missing that I know of. I don't have anything worth taking. You think I've been stealing from Bacon and Hunt?"

"Somebody has."

"Not me. Don't know a thing about it. Don't care. No skin off my butt if somebody's taking their stuff. I'll take care of mine, and they can take care of theirs. I mind my own business."

Gus-Gus and Jackie walked over to Gunnison's dirt driveway and sniffed around at the back of his pickup. One of them started to bark. There was a jon boat in the pickup bed.

"Some nasty oil spots around that truck," Gunnison said. "Those dogs get that oil on 'em, it'll be hard to clean it off."

Rhodes wasn't too worried about the dogs getting oil on them.

They were jumping around the pickup and might scratch it, but Rhodes wasn't worried about that, either.

"I notice you don't have a dog," he said.

"Don't need one," Gunnison said. "I'm not worried about anybody sneaking up on me, and like I said, I don't have anything worth taking. You better watch those dogs of Hunt's, though."

"They won't get any oil on them," Rhodes said. "I'll take them back home now."

"Best way to go is just follow my driveway to the road. Shorter that way, and you won't have to go through any trees."

"Thanks," Rhodes said.

He walked over to the driveway and told the dogs to come along. They barked a bit more and ignored him.

"You like to fish?" Rhodes asked Gunnison, indicating the jon boat.

"Now and then when I have the time. There's good fish in the creek sometimes when it's high like it is now. You?"

"When I have the time," Rhodes said. He called the dogs, and this time they paid attention, running to him and following him down the long, sandy driveway through the trees to the road.

Chapter 10

▼

The road, such as it was, was even sandier than the driveway. The bar ditches were lined with weeds and vines, so there was nothing for Rhodes to do but walk in the sandy ruts. Sand got in his shoes and covered the bottoms of his pants. The sun was warming things up, and Rhodes hoped the top of his head wouldn't blister at the thin spot.

Gus-Gus and Jackie didn't mind the sun or the sand, nor did they stay in the ruts. They romped along the road and through the ditches, and when they scared up an armadillo, they took off across a pasture in full cry. Armadillos were surprisingly fast, and Rhodes didn't think they could catch it unless it got tired and stopped running before they gave up. Even if they caught it, they couldn't do much with it if it balled up and presented its armor to them. He just hoped they'd come back to the road after they'd had their fun.

No cars came from either direction as Rhodes trudged along the road, and he was glad of that. A car or truck would have stirred up the sand, and it would have blown all over Rhodes. He was dusty enough as it was.

He wondered about Gunnison. No watchdog, no worries about being burglarized. It seemed odd, but then people who lived alone in the country were sometimes odd. So were people who lived in town and didn't live alone. Everybody was a little eccentric. It didn't have to mean anything.

After a few minutes Gus-Gus and Jackie came running back. They didn't appear to be a bit tired from their armadillo chase, and they kept right on with their explorations of the ruts and the ditches.

In a few more minutes they came in sight of the Hunts' house. Rhodes felt as if he'd wasted a lot of the morning already, but he still wanted to take a look around the house and barn. If he found something that had been taken from Billy Bacon's barn, then he'd at least feel that he'd accomplished something. If he didn't find anything, that would be useful information, too.

Rhodes saw a pickup parked in front of the house, which was turning into quite a popular spot for visitors that morning. When Rhodes got to the house, Will Smalls, Joyce's brother-in-law, came out the front door and stood on the porch.

"I saw the county Tahoe, Sheriff," Will said. "I was wondering where you'd gone off to."

True to his family name, Will wasn't a large man. He was a good five or six inches shorter than Rhodes, although the sweat-stained straw hat he wore just about made up the difference. He had on a pair of little rimless glasses that hid his eyes under the brim of the hat. At his hip he wore a pistol in a black leather holster.

Rhodes didn't know what every lawman in the state thought about the new open-carry law, but those he did know weren't in favor of it. There had been only one incident in Blacklin County so far, when a man thought that he was being carjacked in the Walmart parking lot by another man who'd simply gotten mixed up about which black Ford pickup was his. Both men had fired shots, but neither had hit his target or anyone else, although a Buick got its back window blown out before the two men had settled down and figured things out with the help of Ruth Grady, who'd arrived on the scene in time to prevent any further damage.

"I've been for a little walk," Rhodes said. He didn't want to mention the prowler, at least not yet. "Giving Gus-Gus and Jackie some exercise."

"I'd think they get plenty of that by themselves."

As if to show he was right about that, Gus-Gus and Jackie sat down and started scratching behind their ears with their back legs.

"They might get plenty of exercise scratching for fleas," Rhodes said. "Anything's possible. But they've been cooped up in the barn all night. They needed an outing. So here we are."

"Well, I'll take over for you now," Will said, coming off the porch. "Joyce told me you were going to feed the boys here, and she felt like she was imposing on you. She asked me to come do it, so here I am."

"They're all yours," Rhodes said. "The food bag's out by the barn."

"I saw it when I was looking for you. I'll feed them, and you can go on back to town."

"I'm going to have a look around first," Rhodes said.

"Well, now, about that," Will said.

He took off his glasses and examined the lenses as if there might be dirt on them. He pulled a handkerchief from the back pocket of his jeans and wiped the lenses, returned the handkerchief to his pocket, and put the glasses back on. Rhodes hadn't known anybody carried a handkerchief anymore.

"Where was I?" Will asked.

"I said I was going to have a look around. You said, 'About that.'"

"Yeah, I remember now. I was gonna say that I don't think you need to be going through the house or the barn unless you have a search warrant. Seems like more and more the government is taking away our rights and doing things that are against the Constitution, like making illegal searches and listening to our phones and spying on us with drones and watching us with hidden cameras everywhere we go."

"The county doesn't have any drones," Rhodes said.

He could have added "yet," because he knew that Commissioner Mikey Burns would love to have drones. The topic hadn't come up, but that's how Burns thought. He liked toys and weaponry.

"That's what you'd like us to believe," Will said.

"We don't have any cameras, either," Rhodes said. "Some of the stores do, but the county doesn't. We're not like Houston and Dallas. For that matter, we aren't listening to your phone calls."

"So you say." Will edged closer to Rhodes. "But you'd do a search without a warrant. You'd violate a man's castle and his property rights."

Rhodes was getting tired of Will's rant, but it wouldn't do to say so. Will might want to fight him, and Rhodes would have to hurt him. Worse, Will might draw his pistol, and that would lead to serious problems.

"I have your sister-in-law's permission to look around," Rhodes said.

"You *did* have her permission, but I educated her about that, and now you don't have it. You might as well get in your big truck that my tax dollars are paying for and go on back to town."

"You're probably right," Rhodes said.

"I know I am. You cops can't just run over everybody like we don't have any rights."

"That's true," Rhodes said.

He thought that it might be time to tell Will that someone else had been there to look around without a warrant, but he decided against it. He didn't have any proof that anyone had been there, nothing that would convince Will, anyway, and maybe whoever it was wouldn't come back while Will was there. If he did and if Will got hurt, Rhodes would try not to feel guilty about it. If Will shot somebody, Rhodes would regret his decision, but Will would do the shooting whether Rhodes warned him or not.

"You take good care of the dogs, you hear?" Rhodes said.

"You don't have to worry about the dogs," Will said. "I'll see to it that they're fed and watered."

Rhodes didn't have any more to say. He got in the Tahoe and drove away. He watched in the mirror as Gus-Gus and Jackie chased the Tahoe about a hundred yards down the road before turning back to the house, where Will was waiting for them.

Blacklin County had quite a few people like Will, Rhodes thought, people who believed that the government was intruding into their lives, watching their every movement, listening to their phone conversations, tracking their computer use, and probably planning to swoop down in black helicopters, raid their homes, take their guns, and lock them away in abandoned Walmarts around the country, all of them connected by a secret network of underground tunnels.

Rhodes didn't know where people got those ideas, whether there was something in the coffee they drank or in the air they breathed or whether they just believed everything they read on the Internet.

Of course, it was possible that Will didn't believe any of those things and that he had another reason for wanting to keep Rhodes out of the house and barn. If there was anything in there that someone didn't want Rhodes to see, it would be gone before too long. Will would get rid of it while the dogs were eating.

There was nothing Rhodes could do about that now. He just hoped Will would feed the dogs.

Rhodes stopped at Walter Barnes's house, which was only half a mile from the Hunts'. Walter wasn't there, and hadn't been there for days. His daughter was, however. She was house-sitting while her parents went on vacation.

"Disney World," Frances Barnes Noble said. "Can you believe it, at their age? Said they'd always wanted to go, though, so they went. First real vacation they've ever had."

Rhodes asked her if she knew the Hunts.

"Just to speak to in passing. Haven't seen them since I've been here."

Rhodes explained why he was asking.

"I'm sure sorry to hear it," Frances said. "He seemed like a nice enough man. I've heard he was a drinker, but I never saw him drunk myself."

Rhodes thanked her for her time and left. Whoever had picked up Melvin, if anybody had, it wasn't Walter Barnes, who was easily eliminated as a suspect.

If there was anybody in the county who was more paranoid than Will Smalls, it was Able Terrell. He was a survivalist who'd built himself a compound surrounded by a stockade fence and moved his family and a few others into it to wait for whatever apocalypse was to come, or whatever one he thought was coming. Rhodes had never been clear about exactly what that was. Nuclear holocaust? Zombie attacks? Plague? It could have been anything. Maybe Able wasn't entirely clear on what it was, either. It didn't matter. Something bad was coming, and Able would be ready for it when it did.

Rhodes had tangled with one of the others living in the compound during an earlier murder investigation, and Able's son, Ike, had turned out to be involved in some things he shouldn't have. The boy had gotten a probated sentence, and he'd been out of trouble ever since, but that didn't make Able any happier about things. It wasn't so much that he was so unhappy with Rhodes in particular as that his displeasure with his son spilled over onto the law Able had moved into the compound to avoid, and Rhodes was the visible representative of that law. That made him suspect in Able's eyes.

The compound was on the way back to Clearview from the Hunts' place, so Rhodes thought he'd stop by and have a talk with Able about the thefts. Rhodes didn't think Terrell had anything to do with them or with Melvin's death, but others had different ideas, at least about the thefts. And then there was Ike. Considering his history, Rhodes wondered about him.

Rhodes turned off the paved county road and drove down a dirt road to the compound. It looked pretty much the same as it had the time he'd single-handedly stormed it and flown over the fence like a comic-book hero. Or that was the way it had been reported on Jennifer Loam's Web site. The fact that it wasn't entirely true didn't matter. There was just enough truth in it to make the story almost believable, and people loved to hear things that were a little bit larger than life, especially when the things were about their local law enforcement. The real thing wasn't nearly as interesting as the exaggeration. Rhodes thought that was the secret behind a lot of what passed for news in the Internet age.

Rhodes parked the Tahoe in front of the stockade gate and waited for the sand he'd stirred up on the road to settle. He read the signs nailed to the gate to pass the time. They'd been changed since the last time Rhodes had been there, but they were just as aggressive as ever. One read DON'T WORRY ABOUT THE DOG. HE JUST BITES. THE OWNER SHOOTS. Another said, TRESPASSERS WILL BE HOGTIED AND TOLD THEY HAVE A PURTY MOUTH. Rhodes was surprised there wasn't one that said SURVIVORS WILL BE SHOT AGAIN.

Something else new was the video camera high on a wooden pole that stood just inside the gate. Able was catching up with the times. Rhodes wouldn't even have to honk to let them know he was there. They'd know already.

Sure enough, the road dust had hardly settled on the Tahoe before the gate swung open a couple of feet and Able Terrell came out. The gate swung shut behind him, so Rhodes wouldn't be going inside. That was fine with him.

Able didn't walk far from the gate. He just stood there, waiting. He was dressed in camo gear, which seemed to be the standard uniform in the compound, and in the crook of his arm he cradled an AR-15, which was also part of the standard uniform.

Rhodes got out of the Tahoe and closed the door.

"Hey, Able," he said. "How are you this fine day?"

"I was doing okay until you turned up on one of the surveillance screens," Able said. "What're you here for?"

He wasn't a big man, but he wasn't small, either. He had a wrinkled brown face and black hair with a white streak down the middle. He didn't wear a hat.

"It's about some things that have been happening down here

in this end of the county," Rhodes said, "and it's about Melvin Hunt."

"What about him?"

Rhodes wasn't ready to tell Able about Melvin yet.

"You know Billy Bacon?" Rhodes asked.

"Banker in town. I don't have much to do with banks."

He didn't add that he didn't have any bank accounts, but Rhodes suspected that was the case. Able wouldn't trust banks. He probably kept his cash hidden in the compound, and Rhodes wouldn't be surprised if there was a considerable amount of gold in there, too, for use when society collapsed.

"Billy's had a lot of things taken from a barn on his property," Rhodes said, "and somebody killed Melvin Hunt."

"Is that right?" Able said. He didn't seem concerned. "How'd it happen?"

"He was in Billy's barn. Somebody shot him."

"That's a shame, but that's what the world's come to, stealing and killing. That's why I got me a fence here. Nobody gets in unless I let them in." He paused and looked at Rhodes. "Not including you, but I've fixed things up a bit since you were here the last time."

"There's a lot of talk in town about who might be doing the stealing," Rhodes said.

Able gave a crooked grin, which caused his face to wrinkle even more. "I'll just bet there is."

"You probably know what's being said."

"I expect so. Everything that happens, they blame on me and mine. People don't like it if somebody's different from them and has a different idea about the world. I've been blamed for a lot of things before, making meth, growing weed, stuff like that. You know as well as anybody that I wasn't guilty of any of 'em."

That was true, as far as Rhodes knew. Or at least it was true about Able. It wasn't so true about his son.

"How's Ike doing?" Rhodes asked.

"He's doing just fine. He's going to the college again, and he's getting good grades. I don't like it that he goes to town, but he says he wants an education, so I'm not going to stand in his way on that. I can promise you he's not stealing from anybody, though. He won't be doing that again. He comes straight back here after his classes, and he doesn't go out again until the next day. If you're looking for somebody to pin those thefts or Melvin Hunt's killing on, I can promise you it's not him or any of my people. I'm keeping a lot closer watch on things now than I used to, and there's no way anybody here is doing anything you'd be interested in."

"You thought that before," Rhodes said.

"Yeah, I did," Able said, "and I was wrong about it. So I've made some changes. I'm sure about everything this time."

Rhodes was sure Able believed everything he said. That didn't mean that Rhodes had to believe it.

"Any chance I could talk to Ike?"

"He's in school today. I don't think you need to talk to him, though. He's on the straight and narrow."

Able had thought that before, but Rhodes didn't see any need to remind him of it again.

"You heard of anything going on down in this part of the county?" Rhodes asked. "Anything that might help me find out who's been stealing or who killed Melvin?"

"I don't hear much. I mind my own business, and I expect other people to mind theirs."

"You and Melvin ever have any trouble?"

Able thought it over. "Years ago, we did. Didn't amount to anything. It was before I moved out here. Got into a little scuffle with him in town once. I don't even remember what it was about. Might have had to do with his wife. I was sweet on her at one time."

Joyce Hunt hadn't mentioned that little tidbit. Rhodes wondered if that was significant. He doubted it.

"Haven't seen Melvin in years," Able continued. "Might not even recognize him if I did."

"What about Joyce?"

"I'd recognize her, maybe, but I haven't seen her in years, either. She didn't understand about what I was planning to do with my life, and we didn't get along too well after I told her."

Rhodes thought he'd gotten about as much out of Able as he was going to get. He could always come back if he had to.

"I'd appreciate it if you'd let me know if you hear anything that might help me out," Rhodes said.

"I'll do that, Sheriff," Able said. "That all you want with me?"

"That's all."

"I'll be going back inside, then."

"I'll be seeing you," Rhodes said.

"I hope not," Able told him.

Chapter 11

▼

As he was about to pull out onto the highway after leaving the compound, Rhodes saw Ruth Grady drive by in a county car on her way to Billy's place. Rhodes had been planning to go back to Clearview and see about the autopsy on Melvin and then talk to Riley Farmer, Melvin's alleged best friend. He also needed to talk to Mika Blackfield, but he'd thought of a thing or two that he wanted to check on at the B-Bar-B. He turned back in that direction and followed Ruth.

She was opening the outer gate when he pulled up behind her. He let the window down and leaned out.

"You can just leave it open," he said. "I'll follow you in."

Ruth nodded and got back into the county car. She stopped at the next gate, got out and opened it, and waited for Rhodes to drive through. He parked at the barn, where she joined him.

"Do you really think we'll find anything else here?" she asked.

"Probably not," Rhodes said, "but I thought about something this morning that we should check on."

"Are you going to keep me in the loop on it?" Ruth asked.

"You've been talking to Hack," Rhodes said.

Ruth grinned. "He claims you never tell him anything."

"And you believe him?"

"Not for a minute."

"You always did show good judgment. Anyway, here's what I'm wondering about. I assumed that because the lock was cut on the front gate, Melvin Hunt came in that way. But what if he didn't?"

"Who cut the lock, then?"

"Suppose Billy Bacon came and found Melvin in the barn. He got angry and shot him. What would he do then?"

Ruth looked down at the ground and didn't say anything for a few seconds. Rhodes let her think about it.

"All right," she said. "Here's what you're thinking. Bacon shot Hunt and went home. Left him right where he was lying. Hunt didn't have a gun, or if he did, we didn't find it, so Bacon couldn't claim self-defense. He didn't know what to do. He talked it over with his wife, and they decided to have Bacon come back and 'discover' the body. He cut the lock himself to make it look as if Hunt had done it."

"We didn't find any bolt cutters," Rhodes said. "Billy slipped up."

"Or?"

"Or it didn't happen like that. Somebody else cut the lock."

"Hunt was here with somebody else?"

"Could be. Or not."

"I'm out of the loop again," Ruth said.

"Somebody cut the lock and came to the barn. What if Melvin either was already there or came in and surprised them?"

"How did Melvin get here?"

Rhodes told her about what had happened that morning. When he'd finished, she said, "You think Will Smalls had something to do with this?"

"Not necessarily. What I think is that someone wanted to look into Melvin's house to see if there was something there that could implicate him. He walked along the creek and came up through the woods. Melvin could have come along the creek in this direction and come through the woods. He might have stumbled into something."

Ruth pushed her hat up on her forehead with her right thumb. "Why would he come here at all?"

"To steal," Rhodes said. "Or maybe he knew something was going on. I don't know the answers. I'm just thinking about what might have happened. What I do know, though, is that we should walk down to the creek and see if we can tell whether Melvin or someone else came here that way. Melvin's truck is at his house, so he either walked or came here with somebody."

"They got into an argument, and his partner killed him?"

"Like I said, I don't know. I'm still trying to figure it out. If we can find out how Melvin got here, that might help."

"What if his wife was his partner?" Ruth asked. "She could have driven here with him, killed him, and gone back home."

"It could be like that," Rhodes said. "Ivy would like it. We need to check out all the possibilities."

"Let's go for a walk, then," Ruth said.

Something resembling a road curved through the trees near the barn and into the pasture. It was really nothing more than ruts with weeds growing between them, like Gunnison's driveway, but rougher. The Tahoe could have traveled it easily, but since Rhodes didn't want to take the chance of missing anything along the way, walking was the only option.

The sandy ruts didn't hold any footprints, however, not from humans anyway. Bacon's cattle had walked in them, and feral hogs had trampled all over them, obscuring any track that Melvin Hunt or anyone else might have left.

The road led up over a little rise, and on the other side were a dozen or so Hereford cattle, all cows and calves, in the pasture. Rhodes didn't see an adult bull. Bacon probably kept a bull in another pasture. The cattle were grazing on the sparse pasture grass and didn't pay any attention to Rhodes and Ruth after looking them over for a few seconds, except for one cow that stretched her neck a bit and mooed. Rhodes wondered if this was Billy's entire herd or if there were more down in the bottoms.

The dam of a stock tank rose up to the right of the cattle, and Rhodes thought that it probably had fish in it. Most of the stock tanks in the county did. There'd been a time when he'd get a chance to go fishing now and then, and he'd even carried fishing gear in the back of his county car. He hadn't wet a hook in so long, however, that he couldn't remember the last time.

"Where are the hogs?" Ruth asked, breaking into Rhodes's thought of catching a lunker bass.

"Maybe we won't see any," Rhodes said. He preferred to think about fish. "In the daytime they hole up in the woods, but they move around a lot. They could have been here last night and today they're miles away. If there are any around they'll be down in the creek bottoms. They won't bother us."

He hoped he was telling the truth. Even in the daytime, an encounter with feral pigs could be dangerous.

"How far is the creek from here?" Ruth asked.

"Another quarter of a mile or so, down there beyond the trees."

They walked on most of the way to the trees, and Ruth stopped, pointing off to the left. "What's that over there?"

A wooded area marked the boundary of the pasture, and Rhodes thought Billy would need to clear off more of his land if he wanted to run any more cattle on it. It wasn't the trees that Ruth was talking about, however. It appeared that there was a clearing among them, but it wasn't quite a clearing. Something was in it.

"We'd better take a look," Rhodes said.

He couldn't see a path to the trees, so they had to cut across the pasture. As they drew closer, Ruth said, "That can't be what I think it is."

"Sure it can," Rhodes said.

Rhodes had seen something like it before, but he knew why Ruth was surprised. The clearing held a large marijuana patch. It was surrounded by two rows of supposedly hog-proof wire, one within the other, so that the feral pigs couldn't run through it without a lot of trouble. It wouldn't have been worth it to them, so that must have been the plan. It seemed to be working so far.

Off on one side of the patch was a water pump with a pipe leading into the woods. Rhodes was sure it went to the creek, which was well filled this year. Nobody would notice if some water was missing. A marijuana patch required a lot of water for irrigation.

"I'm not talking about the marijuana," Ruth said. "I'm talking about *that*."

She pointed to something that hunkered down in a little wallow under the cover of a lean-to by the water pump. Rhodes had to stop and shade his eyes from the sun to get a better look. When he did, he was just as surprised as Ruth was.

"An alligator," he said.

"That's what I think it is, too," Ruth said. "What's an alligator doing here?"

Marijuana patches weren't the only odd things Rhodes had seen in Blacklin County during his career. He'd had to deal with an alligator before, too. He just hadn't seen an alligator and a marijuana patch together. It was an interesting pairing.

"I've read about this," Ruth said.

"You knew it was here?" Rhodes said.

"No, I don't mean that. I mean I've read about marijuana growers using alligators to guard their crops. It seems to be something that happens all over the country. Alligators don't need to be taken care of like dogs do. You can go off and leave them for a while. They can go a long time without food."

Rhodes hadn't heard about the new trend in marijuana-growing security. He didn't think that gators would make very effective guards. While it was true that they were very fast over short distances and that they could clamp down on an arm or a leg and snap bones like toothpicks, they were generally lethargic and not prone to violence unless provoked. Or very hungry. Rhodes wondered when the gator had last had a tasty, nutritious, filling meal.

It wasn't a very big gator, maybe five feet long, and it was quite lean. It might well be hungry. It might also scare off someone who didn't know much about gators, but it didn't bother Rhodes, even if it was hungry, because at the moment it was inside the hog-wire fence and he was on the outside.

"I have a feeling Billy Bacon didn't think we'd come down here," Ruth said.

"He almost certainly didn't," Rhodes said. "He had to call us, though, even if he did think about it, considering that there was a dead body in the barn. He had to take the chance we wouldn't go for a walk in the pasture. The little hill hides this place from the barn, so we wouldn't have seen it if we hadn't come this way."

"He could have fed the body to the gator and gotten rid of it that way," Ruth said.

Rhodes hadn't realized she was so hard-boiled. "He might have been too squeamish for that, and the gator might be too small."

Ruth shrugged. "Maybe. What are we going to do?"

"For the moment we won't do anything."

"Why not?"

"We don't want to alert Billy that we know about it yet. I want to poke around some more while we're here and see if this patch ties in with Melvin's murder."

"You think it does?"

"It could," Rhodes said, "but if it does I don't know how. This whole thing is getting more complicated than I thought it was at first."

"So what's the next step?"

"We'll go on down to the creek and see if there's anything there."

"Sounds good to me," Ruth said. "I don't really want to deal with an alligator right now."

"Me, neither," Rhodes said.

There wasn't much that was helpful at the creek. All they found was the other end of the water pipe. It was obvious that someone had been trampling around it, but whether that someone had come through the woods or from somewhere else was impossible to tell.

While they didn't find anything useful, they also didn't run across any feral pigs. Rhodes considered that to be good news.

"Let's go back to the barn," Rhodes said after he decided they weren't going to stumble onto any clues to either the murder or the marijuana patch. "You can go on patrol, and I'll have Alton Boyd and Buddy come down here and take care of the gator."

"Why don't I stay here and help Alton?" Ruth asked. "Are you trying to protect me just because I'm a woman?"

"Maybe I was," Rhodes said. "I know better than to do that. I wasn't thinking straight. That's a good idea. Three of you working on the gator will be better than two, and it would be a good idea to have someone here to watch the marijuana patch in case the owners show up."

"Where will you be?" Ruth asked.

"I think I'll have a little talk with Billy Bacon," Rhodes said. "I think it's time to mention this little weed patch after all."

On the drive back to Clearview, Rhodes got Hack on the radio and told him to send Alton Boyd and Buddy to the Bacon place.

"Ruth will be at the barn," Rhodes said. "She can tell them what has to be done."

"You going to tell *me* what has to be done?" Hack asked. "Put me in the loop? Or do I have to guess?"

"There's a marijuana patch in the woods," Rhodes said.

"Alton's animal control, not drug enforcement."

"There's an animal with the marijuana."

"I know what you're doin'," Hack said after a pause.

Rhodes wasn't good at pretending innocence, but he gave it a try. "I have no idea what you mean."

"Yes, you do. You're tryin' to keep me out of the loop. That's okay, but Alton and Buddy need to know what kind of animal it is."

"You're right," Rhodes said. "They do. It's an alligator."

"Now you're just makin' fun of me."

"Nope. It's an alligator. Dark green and scaly. Tell Alton it's not as big as the other one he and I wrestled. He and Buddy can handle it with Ruth's help."

"You mean you're not jokin'?"

"I'm not joking. There's an alligator, and it looks hungry. Tell Alton and Buddy to get on down there, but don't tell them the gator looks hungry."

"I'll tell 'em there's a gator," Hack said, "but they won't believe it."

"They will when they get there," Rhodes said.

Chapter 12

▼

The Clearview First Bank was one of the few buildings left in the old downtown area. It had been built well, and while other buildings around it had collapsed, it had held its own, standing tall and straight with its bricks and mortar as firm as ever. The inside had been remodeled, but the floors were still marble, and the sounds were as hushed as they would've been in a church.

Rhodes went straight to Billy Bacon's desk in a glass-enclosed office to the right of the entrance. Bacon stood up, wincing as if his knee bothered him. He seemed surprised to see Rhodes there. He probably was.

"To what do I owe the pleasure, Sheriff?" he asked.

He didn't look as if he really thought it was a pleasure. He wore a gray business suit, a white shirt, and a dark blue tie, looking nothing at all the way he had at the barn the previous day.

"We need to talk," Rhodes said. He closed the office door. "I hope you don't have any appointments."

Billy sat down and looked at his calender. "Not until after

lunch. Have a seat. What do we need to talk about? Have you found out who killed Melvin?"

Rhodes sat in one of the chairs at the front of the desk and leaned back.

"I haven't found the killer," he said.

"Then what?"

"Marijuana."

"Huh?" Billy said, tensing. "I mean, what?"

"Marijuana," Rhodes said. "Pot. Mary Jane. Weed. You know."

"Well, yes, I know what it is." Billy relaxed a little. "I just don't know why you want to talk about it."

"Sure you do," Rhodes said. "You have some growing down at your place in a little clearing in the woods. You even have an alligator there to guard it."

Billy laughed and looked up at the ceiling. "An alligator? You must be joking."

"That's what Hack thought, too."

"Hack?"

"Never mind," Rhodes said. "I'm not joking. When I'm joking, nobody laughs."

Billy stopped looking at the ceiling and looked down at his desk. "Alligators, marijuana. I . . . I don't know what to say. I don't know what you're talking about."

"I think you do," Rhodes told him. "The marijuana's growing on your land. You have to have known it was there. The gator's inside the fence around the marijuana patch, so you'd know about that, too."

"No, that's not true. I never go down there. I never go anywhere but to the barn. The cows come up there when they get fed, which hasn't been often this year, thanks to the rain. If something's not around the barn, I wouldn't know about it. I don't even go down in the pasture to check on the cows, and I certainly don't know anything about marijuana. Much less an alligator." He waved a hand to indicate his office, or maybe the entire bank. "I have a job here. I work every day. When would I have time to grow marijuana? I don't even know how to go about it."

"It doesn't matter what you say you know about growing it. The plants are on your land, and nobody's going to believe you're not the one who's growing them."

"But I'm not," Billy said. He held his hands out over the desk, showing Rhodes the backs and the palms. "Look at my hands. Do they look like I've been cultivating a crop?"

Rhodes had to admit that they didn't. He didn't see any calluses, and the nails were so rounded and clean that he suspected Billy of having had a manicure. If he'd been doing any cultivating, he'd worn gloves.

"If somebody's growing pot on my place, it's not me," Billy said. He looked angry. "You're the sheriff. You have to find out who it is and make them confess. You can't arrest me for something I'm not guilty of."

Rhodes thought it over. Billy sounded convincing, but Rhodes had been lied to for years by suspects and even by victims. He'd come to expect it, and he'd learned how to tell, most of the time, when someone was stretching the truth. He had a feeling that Billy was doing just that, but not by much. There was more to the story, so Rhodes would let it go for now. He'd find out what was going on eventually, but at the moment he had more things to worry about than a small marijuana patch.

"I'm not going to arrest you," he said.

Billy, who'd put his palms down on the desk, pulled his hands back and relaxed. "I'm glad to hear it. I'm innocent, Sheriff. Somebody's using my land for illegal purposes, but it's not me."

"And you don't know a thing about it."

"That's right. Not a thing."

"You know I'll have to burn the field," Rhodes said.

Something flashed in Billy's eyes, but it came and went so quickly that Rhodes wasn't really sure he'd seen it.

"I know," Billy said. "You're the sheriff, and you have to do your job."

Rhodes stood up. "I will," he said.

Clyde Ballinger was the owner and director of Ballinger's Funeral Home, where he lived a sedate bachelor life in what had once been the servants' quarters of the mansion where the funeral home was now located. Rhodes had sometimes wondered what the original owners of the fine home would have thought had they known the purpose to which it would eventually be put, but he'd decided that they wouldn't care, not in their current situations, at any rate. They'd been Ballinger's clients in his old location and were now safely buried in the local cemetery.

Ballinger had at one time been a fan of old paperback books, but he'd taken to reading on a tablet for a while. Then, as he'd explained to Rhodes, he'd gone back to books because he missed them. There were a couple of them lying on his desk when Rhodes walked into his office on the ground floor of the former servants' quarters. The odd thing was that they looked brand-new.

"They are," Ballinger said when Rhodes asked about them. "Seems as if a lot of small companies are starting to reprint things that you couldn't find anywhere, no matter how hard you looked, until the Internet came along. Then you could find them, but some of them were so expensive that you couldn't afford them."

"You could," Rhodes said.

"Well, maybe, but I liked finding them for a quarter at a garage sale. The rare ones never turned up there. Now I can buy them for a few bucks. You take this one, for example."

Ballinger picked up one of the books, a trade-sized paperback, and handed it to Rhodes, who looked it over. The cover was just as tawdry as any of the older ones Rhodes had seen in the office and showed a nude woman diving into a swimming pool where a man waited for her. Two titles adorned the cover along with the nude woman and waiting man: *Lust Queen* and *Lust Victim*.

"Racy stuff," Rhodes said, handing the book back. "Lots of lust. I didn't know you went in for that kind of thing."

"It's not as racy as it looks," Ballinger said. "See, back in the old days a lot of writers, big-name guys sometimes, wrote midcentury erotica because it paid well and they could write it fast."

"Midcentury erotica?"

"Sounds better than soft porn. Anyway, the books were mostly mystery or crime stories with some sex thrown in. Pretty good stuff."

"I'll bet," Rhodes said. "Don't let Buddy catch you with any of those."

Buddy had a puritanical streak, and the naked woman would've been shocking to him.

"I'll keep it out of sight," Ballinger said, opening the middle drawer of his desk and sliding the book inside. "Not that there's anything wrong with it. These stories were all pretty moralistic. The wicked were always punished, usually in ways that gave some business to my profession."

"Speaking of the wicked being punished," Rhodes said, "let's talk about Melvin Hunt. Did Dr. White get here to do an autopsy on him?"

"He did. I have the report for you, and a couple of slugs that he took from the body."

Ballinger took the report and a couple of plastic bags out of a desk drawer and passed them to Rhodes. Rhodes was a little surprised to learn that the slugs were from a .32, but he knew well enough that a .32 could penetrate enough to kill, especially if it hit a vital spot. The first one hadn't, but the second one had. Survivors will be shot again.

Billy Bacon's gun was a .38, or the one that he claimed belonged to his wife was. If that was the only one they had, Billy was in the clear, but Rhodes knew that Billy could have an off-the-books gun, just like a lot of other people in Texas.

Rhodes flipped through the report until he came to the important part. Hunt had indeed died a day before he'd been found. Dr. White had determined this in a couple of ways, one of which was the growth stage of the maggots in the wounds. The blowflies that Rhodes had brushed away had laid eggs, and the maggots had just hatched. If Billy could prove his alibi for the day of the death, the gun wouldn't matter. Rhodes would mark him off the list of suspects. So far he had only his wife to vouch for him, however.

"Anything interesting in there?" Ballinger asked

"Maybe," Rhodes said, "but not anything that's going to help me find out who killed Melvin."

"You'll find out," Ballinger said.

"People keep telling me that."

"You and Sage Barton always come through."

"People keep telling me that, too. I wish they'd stop."

"Not gonna happen."

"That's what I'm afraid of," Rhodes said.

•   •   •

Rhodes's next stop was the jail, where his worst fears were realized. Seepy Benton was there. Rhodes had hoped to see Mika Blackfield, not Seepy, but Mika had already done her report and left. Rhodes was stuck with Seepy.

It wasn't that Seepy was a bad person. It was just that he always wanted to be helpful. Even worse, he *had* been helpful in the past, and that gave him some credibility. After that, Rhodes had consulted with him a couple of times, thus giving Benton leverage, or so Benton thought. Most recently Benton had been operating his ghost-hunting business and had in the process led Rhodes to an important clue in a murder case. Benton wasn't the kind to forget something like that.

Benton, Hack, and Lawton were talking when Rhodes came in. They were so engrossed in their conversation that they hardly looked up, so Rhodes put Hunt's possessions and the slugs in the evidence room and filed Dr. White's report. When that was done he sat at his desk and looked over another report, the one Mika Blackfield had left for him.

She hadn't found anything on Hunt's cell phone. She'd made a list of his calls, but there were only five recent ones. Hunt wasn't the kind of person to do much phoning. Three calls had been to Riley Farmer. The other two had been to Will Smalls. Nothing suspicious about that, although Rhodes wasn't convinced that Smalls was innocent in this case, not after his appearance at the Hunts' place earlier.

Mika had found no social media accounts for Hunt, which wasn't surprising. Rhodes would've been shocked to discover that Hunt even knew what social media were. She also hadn't turned up anything on Hunt by using various search engines. He hadn't left an electronic presence behind.

Rhodes put the report away and thought through everything

that had happened. He was almost sure he'd missed something that would clear things up a bit, but he couldn't quite dredge it up from wherever it was hiding.

"I hear you have another tough case," Seepy Benton said from behind him.

Rhodes turned in his chair to see Seepy standing there.

"Are you going to keep me in the loop?" Seepy asked.

Rhodes looked over to where Hack was pretending to be busy at his desk. Lawton had his hands in his pockets and was looking at the floor as if there might be a speck of dirt there that he could sweep away.

"You're not one of the deputies," Rhodes said. "You're not a commissioner. You're not on the city council. You don't have a place in the loop."

"I'm a citizen of the county," Seepy said. "We citizens need to be in the loop to keep you law enforcers honest. You don't use body cameras, so you need some checks and balances."

"It's a good thing I know you're joking," Rhodes said.

"Okay, I'm joking, but I do want to help out, the way I've done before. You remember, don't you?"

Rhodes nodded but didn't say anything.

"I'll take that as a yes," Seepy said. "So once again I've dropped by to see if can I help out. Do my civic duty. Maybe help you catch an alligator."

Rhodes thought he heard Hack chuckle, but he couldn't be sure because he could see only the dispatcher's back. Lawton's face was impassive.

"My guess is that you're already in the loop," Rhodes said.

Seepy glanced over at Hack, who didn't look at him.

"Maybe I am," Seepy said. "I want to hear about the marijuana patch, if you don't mind. I'm interested in that kind of thing."

Benton looked more like a rabbi than a man who'd be interested in marijuana, not that Rhodes had seen many rabbis in his life and not that he'd know what one thought about marijuana. Seepy had an even bigger thin spot in his hair than Rhodes did. In fact, he didn't have any hair at all on the top of his head, but he did have a nice graying fringe, and he wore a short, neatly trimmed beard. Rhodes didn't see Seepy's hat, but he was sure it was around somewhere, maybe in a chair by Hack's desk.

"Have a seat," Rhodes said, and Benton sat in the old wooden chair by Rhodes's desk. Maybe Seepy could be of help after all. "What do you want to know?"

"First let me tell you something," Seepy said. "You're going to be finding more of those patches all the time."

"What makes you think that?" Rhodes asked.

"Two things. Meth's getting easier to make, and there's cheap meth coming up from Mexico that's taking over the market. It doesn't pay to make it here anymore, not in quantities big enough to sell, anyway, so marijuana's coming back as a cash crop."

"You're a regular bundle of information about drugs," Rhodes said. "How do you know all this?"

"I read the newspapers," Seepy said. "The old-fashioned kind. I get the *Dallas Morning News* every day. You can still learn a lot from newspapers if you're paying attention. That's where I learned about making meth in two-liter soft drink bottles."

Rhodes knew a good bit about that, too. That method of meth cooking was cheap and fast, and now, along with exploding meth houses, Rhodes had to deal with the occasional exploding motel room. Not to mention the time that someone had blown up the men's room at the Walmart. Or the time someone had set fire to the trunk of his car in the parking lot there.

"I've had some practical experience with the meth problem," Rhodes said.

"I know, but those little batches in the soft drink bottles are just for personal use. You can't make enough to sell that way. The meth houses are dangerous and not as profitable as they used to be. Marijuana still is. You've had some trouble with marijuana patches here in the county in the past. Hack and Lawton were just telling me about it."

"That was a while ago. This new patch isn't as big as the one they must have told you about." Rhodes paused. "Where does all this interest in drugs come from, anyway? You're not going to set up a meth lab or a grow room, I hope."

Seepy grinned. "You know me better than that. I'm a law-abiding citizen. Besides, Ruth would handcuff me and lock me up in one of your cells if she caught me growing pot." Seepy looked thoughtful. "The handcuffing part might not be so bad, though."

"I don't want to hear about it," Rhodes said.

"I don't blame you, so forget about the handcuffs. When it comes to drugs, I don't need them to be in a state of euphoria."

Rhodes had to admit that Seepy was relentlessly cheerful, and while Rhodes had nothing against cheerfulness, it could sometimes be a little wearing on him when it was a permanent condition in others.

"A few years ago," Seepy continued, "before I moved here, I was invited to a peyote ceremony that was being held on land sanctioned by the State of Texas for Native American Church ceremonies. I didn't take part because what I experience normally is what most other people experience on peyote. That's what happens to your brain when you live a creative life."

"I'm not a bit surprised," Rhodes said. He'd known for a long time that Seepy's brain didn't work like a normal person's. "But if you're naturally high, why are you so interested in drugs?"

"I'm not interested in drugs for mind-altering purposes," Seepy said. "I'm interested specifically in marijuana because of its medical properties. Here's an old saying that I just made up: 'The weed of crime bears medicinal fruit.'"

"I suppose the Shadow knows," Rhodes said.

"You can count on it, and he'd probably agree with me that every state should legalize marijuana for medical use, or the federal government should. We advocates prefer to call it cannabis, by the way, not marijuana, which has bad connotations."

"If you're waiting for Texas to legalize marijuana, you might have a long wait."

"Cannabis. And maybe the wait won't be as long as you think. The legislature passed a very narrow bill that allows for the use of small doses of a marijuana-derived product with most of the THC removed. The problem is that it can be prescribed only for epilepsy, and a regular doctor can't prescribe it. Only a neurologist or epileptologist can. That's a start, but that's all it is. There's a lot of evidence that cannabis can cure or help with a lot of diseases including several kinds of cancer, but if you're suffering from those things in Texas, you can't get it to help your condition. I just don't think that's right."

"You've done some research," Rhodes said. "It's almost like you're on a crusade."

"I am on a crusade," Seepy said. "My bucket list includes getting cannabis made legal in every state. You want to know why?"

Rhodes didn't think he had a choice. Seepy's eyes were lighting up as if there were a lantern in his head. It wasn't the light of fanaticism, or Rhodes hoped it wasn't, but there was a zeal there that was impossible to miss.

"You're not going to sing that medical marijuana song you wrote, are you?" Rhodes asked.

"I'm glad you remembered it," Seepy said. "It's on my You-Tube channel. I've written a new one, too. You can watch it anytime you want to."

Rhodes didn't know when that time would come. He didn't know enough about YouTube to find the songs anyway.

"Go ahead and tell me about your crusade," he said.

"All right. Here's the story. I have a friend in Arizona who has crippling allergies. She can't leave the house for a lot of the year, and she has to live in only one room the rest of the time. The room's set up with all kinds of air filters that make life bearable but not much more. She's able to get medical cannabis, though, and that helps a lot. My father here in Texas, on the other hand, has the same problem, but he'd be arrested if he tried to get relief the way she does."

"I'm sorry about your father."

"So am I. He's getting treatment, but it's expensive and less likely to give him a good result."

"Maybe the laws will change soon," Rhodes said. "That seems to be the trend."

"I hope so," Seepy said, "and the sooner, the better."

"They haven't changed yet, though," Rhodes said. "I still have to find out who planted that marijuana field, and I have to get rid of it."

"I know. It's your job. You've sworn to enforce the law, but it's a shame you have to do it in this case. Are you going to burn the patch?"

"That's usually how it's done," Rhodes said.

"Can I help? Maybe just watch? Stand downwind and inhale?"

"I thought you said you were on a natural high."

"I am, but it seems like a shame to waste a good opportunity like this to try something new and different."

Rhodes wondered just how new and different the experience would be for Seepy.

"Forget it," Rhodes said.

"If Willie Nelson were here, you'd let him watch."

"He's not here, and I wouldn't even if he were."

"I knew you were going to say that. But seriously, is there something I can do to help with this case?"

Rhodes thought about it for a second. He knew that Seepy couldn't tell him anything about Ike Terrell because of the confidentiality requirements of the college, but he might be able to give him a few hints about what Ike was up to.

"Ike Terrell," Rhodes said. "How's he doing at the college this year?"

"He's in my calculus class," Seepy said. "He's a good student. Does the homework, comes to class. He's not smoking dope in the halls as far as I know."

"There've been a lot of burglaries down in his part of the county. I talked to Able this morning, and he says he and Ike aren't involved."

"Ike does have a past," Seepy said, "but considering his course load, I don't think he has time for burglaries."

"What about growing marijuana?"

Seepy looked thoughtful. "It doesn't take a lot of time or work for that, and you don't have to stand guard if you have an alligator to do the job."

The radio crackled, and Hack listened for a few seconds before turning to Rhodes.

"It's the alligator," Hack said.

"What about it?" Rhodes asked.

Hack grinned. "It got away."

"Uh-oh," Seepy said.

Chapter 13

▼

Rhodes didn't ask how the gator got away because he knew it would take Hack half an hour to tell the story.

"Let them know I'm on the way," he said, starting for the door.

Sometimes it seemed to Rhodes as if every investigation he got involved in was like this one. No matter how hard he tried to go in a straight line, things kept pulling him in different directions. Of course, he could have simply allowed Alton and Ruth and Buddy to deal with the gator problem, but he was the sheriff, and it was his job to be sure that things went smoothly. When things got off track, he was the one who had to get them back on. He supposed that Riley Farmer and the others Rhodes wanted to talk to would just have to wait. As Hack sometimes reminded him, that's why he was paid the Big Bucks.

Seepy Benton followed Rhodes outside and said, "I'm going, too."

Rhodes noticed that Seepy had retrieved his fedora and stuck it on his head.

"You'll just be in the way," Rhodes said.

"I have a personal interest in this," Seepy said. "Besides, you know that I'm good with alligators. You and I have worked together to catch one before."

"You're a private citizen, and I can't order you to stay here," Rhodes said, "but if you get in the way and impede our police work, I'll have to arrest you."

Seepy looked hurt. "I won't get in the way, and I know how to catch alligators."

"You'll have to stay out of the way this time," Rhodes said.

"All right, if that's how you want it."

"That's how I want it," Rhodes said, and got into the Tahoe.

When he'd gone a couple of blocks, he checked the rearview mirror. Sure enough, Seepy was right behind him. Seepy was still there when Rhodes drove through the gate at the B-Bar-B, and he followed right on to the inner gate, which Rhodes got out to open.

"You can close the gate after you drive through," Rhodes called to him. "You might want to wait at the barn. I can't promise you'll be safe from the gator."

"I'm not worried about the gator," Seepy said. "I can handle the gator. I know several alligator-wrestling techniques."

"You told me that the last time we had a gator to catch."

"You didn't let me prove it, though."

"I'm not going to let you prove it this time, either," Rhodes said. "Remember?"

"I remember."

"Good."

Rhodes got in the Tahoe and drove through the gate, not waiting to see if Seepy closed it and followed, but before he'd crested the hill on the way to the marijuana patch, Seepy was behind him again. They stopped in the pasture not too far from the patch and parked beside Alton Boyd's van and Buddy's county car.

"You stay here," Rhodes told Seepy. "I'll see what's going on and tell you when it's safe."

Seepy got out of the Escape. "I'm not worried about my safety."

"Maybe not," Rhodes said, "but I am."

"All right. I'll stay here, but let me know if Ruth is okay."

"I will," Rhodes said, walking away.

Alton, Buddy, and Ruth weren't at the marijuana patch. Rhodes looked around and thought about the situation. If he were an escaped gator, where would he go? The creek, naturally, so Rhodes headed in that direction. In a minute or so he spotted Alton and the deputies through the trees as they stood on the bank of the creek not far from the irrigation pipe.

"What happened?" he asked when he reached them. "Where's the gator?"

"In the water," Alton said around the cheap, unlit cigar he had clamped between his teeth.

"We think," Ruth added. "We didn't see him go in, but he was headed in this direction." She pointed to a muddy spot on the bank. "See?"

Rhodes saw a smooth track in the mud near the water where a gator might have slid in.

"How did he get away?" Rhodes asked.

Nobody spoke up.

"Well?" Rhodes said.

"It was my fault," Buddy said finally.

"Not really," Ruth said. "It was more like my fault."

"They're right," Alton said, removing his cigar and looking at it.

Rhodes thought it was a soggy mess, but Boyd didn't seem to mind. He stuck it back in his mouth.

"What do you mean, 'They're right'?" Rhodes asked.

"I mean it's their fault," Alton said.

Rhodes had just about given up on ever getting a straight story from anybody, not at first. He said, "Tell me what happened."

"I'll tell it," Buddy said. "Since it was my fault."

"More like mine," Ruth said.

"Hold it," Rhodes said. "Let's not start that again. You tell it, Alton."

"Sure." Alton removed the soggy cigar and stuck it in the pocket of his shirt. "You remember that last gator we caught?"

"I remember," Rhodes said.

"Okay. I figured to get this one the same way. Rope it, get its mouth shut, and use the duck tape on it. It's not as big as the last one. We'd just chunk it in the back of the van, and that'd be that."

"It didn't work out that way, though," Buddy said. "It was my fault. I let him get away."

Buddy was short and wiry, but he was stronger than he looked. Rhodes wondered how he'd let the gator escape. Maybe eventually somebody would tell him.

"What happened was that Buddy opened the gate," Alton said. "He should've waited for the professional to do it."

"I thought the gator was asleep," Buddy said.

"They look lazy, but they can run like the wind," Alton said. "Ten or eleven miles an hour if they don't have to run far, and that one didn't. He came charging through those plants and hit that wire gate. Knocked it out of Buddy's hand and knocked Buddy flat on his butt. Knocked Ruth down, too."

"I was standing too close to Buddy," Ruth said. "If I'd been back a little way, I might've been able to stop the gator."

"Nope," Alton said. "You couldn't. Only way to stop one moving that fast is to kill it, and you have to get a pretty good shot at him from the front to do that. He was already headed down to the creek before you could've got out your gun out. Gators need to be in the water, and that one wanted to get back to it as quick as he could."

"Didn't you go after him?" Rhodes asked.

"Sure," Alton said, "but first I had to be sure Buddy and Ruth weren't hurt."

"Were they?" Seepy Benton asked.

Rhodes turned around. "Where did you come from?"

Seepy pointed behind him. "From up there. You didn't come back, and I got worried. I thought I'd better check to make sure the alligator didn't get you."

Rhodes sighed.

"Are you all right, Ruth?" Seepy asked.

"I'm fine," Ruth said. "Maybe my pride is bruised a little bit."

"Not much we can do about the gator now," Alton said. "It's bound to be in the creek."

"If it gets out and eats somebody's cow, they're not going to be happy," Seepy said.

"It's too little to eat a cow," Alton said. "A dog, maybe, it could handle. Besides, it'll have plenty of food in the creek; turtles, fish, stuff like that. If we're lucky, it won't come out on the bank again. And if it does, maybe it won't be in this county."

Rhodes didn't like the idea of letting someone else clean up his mess, but he didn't see any other way to handle it. The gator wasn't in sight, and he wasn't going to ask Alton to go in the water and look for it. If it turned up in somebody's stock tank later on, they'd have to go after it, but maybe that wouldn't happen.

"All right," Rhodes said. "We'll just leave it like it is for now. Buddy, I want you to stay down here and hide out to watch the marijuana patch. I'll send Duke to relieve you later on. I doubt that anybody will show up. If they've heard about Melvin Hunt's murder, they'll stay away for good."

"Okay," Buddy said.

"You can park your car up behind the barn," Rhodes said. "You'll have to walk back down here."

"No problem."

"If you see the alligator," Rhodes said, "give Hack a call."

"You can count on that," Buddy said.

Rhodes had two stops to make in town, three if he counted lunch, but it was already too late for lunch. He supposed it didn't matter. He'd missed so many lunches in the last few years that he'd given up trying to keep up with how many there had been. He didn't mind missing the lunches as much as he minded not losing any weight when he missed them. It seemed only fair that a man who missed as many meals as he did would lose weight. Or if not weight, a few inches around the waist. Neither one had happened.

Not that he was fat. It was just that he wasn't skinny, like Buddy. And as far as Rhodes knew, Buddy had never missed a meal in his life. Yet there he was, not much bigger around than a cedar fence post, whereas Rhodes was going to have to loosen his belt another notch if things didn't change pretty soon. He supposed that was okay. There were a couple of notches left.

Will Smalls lived on the south side of Clearview, on a little side street with older houses that all looked a lot alike. Rhodes parked in front of the house where he'd left Joyce the previous evening. The house was small, with a neat yard that Rhodes envied. He didn't envy the work that went into keeping it neat, however. He wasn't fond of working in the yard, not that he ever had time to do anything like that even if he had enjoyed it.

Rhodes stepped up on the little porch and knocked on the door. Ellen Smalls opened it after a few seconds.

"Good afternoon, Sheriff," she said. "What can I do for you?"

Ellen Smalls suited the last name she'd taken when she married Will. She was only a few inches over five feet tall, unlike her larger sister, and she was whippet thin. Rhodes suspected that she ate as many meals as Buddy did, probably plenty of rich foods, too. Had ice cream for dessert several times a week. Some people just had a high metabolism.

"I'd like to talk to Will," Rhodes said.

"He's not home. He's staying down at Joyce's house for a while."

"That's what I wanted talk to him about. Did he say why he was doing that?"

"Said he needed to take care of the dogs. Jackie and Gus-Gus. They're sweet boys, and they need somebody to look after them. They don't need to be cooped up in a barn all the time."

Rhodes agreed with that, at least, but he didn't think that was the only reason Will was staying there.

"Besides," Ellen continued, "what with all the stealing that's been going on down there, Will didn't think it was a good idea for the house to be left without somebody in it."

That wasn't a bad reason, either, but Rhodes was still suspicious. Will had told him it was all Joyce's idea for him to be at her house.

"Is Joyce here?" Rhodes asked.

"No, she's at the funeral home making the arrangements for Melvin. I'd have gone with her, but I don't like to leave the house with nobody in it. Those thieves could show up here any time at all and kill me like they did poor Melvin. It's so sad that something like that could happen to him. Have you caught the person who killed him?"

"Not yet."

"I hope you do. It's not right that the killer could be loose right here in Clearview. Who knows who he might kill next?"

Rhodes said he hoped nobody else would be killed. He thanked Ellen for her help, though she hadn't been any help at all, and left. He thought about getting a hamburger on the way to Riley Farmer's house but decided against it, even though Riley lived near the Dairy Queen and a Jalitos Ranch Burger would really hit the spot. Sometimes a man had to make sacrifices, though it seemed to Rhodes that he was making more than his share.

Riley lived on the other side of town, not too far from the water tower. Rhodes had spent some time around that area when Seepy Benton had helped him out with the ghost-hunting case, but he hadn't run into Farmer. It was an older section of town, even older than the one where the Smallses lived. Farmer lived on a street that once had been somewhat fashionable. A doctor had lived in the house next door to Farmer long ago, but no one had lived there for years. The doctor had died, and his family had simply boarded up the house after cleaning it out. Weeds and bushes and trees had grown and multiplied and swallowed up the house. It was hardly visible from the street, and most passersby probably didn't even know it was there. Farmer's house, while it wasn't hidden by shrubbery, wasn't in prime condition, and his lawn was mostly dead weeds.

Rhodes parked in the street, got out of the Tahoe, and walked up two concrete steps to the cracked sidewalk leading to the sagging porch. The screen door didn't fit into the frame, and it sagged, too. The windows were covered with venetian blinds that didn't hang any better than the screen did.

Rhodes couldn't see into the house. He knocked on the door and waited. Nobody responded, and Rhodes looked off to the side at the old pickup sitting in the driveway. Unless he was off with someone else, Farmer was at home, so he should have come to the door. Rhodes knocked again.

Once again there was no answer.

Rhodes walked over to the pickup, a Chevrolet from the previous century, and glanced into the bed, which was empty. He looked through the window on the driver's side but saw nothing unusual. The window was open, so Rhodes reached through and honked the horn. That should get Farmer's attention.

It didn't, or if it did, Farmer wasn't going to show himself to Rhodes. After waiting for a minute or so, Rhodes went on around to the back of the house. The backyard looked better than the front, and in the detached garage sat an old pickup. Or it sort of sat in the garage. It didn't quite fit. The back end stuck out into the driveway for a yard or more.

Rhodes went to the back door and knocked on it. Nobody responded, but Rhodes thought he heard a cat howling inside. He thought about that for a while. Did a howling cat give him a sufficient legal reason to enter the house? He thought over some possible rationalizations and decided that the owner of the cat might well be incapacitated. Farmer could have had a heart attack or a stroke. He might have fallen and hit his head.

Rhodes opened the screen and tried the knob on the back door. It turned easily. Farmer wasn't worried that anyone was going to rob him. Rhodes gave the door a little push, and it opened slowly, whining a bit on its hinges.

As soon as there was room, a gray tabby cat shot out past the door, its tail puffed out and a ridge of hair standing up on its back. It fled across the backyard, ran into a hedge, and disappeared. Rhodes was starting to get a bad feeling about things, but he waited until the door was all the way open before calling Farmer's name. When there was no answer, Rhodes went on inside.

The little kitchen where he found himself was clean. No dishes stacked in the sink, no dirt on the floor, no dust on the breakfast table, or none that Rhodes could see. The top of the small gas range was clean. Farmer was a good housekeeper even if his yard and the house itself didn't show any care.

To the right was an entrance to a hallway. Rhodes went into the hall. A bathroom was in front of him. To his right was a bedroom, and another bedroom was to his left. In front of the left-hand bedroom was the living room. Like the Hunts, Farmer had a big new flat-screen TV set. Rhodes walked through the house looking around, but Farmer wasn't there. The house had the feeling that houses do when no one is home. In a way that was a relief. Rhodes had half expected to find Farmer's body.

Rhodes went back outside and closed the door. The cat was nowhere to be seen, but it would probably show up again when it got hungry. Maybe Farmer would be back from wherever he'd gone in time to feed it. Before he went back around to the front, Rhodes took a look in the garage to see why the pickup didn't fit it.

The garage was small to start with, having been built early in the previous century when cars weren't as wide or long as they'd become. It wouldn't be easy for Farmer to open the door and get in and out of the pickup, but he must have been able to manage it.

The pickup wouldn't fit in the garage because most of the space was taken up by gasoline-powered mowers that sat on the dirt floor in various stages of disassembly. A shelf attached to the wall held some greasy rags and tools. Farmer was a tinkerer, and Rhodes recalled that he made a little money by repairing old power mowers for a fee. He also took in mowers that people wanted to get rid of, fixed them up, and sold them. It brought in a little money. Not enough money to afford a new big-screen TV, however. Maybe he had other sources of income.

Rhodes left the garage and walked back around to the front of the house, where a man was standing on the sidewalk.

"Hey, Sheriff," the man said.

He was tall and skinny, with thin white hair and droopy, clean-shaven cheeks. He looked about a hundred years old. Rhodes thought he knew him, but he wasn't quite sure.

"I'm Harry Garrett," the man said. His voice sounded a little husky, as if he didn't do much talking. "Used to cut your hair when you were a just a little shaver." He chuckled. "Little shaver. Some barber humor for you there."

Rhodes recognized the man now. He hadn't seen him in many years, not since the barbershop had closed. There wasn't a barbershop in Clearview now, at least not one like Garrett had owned, three chairs, two barbers most of the time, and on the weekends you could even get a shoeshine. For a second Rhodes had a flashback to sitting on a board set between the two arms of the big barber chair, the smell of shaving cream and hair tonic and talcum powder filling the air.

"Good to see you, Mr. Garrett," Rhodes said.

"Just call me Harry. Good name for a barber, don't you think?"

Rhodes smiled. "A little more barber humor?"

"Right you are. Been a long time since I saw you last. I live across the street there." He pointed to a neat little house that was as old as Farmer's but in much better shape. "I don't get out a lot since I quit cutting hair. Mostly sit at home and watch TV. You watch a lot of TV?"

"Not much," Rhodes said.

"I do. Watch all the time. I like the game shows on the cable. My wife likes the soap operas, but there's not many of those left. We got two TVs, so we don't have any fights about it. I just go in the bedroom when the soaps come on and watch my shows in there. You ever watch the soaps?"

"Never had time," Rhodes said.

"Didn't think so," Harry said. "Anyway, the soaps aren't what I came over here to talk about. You looking for Riley?"

"Yes, I am. Have you seen him?"

"Yep. Don't see much of him. Too busy watching TV. That *Family Feud* is pretty good, but I like *The Chase,* too."

"I'm sure they're good," Rhodes said. "But have you seen Farmer recently?"

"That's what I came over here to tell you, 'cause I figured you were looking for him. I saw him a couple of days ago. It was late in the day. He went off with somebody. Didn't ever see him come back."

"Do you know who he went off with?"

"Nope. Just some pickup truck was all I saw."

"What kind of pickup?"

"Don't know one from the other. Lots of those around. Seems like everybody in town has one."

"Was it new? Old? Did you notice the color?"

"I don't see as good as I once did," Harry said. "I can see well enough to watch TV, though. I like those game shows. Anyhow, I thought you'd want to know Farmer was gone, since you were looking for him."

"I appreciate you telling me," Rhodes said.

"Glad to help out. It was just an accident that I saw him go off. Like I said, I don't get out much. Wouldn't have seen him leave if it hadn't been for me coming out to pick up the newspaper. He might've come back and I just missed him, but since you were looking for him, maybe he didn't."

Garrett turned to leave. He took a couple of steps, but then he stopped and turned back around.

"Come here, Sheriff," he said. "Let me get a look at your head."

"My head?"

"I'll take a look at your haircut. Give you a little free barberly advice."

Rhodes wasn't sure he wanted any barberly advice, free or not, but since Garrett had helped him out a little, he walked over to where the retired barber stood.

Garrett crossed his right arm over his stomach, rested his left elbow on his hand, and fingered his chin with his left forefinger and thumb as he gave Rhodes the once-over.

"Not bad," Garrett said. "Lemme see the back."

Rhodes turned around.

"Got a little thin spot back there," Garrett said.

"I know," Rhodes said.

"Might try some of that Minoxidil on it. Could work. You never know."

"I don't think so," Rhodes said.

Garrett dropped his arms to his side. "I guess not. Anyway, like I said, not bad. Not like a real barbershop haircut, but I guess it'll do."

"I hope so," Rhodes said. "Thanks for your help."

"Glad to do it. I gotta get back now. Don't want to miss too much of *Family Feud*."

"I can't blame you for that," Rhodes said.

As Garrett returned to his house, Rhodes thought about the situation. He didn't know what to make of the information about Farmer. The fact that he'd gone off with someone and hadn't come back didn't have to mean anything sinister. On the other hand, Rhodes didn't think people just went off with someone, leaving the house open, and didn't come back. He didn't know anyone who was related to Farmer, so he didn't know who to call about him. His best friend was Melvin Hunt, and he wasn't going to be any help. Maybe Joyce would know something.

Rhodes got in the Tahoe and started back across town. It would be a good idea to go by the jail and check in to see what was going on around the county before he talked to Joyce. He had a lot more to worry about than Hunt's murder, and though that was the most important, he couldn't neglect the other parts of his job, even if they were insignificant. The voters, he knew, would never forgive him if he did.

Chapter 14

▼

When Rhodes got to the jail, Hack and Lawton were laughing about something. That was a bad sign. Jennifer Loam was there, too, an even worse sign, and she was laughing with them. Rhodes didn't know what they found so amusing, but he was sure it would be on the Internet very soon.

"Hey, Sheriff," Jennifer said when Rhodes came in.

She was young and blond and very bright. Her Web site was probably already making more money than the local newspaper. The owners probably regretted letting her go when they'd down-sized.

Rhodes greeted her. He went to his desk, sat down, and asked what the laughter was all about, knowing that Hack and Lawton would try to make him drag it out of them. He hoped that Jennifer might spill the beans and tell him immediately.

She didn't, and Rhodes thought, not for the first time, that she had fallen in with Hack and Lawton in their conspiracy against him.

"It's about the Baldwins," Hack said. "You know the Bald-wins?"

"Retired schoolteachers?" Rhodes said.

"That's them. They had a problem."

"Not them, exactly," Lawton said.

Hack shot him a look. When Hack started telling a story, he regarded it as his alone and didn't like to be interrupted, much less by Lawton. Lawton just grinned. He enjoyed raising Hack's temperature.

"Did they need our help?" Rhodes asked.

"Sure enough did," Hack said, looking back to Rhodes. "They said they'd been robbed, like all those folks in the southeast part of the county."

Rhodes tried to remember where the Baldwins lived. On a hill out from Mount Industry, he thought, not too far from the chicken farms that had caused so much trouble not long ago. Hundreds of thousands of chickens can make a big stink, and the Baldwins had been some of the chief complainers in the past. The problem had been settled temporarily, but the complaints had started again. Bad odors weren't Rhodes's job, however, but burglary was.

"They wasn't robbed, exactly," Lawton said.

This time Hack did more than look. "Who's tellin' this story?"

"You are," Lawton said.

"That's right." Hack turned back to Rhodes. "What was it I was sayin'?"

"Baldwins. Robbery."

"Yeah. They called to say they'd been robbed. Well, not *they*. It was Mrs. Baldwin that called. She taught in the grammar school. That's what we used to call it, anyway. What do they call it now?"

"Elementary school," Lawton said. "Or maybe grade school. I never can remember."

"Never mind what they call it," Rhodes said. "Just tell me about the robbery."

"He's gettin' touchy again, ain't he, Hack," Lawton said. "Happens a lot lately. You ever notice how touchy he is, Ms. Loam?"

"He seems very calm to me," Jennifer said, grinning at Rhodes. "A little impatient, maybe, but not touchy."

"I'd say touchy myself," Hack told her. "They say that as a man gets older—"

"Don't start that again," Rhodes said.

"See what I mean?" Lawton said.

Jennifer laughed. "Maybe I should be getting a video of this."

"Forget it," Hack said. "I don't want to be on the Internet. Dang it, now you've made me forget where I was."

Rhodes sighed. "Baldwins. Robbery."

"Yeah, anyway, seems they had the grandkids stayin' with 'em last night and one of the girls had some kind of project to do for her school. Some class or other."

"Bread," Lawton said. "She had to make bread."

Hack didn't even bother to look at him. "I said I was tellin' this story. You gonna let me?"

"Sure," Lawton said. "You go right on ahead."

"Robbery," Rhodes said. "Get to the robbery."

"I'm gettin' there," Hack said. "Don't be so touchy. See, Mr. Baldwin, Lonnie's his name, Lonnie wasn't there when they made the bread. The granddaughter didn't want to forget it the next day when she went to school, so she put it in the backseat of the SUV. I think they got a Chevrolet, but it might be a GMC. One or the other."

"GMC," Lawton said, and this time Hack wasn't bothered.

"GMC. She put the bread in the backseat. Today they got ready to go to school and went outside and the bread was gone."

Rhodes shook his head. "They called about somebody stealing bread?"

"You'd call if it was your granddaughter who was goin' to have to tell the teacher somebody stole your homework," Lawton said. "Wouldn't you?"

"The dog usually ate mine," Rhodes said.

"Wasn't no dog," Hack said. "Dog can't open a car door. 'Course, the doors shoulda been locked, but they weren't, and the bread was gone. Della Mae, that's Ms. Baldwin, called right from the cell phone. She was mighty upset."

"Did you send anybody out to check on the theft?"

"Didn't have to," Hack said.

"Didn't have to?"

"Nope. All the cryin' and takin' on caused the thief to confess. Della Mae called back and told me."

"The thief was there?"

"Sort of."

"You might as well tell me who it was," Rhodes said. "I'm not going to take another guess."

"It was Lonnie," Lawton said, and Hack rose up out of his seat.

"Simmer down," Rhodes said. "It's about time somebody got to the point. Finish the story. We have a murder to work on."

Hack sat back down, but he didn't look happy. "What happened was that Lonnie had been out in the yard early that mornin', before anybody was up, and he saw the bread in the backseat. He couldn't figure out what it was doin' there. Nobody'd told him about the project, so he didn't think the bread was for school. He decided he'd put it to some use, so he fed it to his layin' hens."

Jennifer Loam laughed as Hack got to the punch line. So did Lawton.

"I can't decide which is worse," Jennifer said. "Having to explain to the teacher that your grandfather fed your project to some chickens or having to live with the guilt of having done it."

"Or having to live with Della Mae," Lawton said. "It's gonna go hard with Lonnie, I bet."

"Serve him right," Hack said. "Feedin' a little girl's bread to some hens. You gonna put this on the Internet, Ms. Loam?"

"I don't think so. I don't want to make things any worse for the Baldwins. I might put something on there about how the sheriff's dog used to eat his homework."

"That'd be a good story," Lawton said. "Might get him a few votes in the next election."

"Or lose him some," Hack said, as Seepy Benton came through the door.

"I've solved the case," Seepy said.

"What case?" Rhodes asked him.

"The marijuana case. Hi, Jennifer. Hey, Hack and Lawton."

"I need to film this," Jennifer said.

"Hold on just a second," Rhodes told her. "You mean you know who's growing it?" he asked Seepy.

"Well, I haven't gotten quite that far yet," Seepy said.

Rhodes had suspected as much. "Just how far have you gotten?"

"I know who's *not* growing it."

Rhodes supposed that was something. "Who's not growing it?"

"Able Terrell. He's not the one stealing things, either."

"I didn't think he was, but how do you know for sure?"

"I could tell you I made some brilliant deductions," Seepy said.

"But would I believe you?" Rhodes asked.

"I don't see why not. I've made some before. I'm a regular Sherlock Holmes." Seepy looked at Jennifer. "Did you know that I can solve Rubik's Cube in two minutes and twenty-seven seconds? You should get that on video one of these days."

"What does being able to solve a Rubik's Cube have to do with marijuana crops?" Rhodes asked.

"It proves my brilliance," Seepy said.

He had a point there. Rhodes was pretty sure he couldn't solve a Rubik's Cube in under three minutes and maybe not in under three months. Or three years, unless he had some instructions. He wasn't too sure that being able to do it had any practical applications, however.

"I've been teaching a special class in Rubik's Cube and group theory," Seepy continued. "The idea is to introduce bright community college students to the kind of more advanced mathematics they might see at a university. Maybe you'd like to sit in the next time I teach it."

"I'll just concede your brilliance," Rhodes said, "but I still don't see the connection to the marijuana patch."

"It would be nice to see something about that class on your Web site, Jennifer," Seepy said.

"That's a good idea," Jennifer said. "Tell me more."

"Hold it," Rhodes said. "You can do an interview with Seepy after he tells me about the marijuana. I don't want to get in the way of his viral Internet fame, but if he's got information for me, I need to get it."

"Impatient," Hack said. "You were right, Ms. Loam. That's what he is."

"Sounded touchy, too," Lawton said.

Rhodes held up a hand. "That's enough. Let's get to it."

"Okay," Seepy said. "In this class I told you about, there's this one young man who's almost as brilliant as I am. He also knows a little bit about the pot supply in Blacklin County."

"I don't suppose you'd like to give me his name," Rhodes said.

"You don't suppose correctly. He'll remain anonymous. I asked him about local suppliers, and he said that Able and Ike Terrell don't enter into it. Ike doesn't touch the stuff as far as my source knows, and he doesn't sell it, either. In fact, as far as my source knows, there's no marijuana coming out of the southeast part of the county at all. Most of it's small amounts that people grow in their backyards or closets."

"So the crop on Billy Bacon's land is brand-new," Rhodes said.

"That would be my guess. If it's been harvested, nobody's sold anything from it. Not that my source knows about, anyway."

Rhodes thought it over. Even if it was true that Terrell wasn't involved with the marijuana patch, it didn't mean that he wasn't stealing from people or that he wasn't involved in Melvin Hunt's death. It also didn't clear Billy Bacon. It was hard to believe that Bacon didn't know about a crop being grown on his own land.

The phone rang, and Hack answered. He didn't talk long, and when he hung up he didn't waste any time getting to the point.

"You need to get out to Milsby," Hack told Rhodes. "Terry Allison's found a dead man in his pasture."

Rhodes stood up. "I'm on the way."

"You need backup?" Seepy asked.

"I don't think a dead man will hurt me, but it's not a bad idea. Hack, get Buddy and tell him he can leave off watching that marijuana patch. Have him meet me at Allison's place."

"I meant me," Seepy said.

"I know that," Rhodes said, "but it's not a good idea."

"What about me?" Jennifer said. "Freedom of the press."

"I give up," Rhodes said, and went out the door.

Chapter 15

▼

Milsby was north of Clearview and had once been a thriving, if small, community. Not much of it was left of it now except a few skeletal buildings. People lived in the surrounding area, but they thought of themselves as being part of Clearview if they thought they were part of anywhere. Most of them hadn't been alive when Milsby had begun to vanish.

Terry Allison didn't live there. He lived in Clearview, but he had a little piece of property where he had a camp house that he sometimes visited on summer weekends. His property didn't have a gate, just a cattle guard, so Rhodes drove right on in and up the road toward the camp house. Allison was waiting for him when he arrived.

"I sure never expected anything like this when I came out here," he told Rhodes as soon as Rhodes got out of the Tahoe. "I hadn't been here for a while, and I just came to check on things. See if everything was okay with the camp house. I've been hearing about those thefts southeast of here, so I thought I'd better take a look."

Allison had once sold athletic equipment to little schools all over East Texas until he'd retired. He'd traveled a lot and dealt with a lot of school districts, but he'd been loyal to Clearview and was a strong supporter of the local athletic teams. He'd never been an athlete himself, as was clear by looking at him. He was short and round and red-faced and looked like a prime candidate for a heart attack. He must not have seen his shoes in years except when they were off his feet and some distance away from him.

"I don't come out here much these days," he continued. "It was just lucky that I did. Or unlucky. I sure didn't think I'd find a dead man."

"You want to show me where he is?" Rhodes asked.

"Sure. He's easy to spot, though." Terry pointed. "Just look over there past the camp house."

Rhodes looked in the direction that Terry indicated. In back of his camp house was a thick stand of trees. Above the trees six or seven turkey vultures made slow circles in the sky.

"Saw the buzzards," Terry said, "so I thought maybe some-body's dog had wandered into the woods and died, or maybe one of those dang hogs that are all over everything. I wouldn't mind if one of those dang hogs died, to tell you the truth. Or if all of them did. It wasn't a dog or a hog, though. It was a man."

"I'd better go have a look," Rhodes said.

"I'll go with you," Terry said. "Show you where he is." He looked back to the county road where a car was rattling across the cattle guard. "Who's that? Doesn't look like a county car."

"It's not," Rhodes said. "It's probably Jennifer Loam."

"She's the one's got that Web site, *A Clear View of Clearview*, right? Is she going to put me on the Internet?"

"If she doesn't, I'll be surprised."

"Let's wait for her," Terry said. "I always wanted to be on the Internet."

It took only a minute for the little black Chevy Cruze to get to where Terry and Rhodes stood. It stopped, and Jennifer got out on the driver's side. Seepy Benton got out on the other.

"I have a new job," Seepy said.

"I don't want to hear about it," Rhodes said.

"I'm now a part-time reporter for *A Clear View of Clearview*."

"I told you I didn't want to hear about it."

"I know that, but you didn't really mean it."

"Yes I did."

"I needed somebody to help me out with the site," Jennifer said. "I can't cover everything. Seepy's going to be the college correspondent."

"Right now, though, I'm here to help with the reporting on the discovery of a body," Seepy said. He looked at Terry. "Are you the one who found it?"

"Sure am," Terry said.

Seepy looked around. "Let's go over there and stand in front of that house. It will be a nice background for the interview."

"Interview?"

"That's right. I'll interview you about your discovery while Ms. Loam here does a video. Let me get a little bit of information from you."

In response to Seepy's questioning, Terry told Seepy his name and a little about himself. Rhodes sighed. Seepy had been on the job for what? Five minutes? And he was already taking over. Jennifer didn't seem to mind. She was taking video of the circling buzzards.

Rhodes thought this might be a good opportunity for him to

slip away and look for the body without too much interference, so he went off toward the trees. Nobody followed him.

When he got into the trees, he started to wonder just how far the little woods went. If his mental GPS was functioning correctly, something that wasn't always the case, he might be able to figure things out. First, though, he needed to concentrate on finding the body.

It wasn't hard to do. The smell was enough to notify Rhodes of where the body was. He didn't even have to look up to see where the buzzards were. They wouldn't wait around much longer if the humans kept tramping around in the woods.

Not much of an attempt had been made to hide the body. It lay behind a couple of elm trees that had grown together into one large trunk. It didn't appear that the body had even been covered, and small animals had torn the clothing and gotten at it. Whoever had put it there had probably thought the feral hogs would find it and take care of it before Terry Allison showed up, since Terry didn't spend much time on the place.

Within another day or so, the buzzards and hogs would have pretty much done away with the body and left nothing but a few scraps of clothing and some bones, making identification difficult if not impossible. Rhodes had a pretty good idea who it was, though. He wasn't going to rush to judgment, but as far as he knew, only one person was missing from Clearview, and that was Riley Farmer. What was left of the face looked a lot like Farmer, too.

Rhodes got out his cell phone and called Hack. "Is Buddy on his way to Allison's?"

"Yep," Hack said. "Should be there in a little bit. Is there really a body there?"

"There really is," Rhodes said.

Hack didn't ask any more questions, proving once again that

he could be a professional when it counted. Rhodes hung up and took a closer look at the body. Flies buzzed all around it. Ants crawled over it. There were other insects as well, but Rhodes couldn't identify them. It was impossible to tell for sure how Farmer, and Rhodes was now almost sure that's who it was, had died, thanks to the depredations of the animals, but the area of Farmer's back was a mess. Rhodes thought he might have been shot. He patted the back pockets of the pants but found no wallet. No cell phone, either. They'd have to identify the body for certain some other way.

By the time Rhodes had finished his quick examination, he heard Seepy's voice.

"He's right over there," Seepy said. "By that big tree. That's where the smell is, too. Do you want video of him with the body?"

"I don't think my readers are ready for video quite that gory," Jennifer said.

"If it bleeds, it leads," Seepy said. "That's what I've heard, anyway."

Rhodes stepped out from behind the tree. "You've been reading too much about TV news."

"It's true of the Internet, too," Seepy said. "Haven't you heard of clickbait headlines?"

"Do they have anything to do with fishing lures?"

Jennifer and Seepy laughed. Terry looked as if he had no idea what was so funny.

"The Sheriff Walked into the Woods," Seepy said. "You'll Never Guess What He Found There!"

Rhodes could almost hear the capital letters.

"That's a clickbait headline," Seepy said. "You put a few of those on your Web site, Jennifer, and you'll double your hits."

"You're worth every penny I'm paying you," Jennifer said.

"Have we discussed salary?"

"Not yet." Jennifer pointed to where the body lay. "I can see a pair of boots sticking out over by that tree. That's as gory as I'm willing to go. Could I get some video of you standing over there, Mr. Allison?"

"Sure," Terry said. "Why not?"

Terry walked over to the tree, and Jennifer took a few seconds of video while Rhodes looked around the woods, trying to get his mental GPS to clarify things for him.

"Does Crockett's Creek run back there behind the trees?" Rhodes asked Terry when Jennifer was finished with her video.

"Yeah. Runs right across the back end of my property. I don't ever go back there, but I heard it was running pretty high earlier this year."

"How far is it to the creek?"

"Not too far. Half a mile, maybe."

"I'm going to take a walk down that way. Terry, I'd like for you to go back up to the camp house and watch for my deputy. He should be here in a few minutes. Bring him down here and show him where the body is. He'll know what to do."

"Sure thing," Terry said.

He seemed happy about the Internet fame that was about to be his, and he wasn't even panting from his walk, which surprised Rhodes a little.

"Jennifer, you and Seepy can go on back to town," Rhodes said. "Don't go over there and mess up the crime scene while I'm gone."

"What are you going to do?" Seepy asked.

"I'll just look around."

"I know you," Seepy said. "You have a hunch about something. Let's go with him, Jennifer. We citizens have a right to take video of the cops anytime we want to."

"Just as long as you don't interfere with us in the performance of our duties," Rhodes said.

"We wouldn't think of it," Seepy said.

"That'll be the day," Rhodes said.

"John Wayne, *The Searchers,*" Seepy said.

"Buddy Holly," Rhodes said, "but he stole it from the Duke."

Rhodes headed back into the trees. He didn't like leaving the body, but it had been there for a while without anybody watching it, and Buddy would be along in a minute. Rhodes didn't think the buzzards would act before the deputy arrived.

As he walked, Rhodes wondered for the first time if Buddy had been named for Buddy Holly. Maybe he'd ask him.

Rhodes didn't look back to see if Jennifer and Seepy were following him. He didn't have to. He could hear them. They weren't skilled woodspersons, and for that matter neither was he. However, he didn't think he was making quite as much noise as they were.

Seepy was right about the hunch. Now and then Rhodes had one, and it usually paid to check it out. Sometimes he got lucky. Maybe this would be one of those times.

Walking half a mile over open ground was one thing. Walking half a mile through trees wasn't quite as easy, but it didn't take Rhodes very long to find what he'd had the hunch about. He was almost to the creek when he spotted a small cleared area with some marijuana plants growing in it.

Terry Allison was a lot like Billy Bacon, a man who owned some property that he didn't really know what to do with, a man who seldom if ever went past the front half of the land he owned, which happened to back up on Crockett's Creek, a nice water supply for anybody who needed it to grow a little cash crop.

The patch was fenced with the same kind of wire as the one

on Billy Bacon's land. There was a pump with a pipe leading to the creek, but there was no alligator inside the fence. There was a small puddle of muddy water, but that was all Rhodes could see. Although the puddle didn't appear big enough to hold a gator of any size, Rhodes thought he ought to take a look. He had just opened the gate when Seepy and Jennifer arrived.

"Oh, boy," Seepy said. "More pot."

"It's not for you," Rhodes told him.

Seepy looked offended. "I didn't say I wanted it. I'm just glad to see that someone around here is helping me with my crusade."

"What crusade?" Jennifer asked.

"Don't get him started," Rhodes said, but it was too late. Seepy had already launched into his speech about the benefits of medical marijuana and how it should be tested more widely. Rhodes shut his ears and went into the marijuana patch.

He'd taken only a few steps inside the fence when something roiled the water in the puddle. Rhodes stopped where he was and waited.

He didn't have to wait long, as an alligator snapping turtle came waddling out of the water on its clawed, webbed feet. It was as big as a manhole cover, and three ridges of spikes ran down its shell. Its tail was flat and scaly. It opened its beaky mouth, which could easily have held a softball if Rhodes had brought one with him to toss inside. It breathed like a miniature Darth Vader.

"Gosh-gosh-gosh," Jennifer said. "What *is* that thing?"

"Alligator snapping turtle," Rhodes told her. "They aren't usually aggressive, but this one seems to be."

Jennifer already had her camera out. "Will it hurt us?"

"Not if we don't let it. Don't get close. It could snap your leg in two with that beak."

Jennifer backed up, but she kept the camera running. "Are you going to do anything heroic?"

"Are you asking me or Seepy?" Rhodes looked around. "Where is Seepy, anyway?"

Seepy stood well outside the fence and didn't appear interested in coming inside.

"I guess you were asking me," Rhodes said, "and I'm not going to do anything heroic. I'm not going to do anything at all unless I have to. I don't want to shoot the turtle. It's considered a threatened species in this state."

There was more to it than that. In addition to the fact that the turtles were protected, Rhodes happened to like turtles. Not this particular turtle, but other, smaller, ones. He associated them with good luck and felt they'd helped him out a number of times. He liked to think he was a rational person, so he never told anybody about him and turtles. He certainly wasn't going to tell Seepy, even though Seepy would have understood. Seepy had a mystical side and even believed in ghosts.

"People make soup out of turtles like that," Seepy called from his position outside the fence. "Just one more good reason to become a vegan."

While the conversation had been going on, the turtle had lumbered closer. It didn't appear to have any intention of stopping. Rhodes had seen several snappers in his lifetime, but he'd never seen one like this. They were usually shy and incurious. This one didn't appear to be either.

"If they bite down on your arm or leg," Seepy called, "they won't let go until it thunders."

"That's just an old wives' tale," Rhodes said. "Don't worry about that. Besides, if that thing bites you, it won't have to hold on. It'll cut right through bone and all. We'd better get out of here, Jennifer."

He didn't have to tell her twice. She was already on the way out. The turtle kept right on coming.

"Shut the gate," Seepy said when Rhodes and Jennifer were outside the fence, but Rhodes wasn't listening. He was looking around for a fallen tree limb. He'd decided to do something after all. He saw a limb about the size of a baseball bat not too far away and went to pick it up.

"He's coming out the gate," Seepy said.

"You could use one of your karate moves on him," Rhodes said. "The ones you learned from Professor Lansdale."

"Not karate," Seepy said. "Chen Shuan. And he didn't teach me how to fight turtles. I don't know where the pressure points are."

Rhodes picked up the limb and swished it through the air.

"You going to hit him with that thing?" Buddy said, walking up through the trees. "Because if you are, I'll have to arrest you."

"You're supposed to be working the crime scene," Rhodes said.

"Terry told me you were wandering around in the woods, and I thought you might need some help. Sure enough, you do."

"What about the buzzards?"

"I told Terry to stand by the tree and scare 'em off if they decided to pay a visit. I told him to be careful about the crime scene. He's already walked around there anyway."

"You have any ideas about this turtle?" Rhodes asked.

Buddy patted the big Magnum at his hip.

"That would be a lot worse than hitting him with this stick," Rhodes said. "I'd be the one who'd have to arrest somebody if you shot him."

"Better call Alton Boyd, then. He's the animal expert."

Rhodes wasn't going to call Alton. He thought he could handle the turtle by himself. It had stopped moving. Maybe it was tired. It was about ten feet from Rhodes, and it looked right at him as if daring him to come closer.

"I've just never seen anything like that before," Jennifer said. "It looks like something that escaped from Jurassic Park."

"Only smaller," Seepy said.

The turtle took a step forward.

"Not small enough," Jennifer said. She started the camera again.

Rhodes took a step toward the turtle and extended the tree limb. The turtle's head flashed out like a striking snake, and its beak bit down on the limb.

"Gosh-gosh-gosh," Jennifer said. "That's really scary. I'm glad I got it on video. It'll look great on the Web site. It might be a little shaky, though."

"Heroic Sheriff Confronts Prehistoric Beast," Seepy said. "What Happened Next Will Amaze You!"

"Great clickbait headline," Buddy said.

"What *will* happen next?" Jennifer asked.

The turtle hadn't broken the limb, and true to the old wives' tale, it was hanging on. Rhodes started to drag it.

"I'm going to see if I can get it to the creek," Rhodes said. "It will be a lot happier there than it was in that puddle."

"What if it decides it would rather clamp down on you instead of that limb?"

"I'll make a run for it," Rhodes said. "I might be slow, but I think I can still outrun a turtle."

"Have that camera ready, Jennifer," Seepy said.

"I'm ready."

"Let the games begin," Seepy said.

Chapter 16

▼

The turtle proved cooperative for most of the short distance to the creek. It didn't let go of the limb, and it didn't dig in with its claws and try to prevent Rhodes from dragging it. Once it even walked forward a couple of steps on its own. Rhodes thought later that he should have known it wouldn't be that easy all the way to the creek.

Rhodes had seen a place where the bank had a little cut in it that would allow him to walk down close to the water's edge. There were some cow tracks in it.

Rhodes thought that if he left the turtle at the top of the cut, the turtle would figure out for itself that being in the creek was preferable to being in a mud hole. The creek would have fish and frogs in it, and the turtle could fend for itself rather than depending on someone to bring it some food. It occurred to Rhodes that it might be hungry. That might explain why it was so aggressive.

Rhodes's foot slipped as he started down the bank. There was nothing to grab hold of, and he couldn't stop himself as he slid down to the creek. He'd kept his hold on the limb, so the turtle was coming right along with him. However, just as Rhodes's feet touched the water, the turtle decided it was time to let go. Because it was also sliding at that point, it was sliding straight toward Rhodes.

Rhodes's feet didn't find any purchase in the slimy mud of the creek bottom. He looked at the turtle and saw that it was heading directly for his face, its mouth wide open.

In the past Rhodes had never given much thought to his nose. It just sat there in the middle of his face, and he didn't even notice it anymore when he was shaving. It occurred to him now, however, that it wasn't such a bad nose and that he was rather fond of it. He'd hate to have it bitten off by a turtle.

A scene from an old movie flashed through Rhodes's head, and he pictured Lee Marvin with a silver nose in place of the one that had been bitten off in a barroom brawl. It was a look that Marvin could pull off, but Rhodes was no Lee Marvin. He didn't think the look would be good for him.

Rhodes rolled to the side, kicking his feet in the water. He barely managed to move far enough to let the turtle slide by. The hard shell grazed his shoulder.

When the turtle splashed into the muddy water, it remained still for a second or two. Then it turned its head to allow its hard marble-sized eyes to look at Rhodes, who, if he'd been a mystical person like Seepy, would have sworn that the turtle was smiling. That was impossible, and Rhodes knew it, but he did think it was likely that the turtle was glad to be in the creek, if turtles could be glad. Maybe it was thanking him, if turtles could be thankful.

Rhodes crawled up onto the bank. He was muddy all over and wet from his knees down. His clothes were a mess.

"Did you get all of that on video?" he asked Jennifer.

"I think so," she said, grinning.

"What Happened Next Amazed Me!" Seepy said.

"You know he's armed, right?" Buddy said.

"He wears that ankle holster," Seepy said. "His pistol's all muddy and wet, so I think I'm safe."

"For now," Rhodes said.

"I could shoot him for you," Buddy said. "There's always room for another body in the woods. Or we could feed you to the turtle."

"Better not," Rhodes said, nodding at Jennifer. "There's a witness, and she has a video camera. You'd have to shoot her, too."

"That's how it is," Seepy said. "You kill one person, and it just leads to more killing." He turned serious. "The man by the tree is the second murder in two days. Was he killed because of the first one?"

"I don't know the answer to that," Rhodes said. "It's possible that the two are connected, but we'll have to wait for more information before I can say for sure. That means you need to start working the crime scene, Buddy. I think I'll go home and change clothes."

"I think I'll edit some video," Jennifer said.

"I'll stay here with the cannabis patch," Seepy said.

"No you won't," Rhodes told him.

Rhodes had been messy and muddy before, more than once, so it wasn't a new experience. He'd never been caught on video before, but that didn't really bother him. It was about time that he was shown doing something antiheroic, even comical. Maybe that would put an end to some of the Sage Barton comparisons. It was something to hope for, anyway.

After making sure that Jennifer and Seepy had left and checking that Buddy was working the crime scene, Rhodes talked to Terry, who was a little surprised at Rhodes's disheveled appearance.

"It's a long story," Rhodes told him when he asked about the muddy clothes. "A snapping turtle was involved. Let's leave it at that."

"A snapping turtle?"

"Yes, but never mind him. Have you had any reports from your neighbors around here of people coming onto your place?"

Terry shook his head. "Nobody's said a thing to me. If you look around, though, you can see I don't have many neighbors."

That was true. Houses were not exactly a feature of the landscape on the dusty county roads around what had once been Milsby.

"I did a little poking while you were down at the creek," Terry went on. "I didn't see any tire tracks or anything, and I didn't find anyplace where somebody had parked."

Rhodes should have cautioned Terry about poking around, but it wasn't likely that he'd disturbed any clues. If there were any, Rhodes hadn't spotted them.

"It's like that body was just dropped out of the sky," Terry said.

Rhodes looked up at the sky. The buzzards were still circling, but they were sailing up higher, small black figures against the white clouds and blue sky. They were going to have to look somewhere else for food because Buddy would soon be calling the ambulance to take the body away.

"It didn't fall out of the sky," Rhodes said.

"I know, but I can't figure out how it got there."

Rhodes couldn't figure it out, either, but the body was there, nevertheless. Sooner or later he'd have an answer as to how it got there. Right now he just wanted to be sure who it was, Riley Farmer or someone else.

"Is there anything else you want to tell me about?" Rhodes asked Terry.

Terry gave him a puzzled look. "Like what?"

"Like the marijuana patch down by the creek."

Terry laughed. "That's a good one, Sheriff. You ought to know me better than that. I don't even know what marijuana looks like, much less how to grow it."

"Somebody does," Rhodes said. He wasn't laughing.

"You're not joking?"

"Not even a little bit."

"It must just be some wild stuff. I think I've heard that it can grow wild. Maybe birds dropped some seeds back in there. Like I said, I don't know all that much about it."

"It's not growing wild," Rhodes said. "There's even a nice little fence around it."

Terry no longer looked amused. He looked worried. "I don't know anything about it. Really. A fence? How could there be a fence? I didn't build one. I don't even go down to the creek. I just come out here to sit in my little camp house and read a book or listen to the radio. My wife comes with me sometimes. She likes the birds and squirrels. We get away from town, relax a little, you know how it is."

Rhodes didn't really know how it was. He'd tried to relax only a day ago, and it hadn't turned out well. Maybe if he had a little place in the country with a camp house, it would be different.

"Are you going to arrest me?" Terry asked.

"Not today. Maybe you're telling the truth. Maybe you didn't know anything about the marijuana."

"I didn't," Terry said. "I swear it."

He sounded as if he were telling the truth. Rhodes had been watching his eyes, waiting for the glance upward and to the left, supposedly the telltale sign of lying. Terry's eyes were right on Rhodes and didn't move.

It was a curious coincidence, though. Two marijuana patches, two dead men. Both patches and both dead men on an area of property that the owners said they never looked at. Both dead men discovered by those owners. Could Billy Bacon and Terry Allison be involved together in a marijuana-growing conspiracy? It didn't seem likely, but then nothing about the whole situation was likely. The possibility of a conspiracy between Billy and Terry was something Rhodes would have to consider. Along with a lot of other things.

"Do you own a gun?" Rhodes asked.

"Damn," Terry said. "You've already accused me of farming marijuana. Are you going to accuse me of murder now?"

"I haven't accused you of anything," Rhodes said. "I'm just asking questions."

"Right. Like those talk-show guys on the radio. 'Is our president secretly working with the radical underground to destroy our nation? I'm not saying he is. *I'm just asking.*'"

Rhodes thought of Will Smalls and Gene Gunnison. Terry was like a combination of both of them.

"It's not like that at all," Rhodes said. "It's my job to find things out when somebody's killed. You have to admit that the situation's . . . interesting."

"Well, I didn't plant the marijuana, and I didn't kill anybody. And to answer your direct question, I don't own a gun. I used to have a pistol that I carried with me in the car when I was traveling, but I sold it when I retired. Sold it legally, in case you were wondering. To a dealer. With paperwork and everything."

"I'm glad to hear it," Rhodes said.

"Besides, I wouldn't have called you about the dead man if I'd put him there. I'd have let the buzzards and the hogs take care of him."

"I don't think you have anything to worry about," Rhodes said, "but I have to ask the questions. If I didn't ask them, I wouldn't be able to find anything out."

"I guess I can understand," Terry said. "I just don't like being accused."

"I wasn't accusing, remember. Just asking."

Terry grinned. "Okay, I get it. It's your job. You have to ask questions, no matter who it is you're asking."

"You're right, and I appreciate your help. If you get any ideas about that marijuana patch or if you hear about anybody coming onto your property, you give me a call."

"I'll do that," Terry said.

"I might have to ask you some more questions later."

"Okay," Terry said. "As long as you're just asking."

Rhodes drove home and put the muddy clothes in the hamper. He took a shower and changed, then got out his gun-cleaning kit. He spread a plastic garbage bag on the kitchen table, put newspapers down on top of it, and got some paper towels.

Yancey danced around, watching the preparations as excited as if he'd never seen anything like them before, although Rhodes had cleaned his pistol many times in Yancey's presence. The cats took no interest in the proceedings at all. They weren't interested in much of anything other than eating, grooming themselves, and having a good nap. Not necessarily in that order.

Rhodes sat at the table to clean the gun. As soon as he opened the solvent, Yancey left the room. The smell must have bothered him. If it bothered the cats, they didn't show it. They continued to sleep in their usual spots.

The pistol didn't seem too much the worse for its dip in the creek. It had been protected in the holster, which was fabric and easily cleaned, and it wasn't muddy. Rhodes knew that rust was always a possibility, however, so a good cleaning and oiling seemed called for.

While he worked on the pistol, Rhodes thought things through. If the body at Terry Allison's place was indeed Riley Farmer, and the odds were certainly in favor of that, then there was undoubtedly some connection between his death and the death of his friend Melvin Hunt. Just what the connection was, Rhodes didn't know. Yet. He'd have to figure it out. The only way to do that was to keep on asking questions, even if it irritated people like Terry Allison.

So far nobody was admitting to anything, as was almost always the case, but somebody was guilty. It might be somebody that Rhodes hadn't even talked to yet. He didn't think so, but it could be that way. He'd have to find out more about Farmer's friends and acquaintances if he could, although Farmer might not have had many friends other than Hunt. He seemed like a man who kept to himself. He did have a nice new TV set, which was something that Rhodes was still puzzling over. It wouldn't have seemed so odd, he supposed, if Hunt hadn't also had one. Both men had come into money some way or another.

At the moment, Rhodes had more questions than answers, but that was often the way things went. He'd at least heard and seen a few things that had given him some ideas. That was usually how his cases worked. They weren't so much mysteries as they were puzzles. He had a lot of the pieces. He just had to find out where they fit. At first they were scattered all around. He'd try one piece here and another one there, and for a while the whole picture would be more or less a jumble. If he kept at it long enough, however, the pieces would start to fit together.

That wasn't the whole story. Sometimes pieces of the puzzle were missing. The picture would start to look like something, but it would be incomplete. Rhodes would have to go looking for the missing pieces, which might turn up anywhere. He'd find one here and one there, and sooner or later there would be a complete picture, clear as could be. Or clear enough for Rhodes to make an arrest, at any rate.

The marijuana patches were obviously connected to each other, even if the murders weren't, yet. They both had the same kind of fencing, and both were guarded by formidable reptiles that would scare just about anybody who happened on them. That wasn't a coincidence.

Rhodes still wondered about Allison and Bacon. Both of them said they never went to the back of their holdings, but was that really likely? He could see that it might be in Terry's case, since Terry didn't have any cattle and didn't look like a man who'd do much walking. Billy didn't do much walking, either, because of his bad knee, but he could drive to the creek if he wanted to.

The sign Billy had nailed on his post was another thing that made him look like a good suspect, which was why Rhodes kept coming back to it. SURVIVORS WILL BE SHOT AGAIN. If Melvin had been shot only once, the sign wouldn't have seemed too incriminating. Billy hadn't helped himself by pulling the sign down and hoping Rhodes wouldn't see it. Had he removed the sign because he knew it was practically an admission of guilt? Or was the sign just a coincidence? Rhodes didn't care for coincidences, though from time to time he was forced to admit their existence.

The failure to report the body at first was another strike against

Billy, and Rhodes was sure Billy was guilty in that instance. The extra day would have given Billy time to get to Farmer's house, get him into his pickup on some pretense or other, and kill him. Getting him into the woods on Terry Allison's place wouldn't have been easy, but Billy could have done it. Rhodes wasn't sure how he could have done it, but there was no doubt that it was possible.

Ivy had said that Joyce Hunt had to be Melvin's killer simply because she was Melvin's wife, but maybe Ivy would change her mind now that there had been a second murder. Rhodes would have to ask her.

And what about Will Smalls? He was the main person Rhodes wanted to talk to again. He was next on the list.

When Rhodes finished cleaning the pistol and thinking things over, he realized that once again he'd missed lunch. He pulled one end of the garbage bag over the newspapers and paper towels left on the table and bagged everything up. He took the bag out to the trash bin and tossed it in.

Speedo, the border collie who lived in the Styrofoam igloo in the backyard, was lying in the shade of a pecan tree. He came over to Rhodes for a head rub and looked around as if he thought something was missing.

"Yancey's in the house," Rhodes said. "I don't have time to play."

Speedo gave him a reproachful look and went back to lie down in his shady spot. Rhodes went back inside and washed up before taking a look into the refrigerator.

What he saw there didn't encourage him. Ivy had been on a healthy-eating kick for a long time now, and while Rhodes couldn't really tell much difference between turkey bologna and what he considered the real thing, the thought of it put him off. There wasn't much else to be had, however, so he made a sandwich with the turkey bologna on 100 percent whole wheat bread, adding light mayo and reduced-fat cheese. It was better than nothing, but not by much. If he'd had a Dr Pepper, that would have improved things, but he hadn't given in on that principle yet.

He cleaned up the kitchen and decided that there was plenty of time left in the day to drive back to the southeast side of the county and talk to Will Smalls again. If someone had come back to the house to snoop around, maybe Smalls had seen him. Or shot him, for that matter. It would be a good idea to find out if either of those things had happened. It might be a good idea to talk to Gene Gunnison again, too, while he was in the neighborhood.

It was time to start fitting some of those puzzle pieces into their correct places.

Chapter 17

▼

Gus-Gus and Jackie were glad to see Rhodes again. Will Smalls was not. The dogs ran out from under the porch and came to greet Rhodes with wagging tails and toothy dog grins. Rhodes rubbed their heads while Will sat on the porch in a metal folding chair and glowered.

"I don't see why you came back here, Sheriff," Will said by way of greeting. "Not unless you brought a warrant with you."

"Don't bother to get up," Rhodes said, even though Will had made no move to do so. "I won't take up much of your time, and I don't have a warrant."

Gus-Gus and Jackie saw that Rhodes wasn't going to play with them, so they went back under the porch where it was shady. Rhodes stood in the yard while he talked to Will.

"If you don't have a warrant, you're just wasting your time," Will said.

"Maybe not. You know Riley Farmer?"

"Yeah, I know him. He's Melvin's buddy. Why?"

"Somebody killed him," Rhodes said.

Will leaned forward in the chair. "The hell you say."

Genuine surprise or just good acting? Rhodes liked to think he could tell the difference, but this time he wasn't sure.

"Just like Melvin," Rhodes said. "You know anything about growing marijuana?"

"Sheriff, I don't know what you're talking about or what you're getting at. Marijuana? Somebody's killed Riley? Sounds like you have yourself a real crime wave to handle, but it's got nothing to do with me."

It was hot in the late afternoon, but Will seemed to be sweating from something besides the heat.

"I wish I was sure of that," Rhodes said. "You've already lied to me once."

"Dammit, Sheriff, you can accuse me of a lot of things, but you better not call me a liar."

"I just did," Rhodes said. "You might call it 'misspeaking.' You told me that Joyce wanted you to stay here and keep an eye on things, but that wasn't the truth."

"The hell you say."

"You sure do like that expression."

Will stood up. "I'm getting real tired of you, Sheriff. You aren't near as funny as you think you are."

"People tell me that all the time," Rhodes said.

"Well, they're damn sure right. You better leave now. I don't have anything else to say to you."

"You don't want to tell me why you were lying to me?"

"I wasn't lying. Joyce told me to come out here. You can ask her."

"I will," Rhodes said, but he knew that as soon as he got out of sight, Will would call her so they could get their stories straight.

"Joyce said you had a key to the house," Will said. "You might's well give it to me."

Rhodes knew he wasn't going to have a use for the key, not the way Will was talking, so he fished it out of his pocket and handed it over.

"Riley Farmer went off with somebody in a pickup a couple of days ago," Rhodes said, after he'd given Will the key. "It looked like yours."

It turned out that Will did have something else to say after all. "Give it up, Sheriff. I haven't seen Riley Farmer in a long time, and there's a lot of pickups in this county that look a lot like mine."

Rhodes hadn't thought he'd be able to get Will to break down and confess with such a transparent gambit, but it didn't hurt to try. It was time to change the subject.

"Anybody come snooping around the place while you've been on guard?" Rhodes asked.

Will sat back down. "Not that it's any of your business, but no. It's been real quiet, and I'd like it to stay that way. You go on now. I'm tired of talking to you."

Rhodes was tired of talking to Will, too, and he didn't have any more questions at the moment, so he just said, "Thanks for your hospitality," and left.

Gus-Gus and Jackie came running out from under the porch to see him off. It was nice to know that he still had at least two friends.

Gene Gunnison wasn't sitting on the porch when Rhodes drove up to his house. He was nowhere in sight. He was around somewhere, Rhodes knew, since his pickup was still sitting where it had been earlier. The boat had been removed from the bed and wasn't in sight. Maybe Gunnison had dragged the boat down to the creek and gone fishing. Rhodes walked to the pickup and looked around. There was a worn track down to the woods, and there was a little boat trailer beside the barn. It would be easy for someone Gunnison's size to get the boat on the trailer and pull it down to the creek, but it didn't seem likely that he'd take the trouble to pull the trailer back up to the barn. It didn't seem likely that he'd go fishing, for that matter.

"Sheriff?" Gunnison called from the front porch. Rhodes hadn't heard a door open or close. Gunnison was the quiet type. "What're you doing back here? I thought I told you I wasn't too sociable."

It seemed like hardly anybody was ever glad to see the sheriff.

"I thought of a few more questions," Rhodes said, and he walked back to the front of the house. By the time he got there, Gunnison was sitting in his chair with his booted foot on the up-turned bucket.

"Must be nice to have a job like yours," Gunnison said. "Driving around all day, pestering people and asking them questions."

"It's not bad," Rhodes said, "but it might be too sociable for you."

"Ha ha."

Rhodes had found yet another person who didn't think he was funny. Come to think of it, those people far outnumbered the ones who appreciated his little jokes by a few hundred to one. He wasn't even sure there was one. Sometimes Ivy laughed, but she might have been doing it just to make him feel better.

"I was wondering if you knew Riley Farmer," Rhodes said.

"Don't know that I do. Why?"

"He's had a little bad luck," Rhodes said.

Gunnison raised his foot about an inch off the bucket. "Haven't we all."

"Riley's a little bit worse off than you," Rhodes said. "He's dead."

Gunnison lowered his foot. "That's too bad. You want to tell me why I should care?"

"Seems to me that whoever killed Riley might've killed Melvin. Melvin was your neighbor, so I thought you might've noticed some things going on around here. There's been a good bit of stealing, so that ties in with it, too, maybe. It's getting downright dangerous down here in this part of the county."

"I'm not worried," Gunnison said. "Nobody's gonna bother me."

"Somebody bothered Riley Farmer. Met him outside his house and took him off and killed him."

"Thing is," Gunnison said after a few seconds passed in silence, "I didn't know Farmer very well. Just knew him to say hey to if I saw him, which was mighty damn seldom. It's too bad he's dead, but it's not like we were buddies or anything. Me and Melvin weren't, either. I don't know who killed 'em or why, but I won't miss 'em. I just want to be left alone."

Some jays were cutting up down in the woods, but that was the only sound Rhodes heard. They were too far from the highway to hear the cars that passed, and if there were any cattle nearby, they were keeping quiet.

"Seems like you're pretty much alone, all right," Rhodes said.

"Yep, and that's the way I like it. Hint, hint."

"I take it you're bored with this conversation," Rhodes said.

"You got that right."

"In that case, I guess I'll be going."

"Don't hurry back," Gunnison said.

Rhodes had a lot to think about as he drove back to Clearview. He called Hack to let him know he was going off duty, and Hack didn't even question him about the body at Terry Allison's place. Rhodes figured that Buddy had come in and kept Hack in the loop.

It was just about time for supper, so Rhodes stopped at his house to see if Ivy had started to cook anything. She hadn't, because she was out in the front yard sweeping off the sidewalk.

"Working hard?" Rhodes asked.

"No. Just doing a little tidying up," Ivy said.

"That can be hard work," Rhodes said. "Why don't we go out to dinner again."

To his surprise Ivy said that sounded like a good idea, so he decided to push his luck.

"How about going to the Round-Up?" he asked.

Ivy thought it over. "Well, all right. I suppose we can find something healthy on the menu there."

Rhodes thought she was wrong about that, but he didn't say a discouraging word.

"You go out and play with Speedo," Ivy said. "I'll get ready. It won't take a minute."

She took the broom into the garage, and Rhodes went inside, figuring it would be more than a minute but not much. Ivy wasn't one to dawdle. Yancey was in the kitchen, and he hopped around and yipped to show how thrilled he was to see Rhodes. It was as if Rhodes had been away for years instead of a few hours. Rhodes knew that what really had Yancey excited wasn't that Rhodes had come home. It was that Yancey knew he'd get to go out into the backyard and torment Speedo for a while.

"That's right," Rhodes said. "I came in to get you. Are you ready to go out?"

Yancey's yipping increased in volume.

"I thought so. Come on."

As soon as Rhodes opened the screen door, Yancey shot past him, down the steps, and out into the yard, looking for the squeaky toy that the dogs played with. Speedo didn't have a chance. He was lying under the pecan tree, and he got up as quickly as he could, but Yancey had the advantage of knowing where the toy was. He ran to it and scooped it up before Speedo could get started.

Rhodes sat down on the top step and watched the dogs. Yancey was so small that he had trouble running in the grass, which Rhodes had to admit should have been cut a few days earlier. Speedo was much bigger and faster than Yancey, but he didn't catch up to the smaller dog too soon. It was as if he were considering his strategy or letting Yancey have his fun while he could.

Yancey tired out quickly and dropped the squeaky toy, which was a well-chewed yellow duck. Rhodes had two or three spares in the house, and it would soon be time to break out another one.

Yancey stood guard over the duck, panting a little as Speedo came up to snatch the toy away. When they played this game, sometimes he got it, and sometimes he didn't. This time he did, and he took off at a lope, running around the yard so fast that Yancey couldn't keep up, not that Yancey really tried. He was mainly interested in waiting until Speedo dropped the duck so he could swoop in and grab it.

Speedo pulled a dirty trick, however. He ran over and dropped the duck at the foot of the steps for Rhodes to pick up and throw to him. Rhodes picked it up and threw it as high and as straight up as he could.

"Jump ball!" he said.

The dogs both timed it pretty well and jumped together. Speedo was so big that he knocked Yancey a yard or so away and grabbed the ball in the air. Yancey rolled over and attacked.

Ivy came out the back door. "Sometimes I think you have more fun with that toy than those dogs do."

Rhodes stood up. "I probably do. Come on, Yancey. Time to go inside."

Speedo dropped the duck and trotted back to his favorite spot. Yancey did something that he'd never done before. He snatched up the duck and headed for the back steps at his top speed. Rhodes grinned and opened the door as Yancey bounded up the steps and into the house. Speedo took no notice, but Yancey didn't seem to care.

"He thinks he put one over on Speedo," Rhodes said.

"Speedo let him," Ivy said. "Sometimes it's easier that way."

Rhodes thought there might be some hidden meaning there, but he couldn't figure out what it was. He said, "This isn't official business, so let's go in the Edsel. I haven't driven it lately, and I need to be sure the battery's okay."

"That's fine with me," Ivy said.

Rhodes had come by the Edsel at the same time he'd come by Yancey in the investigation of a murder case. It was kind of a package deal. The old car had been well maintained, and Rhodes liked to drive it now and then to be sure it stayed in working order. It was considered by a lot of people to have been one of the auto industry's biggest failures, but Rhodes liked it for its peculiarities, like the fish-mouth grille and the push-button automatic transmission with the buttons in the center of the steering wheel.

The Edsel hadn't been driven for a while, but the battery cranked the motor after a couple of seconds, and Rhodes backed the car out of the garage. As they drove to the restaurant, he told Ivy about the discovery of Riley Farmer's body.

"He's not married," Rhodes said, "so his wife couldn't have killed him."

"Melvin Hunt's wife could have," Ivy said. "It's always the wife. If Riley was Melvin's best friend, then she might have had to kill him to cover up the first murder."

"Anything's possible," Rhodes said.

"But you don't believe it."

"I didn't say I didn't believe it. It could have happened that way. There are some things that make me wonder."

"What things?" Ivy asked, and Rhodes told her about Will Smalls.

"What if Joyce is the one who lied?" Ivy asked when he was finished.

"Her sister's the one who told me, not Joyce."

"Well, then. Everybody makes mistakes."

"I thought I'd made a mistake once," Rhodes said, "but I was wrong."

Ivy laughed.

Rhodes laughed, too. It was about time somebody appreciated one of his jokes.

Chapter 18

▼

Rhodes found out that the joke was on him when he arrived at the Round-Up. The sign in front had formerly said ABSOLUTELY NO CHICKEN, FISH, OR VEGETARIAN DISHES CAN BE FOUND ON OUR MENU! Now it said TRY OUR NEW CHICKEN AND VEGETARIAN DISHES!

"You knew, didn't you," Rhodes said when he'd parked the Edsel on the asphalt lot.

"I'd heard that there'd been a menu change," Ivy said, giving him an innocent look. "I wasn't sure how drastic it was."

"Pretty drastic," Rhodes said, getting out of the car and looking at the sign again. Underneath the main message was TODAY'S SPECIAL: GRILLED CHICKEN BREAST WITH GARLIC HERB DRESSING, RICE, AND GREEN BEANS. Underneath that it said FREE WI-FI!

Rhodes sighed.

"Don't take it so hard," Ivy said. "I doubt that we'll see a single person with a computer on the table."

"It's not computers that worry me," Rhodes said.

Ivy grinned. "I didn't really think so, but you don't have to order the chicken breast. I'm sure you can find plenty of things that will clog your arteries."

Rhodes hoped that was true, but he didn't think it would be a good idea to say so. They went inside, where they were greeted by Mary Jo Colley, one of the servers. Rhodes knew her, and not just because he was a regular customer. She'd been on the periphery in a couple of his cases.

"Good evening, folks," she said. "I see you've had a tough day, Sheriff, but you handled it all well."

"What do you mean?" Ivy asked.

Mary Jo gave her a quizzical look. "He hasn't told you?"

"He never tells me anything."

"You're starting to sound like Hack," Rhodes said.

"Let me get you seated," Mary Jo said. "Then I'll tell you the news. I'll even show it to you."

She led them to a seat in a booth by one of the front windows. Several people waved or nodded to Rhodes and all of them seemed to be grinning. Rhodes wondered what was going on.

"Let me get y'all some water," Mary Jo said after they were seated. "I'll be back in a jiffy."

The restaurant's soundtrack was something that was called "classic country," which was fine by Rhodes. He wasn't fond of the current music masquerading as country, but he liked the old stuff. At the moment, Roy Drusky was singing "Red, Red Wine."

Mary Jo returned in the jiffy she had promised, and in addition to the water she carried, she had an iPad stuck under her arm.

Wi-Fi, Rhodes thought. Trying to put off what he was sure was coming, he said, "When did the policies change around here?"

Mary Jo set the water and the iPad on the table. It was in a black case. "Last week. Had too many people coming in and complaining about the menu and asking about the Wi-Fi connection. I guess Clearview is growing up."

"That's one way to look at it," Rhodes said.

"We might even have some gluten-free items before long," Mary Jo said. "Clearview is getting more like California all the time, but you can still get a steak and a baked potato with butter and sour cream, though."

That was the best news Rhodes had heard all day.

Ivy tapped the iPad. "What's that for? Do we order with that now?"

Mary Jo laughed. "Nope. That might be coming down the pike, but that's not what it's for. There's some video I want to show you. Your husband's a real hero, you know that?"

"In general, yes, but not specifically. Are you talking about the loaf-of-bread incident?"

"Well, there's that," Mary Jo said, "but that's yesterday's news, and there's no video. I was thinking about the Jurassic Turtle."

"Jurassic Turtle?" Ivy looked at Rhodes, who shrugged. He remembered that Jennifer had said she was going to "edit some video," but he didn't know exactly what she might have done.

"Let me show you," Mary Jo said.

She opened the iPad case's cover and found *A Clear View of Clearview*. She opened a link, and a video started. Mary Jo was standing on Ivy's side of the booth, so the video was upside down from Rhodes's side. He couldn't tell much about what was going on, but he could see that he and the turtle were involved.

"I found some muddy clothes in the hamper," Ivy said when the video was over. "Little did I know they'd been worn by somebody who's not afraid of taking on a fight with a really big turtle."

"That's an alligator snapping turtle," Mary Jo said. "One of those things can take your fingers right off if you aren't careful. I had a boyfriend one time that lost a pinkie finger to one of those turtles when he was out fishing and hooked it by accident. Tony Spano. That turtle wasn't one bit grateful when Tony tried to get the hook out of its leg. Tony had a beer cooler with him, so he put the finger on ice. The doctors reattached it, and it worked as good as new. Well, almost."

She pushed something so the video would replay, turned the iPad around, and shoved it over to Rhodes's side of the table. He didn't want to watch, but he felt he had to. Sure enough, the headline said JURASSIC TURTLE, and the way Jennifer had edited the video made him seem much more in control of the situation than he had been in reality. She even made it look as if his face-to-face confrontation with the turtle on the creek bank had been both brave and deliberate. In fact, the video looked to Rhodes like something out of an old *Jungle Jim* movie, the ones Johnny Weissmuller made after he'd gone a little bit to seed and gotten a tad too heavy to play Tarzan. He still looked pretty good, though, and so did Rhodes, who now understood why everybody had been so friendly to him as he walked through the restaurant. Most of them had probably seen the video.

"I'd like to see Sage Barton do it any better," Mary Jo said.

"Has everybody in town read those books?" Rhodes asked, closing the cover on the iPad case.

"Just about," Mary Jo said. "Those two women who write 'em really do know you."

"They don't know me at all," Rhodes said. "I'm not anything like Sage Barton. More like Johnny Weismuller."

"Who?"

"Never mind. Let's just leave it that I'm not Sage Barton."

"That's the truth," Ivy said to Mary Jo. "He's a whole lot better than Sage Barton."

Mary Jo gave Rhodes an admiring look. "I'll just bet he is."

Rhodes reached for a menu from between the napkin holder and the ketchup bottle next to the wall, and Mary Jo took the hint.

"I'll give y'all a minute to look things over," she said. "The menu's a little different."

"That's what I'm afraid of," Rhodes said.

Mary Jo laughed, picked up her iPad, and left. On the speakers Loretta Lynn was singing about how nobody was woman enough to take her man.

"Were you going to tell me about the turtle?" Ivy asked Rhodes.

"I hadn't thought about it. It wasn't a big deal."

"It looked like a big deal to me."

Rhodes handed her a menu. "It's all in the editing."

Ivy opened her menu. "Editing?"

"Never mind," Rhodes said.

"What are you going to have?" Ivy asked, looking at the menu.

"Not the chicken," Rhodes said. "What about you?"

"I wonder if they have turtle soup," Ivy said.

Rhodes had a New York strip and a loaded baked potato, which was a very satisfying end to a not very satisfying day. He was thinking about having dessert when he saw Mikey Burns approaching the table.

Rhodes had to answer to all the county commissioners, but Burns was the only one who called him in for little talks with any kind of regularity. Burns always had some new idea or proposal that he wanted Rhodes to consider, and in spite of the fact that Burns frequently wore colorful aloha shirts and looked like a smaller, more benevolent Santa Claus except with a shorter beard, the proposals almost always involved heavy-duty ordnance of one kind of another.

This evening Burns wore a shirt just a bit less brightly colored than those he usually sported. This one was navy blue and covered with guitars of various sizes. It was still a shirt that stood out in the Round-Up, or for that matter in Clearview itself, which was a town of more traditional dressers. Rhodes had always thought that the shirts were part of a carefully crafted image, something that set Burns apart from anyone who might dare to run against him for his position. How could anybody vote against a man who wore shirts like that?

"Good evening, Sheriff," Burns said when he reached the booth. "Good evening, Ivy."

"Good evening," Ivy said, and Rhodes nodded, thinking that it was good-bye to dessert.

Burns didn't wait for an invitation to join them. He pulled a chair away from a vacant table and sat down at the end of the booth.

"Great job with that robber at the convenience store," he said when he was seated. "With that turtle, too."

"Thanks," Rhodes said. "That's what the county pays me for."

"You've handled things well." Burns paused. "Any progress on those killings?"

"I can't really talk about an investigation in progress," Rhodes said, using the cliché to cover for the fact that he hadn't arrived at a solution yet. "Not even with a commissioner. I have a few ideas I'm following up on."

"What about those marijuana fields?"

"They aren't really fields. Just small patches."

It occurred to Rhodes that they were small because that made them easier to hide. The small size might also explain why there were two of them. Spread them around so that if one was found, the other might remain undiscovered. But if there were two, why not three? Or four? It was something to consider.

"You know what we need, don't you?" Burns said.

Rhodes had a feeling that he knew what Burns was going to say, but he pretended not to. "I have no idea."

"Drones," Burns said. "We need drones."

"Why?" Rhodes asked.

"You know why. We could spot those marijuana fields from the air a lot easier than you can stumble across them when you're investigating something else."

"It's not like we have a lot of marijuana patches," Rhodes said.

"Even one is too many. We don't want people to think this is a sanctuary county for marijuana growers."

"I don't think anybody would get an idea like that," Rhodes said. "Here's what we can do. We can call it *cannabis*. That's the name some people prefer. That way it won't have the bad connotations."

Burns thought it over. "I'm not sure that would work. We need some drones."

Rhodes tried another tactic. "If we fly a bunch of drones around the county, people are likely to get the idea that we're spying on them. Plenty of folks around here are suspicious of things like drones. Some of them already think we have cameras on every street corner in town."

Burns brightened. "Those cameras might be a good idea. It wouldn't take many of them. It would cut down on crime."

As far as Rhodes could recall there hadn't been any crime downtown in years, mainly because there was hardly any downtown left.

"We'd have to hire people to maintain the cameras, watch the video, fly the drones, write up the reports," Rhodes said. "It would be a big strain on the budget, and the results might not be worth it. It might cost us some votes, too."

Burns didn't look happy about that. Drones might be dear to his heart, but votes and money were more important.

"Maybe you're right. We don't want to upset the voters or go over our budget." Burns stood up and pushed the chair back to the vacant table. "I'd better get back to my booth. Mrs. Wilkie might start feeling lonesome. You keep up the good work, Sheriff. Y'all have a good evening."

"Is he going to marry Mrs. Wilkie?" Ivy asked as Burns walked away and Willie Nelson was singing about a redheaded stranger. "They've been dating for a good while now."

Rhodes didn't know how to answer that. At one time Mrs. Wilkie had had her eye on him, but that hadn't worked out because Rhodes had met Ivy. Later Mrs. Wilkie had become Burns's secretary, and eventually they'd begun dating. Rhodes didn't think it was a serious affair, at least not on Burns's side, but he wasn't a very good judge of that sort of thing.

"He doesn't talk about it," Rhodes said.

"I think she'd like to get married," Ivy said. "That's what I heard at the beauty shop."

"Well, that settles it," Rhodes said, thinking that Mikey Burns was as good as hitched, although he might not know it yet.

After they left the restaurant without having dessert, which was a bit of a disappointment, Rhodes took Ivy home and put the Edsel in the garage.

"I'm going to visit a few people," he said before Ivy went in the house, "and I need to go by the jail. Official business, so I'll take the Tahoe."

"It's getting late," Ivy said.

"I'll try to be home in time to watch the news at ten."

"You never watch the news."

"There's always a first time," Rhodes said, climbing into the Tahoe.

At the jail the first thing Rhodes did was ask Hack if he was in the loop.

"No thanks to you," Hack said. "Buddy filled me in, though."

"I thought he would. Did he find anything at the crime scene?"

"Said he didn't. Animals had pretty much messed everything up."

Rhodes had thought that might be the case, but there was always the chance that the killer might have overlooked something. Too bad it hadn't happened like that.

"Buddy had the JP come out and then called to have the body picked up and taken to Ballinger's," Hack said. "Dr. White'll do the autopsy when he gets around to it. Maybe tonight."

"Anything else going on that I need to know about?"

"You feelin' out of the loop?"

"Don't start that," Rhodes said. "Just tell me if there's anything I need to know."

"Depends on what you think you need to know."

Rhodes wasn't in the mood to play any of Hack's games tonight.

"Major crimes only," he said. "Pretend nothing else has happened."

"Then there ain't a thing you need to know about."

"Good. Now I have a question for you. Departmental business. Who has a jon boat and a trolling motor that the department can borrow?"

"That's an easy one," Hack said. "Lawton."

Rhodes was a little surprised that he hadn't known about Lawton's boat.

"He don't ever use it," Hack continued. "Bought it years ago when he thought he was gonna be a fisherman. Never took to it, though, and put the boat in his garage. It's still there, and the trolling motor is, too. You plannin' to go fishin' on department time?"

"I'm planning to do a little reconnaissance," Rhodes said.

"A little intelligence operation?"

"With me doing it, there might not be much intelligence involved. You tell Lawton I want to borrow that boat. Tell him I'll be at his place tomorrow morning at seven o'clock, and tell Buddy to meet me there."

"Where you plannin' to go?"

"On a little cruise down Crockett's Creek."

"Business trip?"

"Looking for marijuana patches," Rhodes said.

"Think you'll find any?"

"You never know," Rhodes said.

Chapter 19

▼

After leaving the jail, Rhodes drove to the Smallses' house. He wanted to talk to Joyce and her sister, and to Will, too, if he was there, although Rhodes thought Will was probably going to be spending the night at Joyce's house in the country. Rhodes liked to go by in the evening to talk to people because nobody expected to see him then. It wasn't quite as if he were the Spanish Inquisition, but he did sometimes get some answers that he might not have gotten otherwise.

This time it didn't work. Will wasn't there, and Joyce and Ellen, while they were civil enough, made it clear that they didn't want to talk to Rhodes. When he pressed them, they stuck to the party line, telling Rhodes pretty much what Will had told him earlier.

"It's just that I thought I needed somebody to watch the house," Joyce said. "Those thieves and all. You know."

"Ellen, you told me that it was Will's idea to watch the house," Rhodes said.

"Did I say that?" Ellen asked. "I didn't mean to. I must have been mixed up."

What was more like the truth of the matter was that she'd had a call from Will, who'd told her to change her story.

"Okay," Rhodes said, "but I still don't see why you'd have any objection to me searching the house."

"It's personal," Joyce said, avoiding his eyes. "Melvin wasn't hiding anything, but I just don't like the idea of anybody going through his stuff. It doesn't seem right. You know?"

Rhodes knew, but privacy didn't matter when it came to murder. "I can get a search warrant."

Joyce looked at her sister.

"You don't need to get a warrant, Sheriff," Ellen said. "I told Will I didn't want him staying out there anymore after tonight. He'll be back tomorrow, and you can do whatever you want to, warrant or no warrant."

Rhodes knew what that meant. Will would have gone through the house and removed or destroyed whatever it was that the family might have been worried about. Or whatever *someone* had been worried about. Rhodes still didn't know for sure whose idea it had been for Will to go to the house in the first place, though he was pretty sure it wasn't Joyce's.

"That's fine," Rhodes said. "I'll go by as soon as I get a chance now that I have permission. I do have permission, don't I?"

"Yes," Joyce said. "You have permission."

"I'll need a key if the place is locked. I gave the one I had to Will."

"I'll get it for you," Joyce said.

She left the room, and Ellen and Rhodes looked at each other. Rhodes didn't have anything to say, so he didn't say it. Neither did Ellen, and in a minute or so Joyce came back with the key. She handed it to Rhodes.

"Thanks," Rhodes said, knowing that he likely wouldn't go by the house at all. There wouldn't be anything useful to find, not after Will had cleaned the place up, and Rhodes had other things to do now. Still, he wanted Joyce and the others to think he'd gone by. He was sure they were hiding something, and he didn't want them to get too comfortable.

"I wanted to make sure of something," he said. "Didn't you tell me that Melvin's welding rig was insured?"

"Yes," Joyce said. "We got a little insurance money for it, and that helped us out a lot."

"I thought I remembered that." Rhodes turned to go, then turned back. "If Will's coming back to town, who's going to take care of the dogs?"

"Will's bringing them to town until after the funeral," Ellen said. "We have a good fence in the back, so they'll be fine for a few days. When Joyce goes home, we'll take them back."

Rhodes felt a little better about things knowing that the dogs would be taken care of. That was one less thing for him to worry about.

He thanked Joyce and Ellen for their help, though they didn't deserve it, and left.

Ivy acted surprised to see Rhodes when he got home. She wasn't nearly as excited as Yancey, however.

"I told you I'd get home in time to watch the news," Rhodes said, with Yancey prancing around his legs.

Ivy bent down and tried to calm Yancey. It took a few seconds of sweet-talking and head stroking, but it finally worked. Yancey rolled over and wanted his belly rubbed. Ivy complied, told him what a good dog he was, and stood up. Yancey ran into the spare bedroom where he slept.

"I didn't say you wouldn't be home," Ivy told Rhodes. "What I said was that you never watched the news."

"And I said that there was always a first time. It won't be tonight, though. I don't need to hear any talk about any car wrecks or parking-lot shootings. I get enough of that in my job."

"We don't have shootings in the parking lots in Clearview," Ivy said.

"We might as well have. We have bulls running loose in them."

"That was months ago, so it's not like it happens all the time. When it does we have a heroic sheriff to take care of things."

Rhodes wished he hadn't said anything about parking lots. The incident with the bull was yet another video that had been published on Jennifer Loam's Web site, and everybody in Blacklin County had seen it. What bothered Rhodes even more than that was the fact that people outside the county had seen it. He wasn't comfortable with being made out to be a hero. He just wanted to be left alone to do his job.

"Well?" Ivy said.

"Well, what?"

"Are you going to watch the news, or aren't you?"

"Can't you think of something better for me to do?"

"As a matter of fact," Ivy said, "I can."

The next morning Rhodes got up early and went to the funeral home at six thirty. Clyde Ballinger was an early riser, and Rhodes thought he could find him in his little apartment, either eating breakfast or reading a book or both.

Rhodes smelled bacon when he got out of the Tahoe and was a little disappointed when he found that Ballinger had already finished with his breakfast.

"If I'd known you were coming," Ballinger said, "I'd have baked a cake."

"What?" Rhodes said.

"It's an old song. My grandmother used to sing it. I can't bake, but I could have saved you some bacon. You like bacon, don't you? I could go fry you up a strip or two."

Rhodes did like bacon. Real bacon, that is. He wasn't too fond of the turkey bacon that Ivy bought, and he wouldn't have minded if Ballinger had saved him a piece of the real thing. That wasn't the purpose of his visit, however.

"Thanks for the offer," he said, "but I just wanted to check on the autopsy."

They were in Ballinger's office, and Ballinger opened a desk drawer and got out the report, along with a plastic bag holding the bullets that Dr. White had recovered from the body. Rhodes took the report and asked if Dr. White had found any identification on the corpse.

"It was Riley Farmer," Ballinger said.

"He didn't have a billfold," Rhodes said.

"No, but he had a tattoo on his left biceps. Dr. White was Riley's doctor at one time, and he recognized the tattoo. It's all in the report."

Rhodes flipped through the report and noted that Farmer had been shot with a .32. He'd have Mika do a ballistics comparison, but he'd have been willing to bet right now that the bullets would match the ones that had killed Melvin Hunt.

He'd also been right that Riley hadn't been killed where he'd been found. He'd been dead a while before he was dumped under the tree.

When Rhodes was through looking at the report, Ballinger handed him the plastic bag. "I hope you catch whoever killed those fellas, Sheriff."

"So do I," Rhodes said.

Rhodes dropped off the report and the evidence at the jail and drove to Lawton's house, where he and Buddy loaded the jon boat into the back of Rhodes's pickup. Rhodes hadn't wanted to try to shove the boat into the Tahoe. It might have fit, but he didn't want to take a chance on scratching the Tahoe, not while it was still new, at any rate.

"Y'all be careful with my boat, you hear?" Lawton said. "I might decide to retire one of these days. Might take up fishin' like I started to do before, and I'll need the boat for that."

"We'll be careful," Rhodes told him, thinking that Lawton was like Hack and would never retire. "Is the battery for the trolling motor charged up?"

"Sure is. Got it on a charger in the garage. It's a little too heavy for a weak old guy like me to carry, though."

"Buddy can handle it," Rhodes said. "Right, Buddy?"

"Easy," Buddy said. "I'll go get it."

Buddy went into the garage. Rhodes and Lawton waited. In a couple of minutes, Buddy came back out with the battery.

"Doesn't weigh more than ten or twelve pounds," he said.

"Yeah," Lawton said. "I know. I'm more lazy than weak."

Buddy gave Lawton a disgusted look. He put the battery in the pickup bed and shoved it as far back as he could under the slanted boat. He went back in the garage and got the trolling motor and slid it in behind the battery.

"That's it," he said, dusting his hands.

"I hope you can navigate that creek," Lawton said, giving Rhodes a critical look. "It's deeper than it's been in years, but with a good bit of weight in it, the boat might get hung up on some mud or an old stump."

"If we start sinking in the mud, I'll make Buddy get out and push," Rhodes said.

Lawton smirked. "I don't think it'll be Buddy that's weighin' you down."

"I was joking," Rhodes said.

"I wasn't," Lawton said. "I don't want you to get the propellor stuck in the mud on the bottom of the creek and burn up my motor."

Rhodes wondered if he should start having the grilled chicken breast the next time he went to the Round-Up, but he knew he wouldn't.

He thought of something else they needed. "Do you have any paddles? We'll need them at first, and I don't want Buddy to have to push if the battery plays out on us."

"You don't want to be up the creek without a paddle," Lawton said. "I got some in the garage, not too far from where Buddy got the battery."

Buddy went back into the garage and came out with a couple of old wooden paddles that he shoved into the back of the pickup.

"Ready to go?" he asked.

Rhodes looked at the sky to the north and west where some black clouds were building up.

"We might be in for a little rain," he said, "but we won't melt if we get wet. Let's get started."

"Y'all be careful," Lawton said. "Don't fall overboard. Don't burn up my motor, either."

"We don't plan to," Rhodes said, getting into the pickup.

"You know what they say about plans," Lawton called as Rhodes started the pickup, but Rhodes didn't answer him.

Not too far from Terry Allison's place there was an old wooden bridge across Crockett's Creek. Rhodes drove to the bridge and pulled off the road into the weed-lined bar ditch. He and Buddy wrestled the boat out of the pickup and down to the creek, then went back for the battery, motor, and paddles. They got the motor clamped on the mount and hooked to the battery, and Rhodes tossed the paddles into the boat. The clouds were thicker and closer now, and a low rumble of thunder rolled out of them.

"I kinda wish I'd brought a slicker," Buddy said.

"Maybe you won't need it," Rhodes said. He looked at the boat. "I'll get in first."

Since the trolling motor was in the front, Rhodes thought it would be best if he was in the back. That way the front end of the boat would be a little higher, and maybe the motor wouldn't get stuck in the mud. Rhodes didn't think there was any chance of that, but he didn't want to upset Lawton.

Rhodes stepped into the boat, which immediately sank deeper into the water, and made his way to the back. He sat down, and Buddy pushed the boat off into the creek. He jumped in at the front, and Rhodes grabbed the sides of the boat to avoid falling out. Buddy got seated and used one of the paddles to turn the boat downstream.

Rhodes picked up the other paddle, and they got the rowing arrangements settled, paddling for a few yards before letting the boat drift. The creek didn't have much of a current, but it was enough to move the boat after a little momentum had been established.

Rhodes's plan was to move slowly down the creek, all the way across the county, looking for likely spots for marijuana patches. On the return trip they could use the trolling motor and make better time since they wouldn't have to be watching the shore.

The trees along both sides of the bank were thick and tall and grew far out over the creek, covering it completely in many places. The thunder rumbled above them and shook the leaves in the trees.

With the clouds and the trees it was almost dark along the creek. The humidity made Rhodes's shirt stick to his back, and he smelled the mud along the banks and the oncoming rain. Gnats swarmed over the muddy water, and a few mosquitoes hummed near Rhodes's ears.

Rhodes looked for the snapping turtle and the alligator, but he didn't see either of them. A few small turtles stuck their heads out of the water now and then, but they ducked back down when the boat came near. The snapping turtle could have eaten one of them in a single bite.

"That slicker might have been a good idea after all," Rhodes said as a loud clap of thunder rattled the tree limbs.

"Too late now," Buddy said.

The rain started to fall, widely spaced drops the size of dimes dimpling the water. Once again Rhodes wished that he wore a hat. He needed to get over his vanity and wear one for practical purposes, but he couldn't quite bring himself to do it. However, a hat would both cover the thin spot and protect him from rain. That was something worth considering.

The rain began to come down harder but in smaller drops

that were closer together. The trees blocked some of it, but not enough. Rhodes thought he and Buddy would be soaked before long.

"Just what are we looking for, anyway?" Buddy asked. "Besides a house we can get into, I mean."

"There won't be any houses," Rhodes said, wiping the rain off his face. He wouldn't have minded finding some cover, either. "Nobody has ever built near the creek. We're looking for a place on the bank where a boat might have put in, with a trail up into the trees."

The rain had brought a little breeze along with it, so the boat was moving along just fine without any effort from Buddy and Rhodes. All they had to do was guide it with the paddles and keep it in the middle of the creek. The bad news was that Rhodes was already starting to feel chilled. The weather might be warm, but the rain wasn't.

The boat passed Allison's place, and they were another mile along when the rain stopped. The sun came out almost at once, and while not much of it filtered through the trees, Rhodes started to warm back up. He'd gone from hot to cold to warming up, which was probably not good for his system. He hoped he didn't catch a cold.

"Look over there," Buddy said, pointing at the bank on the right.

Rhodes looked and saw a narrow opening where a boat could pull in. A muddy trail led up into the trees.

"Let's get out and take a look around," Rhodes said, and Buddy used his paddle to turn the nose of the boat toward the bank.

They nudged into the mud, and Buddy jumped out of the boat. A rope tied to the bow was in his hand. He slipped and slid his way up the bank and wrapped the rope around a tree trunk.

Rhodes followed along behind him, nearly falling twice but each time catching his balance before pitching headfirst into the mud.

"Looks like somebody's been here, all right," Buddy said. "There's the irrigation pipe, and your marijuana patch is right over there."

It was smaller than the other two patches, but that was probably because the trees here were thicker and there wasn't any room for a bigger one. It had the same kind of fence as the others, so it had likely been planted by the same person or persons unknown. Rhodes and Buddy walked over to it to have a look.

The first thing Rhodes wanted to check was whether the patch was guarded by an intimidating reptile, but this time there was no reptile of any kind to be seen. Rhodes thought he knew why, but to check he took a short walk up in the direction of where a road was likely to be. He was in the trees all the way to the road. Nobody had put a cabin or a house or a barn on this property. The marijuana grower, or growers, must have assumed they were safe from scrutiny. You'd have to be looking for the patch to find it, and nobody but a snoopy lawman would cruise along the creek for that purpose, and how likely was that? No need for a guard here.

Rhodes returned to the patch, where he didn't see anything helpful. Nobody had been thoughtful enough to leave him any clues, so he and Buddy returned to the boat. They drifted all the way down the creek past Billy Bacon's land and found only one more small patch of marijuana. It was also on entirely wooded property. There wasn't a lot of land like that in this part of the county. Most of it had been farmed at one time or was being used for ranching now, so it had been cleared. Mesquites and other trees were returning to take it over again in some cases, but they weren't thick enough to hide anything yet. Trees grew all along the creek bank, of course, but the land beyond them was cleared and in use most of the way along the water. Whoever was growing the marijuana didn't have a lot of choices for hiding places, at least in this end of the county.

Rhodes and Buddy turned the boat around, and Buddy lowered the trolling motor into the water. It worked smoothly and quietly after he started it, so they started back up the creek. A bit of water left over from the rain sloshed around in the bottom of the boat, but it wasn't too bad. Rhodes's clothes had dried, and he was fairly comfortable. The slight breeze didn't chill him, and it didn't appear that the motor's propellor would get stuck in the mud. Rhodes was sure it would be fine all the way.

When they passed over the Deep Hole, Buddy said, "Kinda wish I'd brought some fishing gear along. I've heard there's big fish in here."

"Used to be," Rhodes said, wishing he'd brought some fishing equipment himself. "I don't know about now."

"Guess we don't have time for fishing, though," Buddy said. "Gotta fight crime and keep the citizens safe."

"That's the job," Rhodes said.

"Too bad you didn't find out anything from those marijuana patches."

"At least we found them," Rhodes said.

"Yeah, but that's all we found. We still don't know who the growers are. Maybe this wasn't a wasted trip, but we didn't really learn much."

"You might be surprised," Rhodes said.

"You see something you're not telling me about?"

"No. I'm just shoving some puzzle pieces around. Some of them are starting to fit. Or maybe I'm forcing them where they don't belong. We'll have to wait and see."

"We gonna burn those marijuana fields?"

"Eventually. We need to settle some other things first. I don't think there's going to be a harvest anytime soon."

"You gonna let Seepy watch the burning?"

"Not a chance," Rhodes said.

Chapter 20

▼

After Rhodes and Buddy returned Lawton's boat and motor, Rhodes dropped Buddy off at the jail and went home to get the Tahoe. He'd decided that he'd visit the Hunts' house after all. Will might not be an expert at removing things, so maybe he'd overlooked something that would help Rhodes to put some more of the puzzle pieces in the right places. Rhodes thought he'd found some of the missing pieces. The picture was starting to shape up, but it still had some big gaps in it. Finding a few more pieces would help a lot.

Rhodes realized that there had been times when he hadn't been able to complete the puzzle. However, even though the picture he wound up with wasn't whole, there was enough of it for him to recognize what he was looking at. The pattern was clear even with the missing pieces. Sometimes that had to be enough.

Rhodes called the jail to let Hack know where he'd be. Hack didn't have any major crimes to report, just a squabble between a woman and her son, whom she accused of stealing her postage stamps.

"I don't think you need me to handle that one," Rhodes said.

"Nope. Stamps might be a federal crime, anyway."

"Good thought. You planning to call the FBI?"

"Nope."

"Probably not a good idea," Rhodes said. "I'll check in again later."

"That's right. You just go on and do whatever you want to," Hack said. "Don't bother to tell me what you found out this mornin' on your little river cruise."

"Buddy's filled you in, I expect," Rhodes said.

"That's right. I'm glad I can count on some people."

Rhodes signed off with a laugh.

This time when Rhodes arrived at the Hunts' house, there were no dogs under the porch, and Will's pickup was gone. Rhodes went out to the barn first. It wasn't locked, so he went in and looked all around. He found some old pieces of rope and quite a few scraps of metal. A broken-down riding lawn mower sat in one corner of the barn, where a few tools hung on the wall. The tools didn't look like they'd had a lot of use, and they didn't seem good enough to have been stolen from anywhere. A gas can sat near the mower, but it didn't hold diesel fuel like the ones stolen from Billy Barton.

Among the tools was a pair of bolt cutters. Rhodes took them down and looked them over. They didn't appear to have had much use, but if they'd been used to cut the lock on Billy Bacon's gate, it should be possible to match them to the cuts. Rhodes took the bolt cutters to the Tahoe and tagged them.

After dealing with the bolt cutters, Rhodes went back to the house and searched the rooms. He didn't find anything that looked to be of any help there, either. If there had ever been anything to find, Will had removed it.

There were very few hiding places. The closets were practically bare, and the cabinets in the kitchen and bathroom held only what might be found in anybody's house, none of it new. Rhodes looked in the little jewelry box on top of the dresser in the bedroom that Joyce and Melvin had shared, but he saw only a cheap watch and some costume jewelry, nothing that had turned up on any list of stolen items.

Rhodes remembered to check in the cabinet to see if the pistol Joyce had mentioned was there. It was, and Rhodes picked it up to examine it. Either Melvin hadn't had it with him when he was killed, or it had been returned to the cabinet. Rhodes thought it was more likely that it hadn't left the cabinet in quite a while. It wasn't loaded, and Rhodes didn't see any cartridges for it. He put it back where he'd found it and went back into the room with the new TV set.

Rhodes sat in the rocker where Joyce had sat when he told her about Melvin's death and thought things over. The way Rhodes had arranged the puzzle pieces had Melvin behind the thefts of all the various items that had been taken. Melvin had been down on his luck for a while, and maybe the thefts had been the only way he believed he could turn things around. It had worked, as the big TV set and satellite dish proved.

In the sequence of thefts, some small things had been taken first, and then Melvin's welding rig had been spirited away. Except Rhodes didn't think that the welding rig had been stolen at all. He'd been suspicious from the first because of the dogs. There was no way that Gus-Gus and Jackie were going to let anybody slip around the property without alerting everybody in the house. They might even attack a stranger, as they'd almost attacked Rhodes on his first visit.

Add to that the fact that the welding rig had been insured. Rhodes believed that Melvin had done some smaller thefts and then pretended that the welding rig had been stolen so he could blame it on whoever committed the earlier crimes. After collecting the insurance money, he had to keep on stealing things for a while to make sure that nobody suspected that he was the guilty party. It had been a successful plan up to a point, but then somebody had killed him. That was as far from successful as you could get.

Billy Bacon had a motive for the killing. He'd been pretty hard hit, and the thief had kicked in his well and taken his father's saddle and saddle stand besides. In spite of Joyce's high opinion of her husband, Rhodes was pretty sure that Melvin was the thief and also the one who'd kicked in the well just for meanness. It was an excellent theory, and it was too bad Rhodes had no evidence to support it.

Evidence. That was the problem. Where was the evidence? Rhodes was sure that Melvin could have disposed of most of it easily enough. Houston and Dallas weren't that far away. Just stick the stolen goods in the back of a pickup and take off for the big city. A flea market would be a quick and easy place to get rid of just about anything. Pay for a booth, drive the truck onto the grounds, and start selling.

The thing was that Joyce didn't seem to know anything about the thefts. She would almost have to have known if Melvin had been going to the city to sell the goods. That meant that someone else was selling them instead of Melvin.

That's where Riley Farmer came in. He was Melvin's best

friend, maybe his only friend, and was therefore most likely to have been Melvin's partner. Rhodes hadn't found anything on Farmer's property, though, and it was hard to believe that the two men could have gotten rid of everything.

That left Will Smalls. Rhodes had a feeling Will was a part of the scheme as well. Rhodes didn't know if Will had somewhere to store the stolen items, but he must have known what was going on. Otherwise he wouldn't have been so determined to keep Rhodes away from the Hunts' house.

Rhodes thought that Ellen and Joyce had been kept out of the loop, as Hack would have put it, maybe because they would have objected to the criminal activity or maybe because it was just safer to keep them in the dark. Joyce was acting so differently that she might have been told at least a little of the story. Ellen, too. Rhodes wondered if there was a place at the Smalls house where stolen goods could be stored.

Rhodes realized that he'd started rocking in the chair. It didn't make much noise, and the rocking motion was comforting in a way. He didn't want to get too comfortable, however. He needed to come up with some answers, not rock and relax.

It was then that he thought about the storm cellar. It would've been easy enough for Melvin to come home with a pickup full of what he could have told Joyce was "welding supplies" that he had to put in the barn. He could put them in the storm cellar instead, knowing that there was no way Joyce was going into it. He could keep things there until he got a chance to pass them along to someone else, either to Will or to Riley. Of if either of those two had been with him when he stole things, they could simply have taken them away almost at once and sold them within hours.

That theory still left some things unexplained, such as why there had been no vehicle at Bacon's barn after Melvin was killed.

Had Riley taken him there? Or had it been Will? It wasn't out of the question that Melvin had walked, but that wouldn't explain the lock that had been cut on the gate chain.

Rhodes stood up. He needed to have a look in the storm cellar. He went out the back door and into the yard. The roof of the storm cellar was concrete, and a small, rusty vent pipe stuck up from the back end. The doorway was almost flat on the ground, thick wood covered with shingles, and it had a hasp and a padlock on it. That was interesting, since locking a storm cellar door from the outside didn't make any sense. People needed quick access to the cellar in case of a storm, so nobody ever locked the door. Not from the outside, anyway. Storm doors locked from the inside so the doors wouldn't be flung open by the wind, causing whoever was inside to be sucked out into the storm.

Rhodes didn't think it was a good idea to use the bolt cutters he'd found, but there'd been a screwdriver in the barn. He got the screwdriver and knelt on the ground to remove the screws that held the hasp. He justified what he was doing by telling himself that he had permission from Joyce to search the house, with Ellen as a witness. He hadn't been told that he could break into the storm cellar, but he considered that doing so was part of a reasonable search. He'd replace the hasp when he was done if that turned out to be necessary.

Rhodes set the screwdriver and screws on the roof of the cellar when he'd finished. He stood up, stretched, and then bent over to grasp the edge of the door. He pulled it upward. The door was heavy, all right, but not too heavy for him to lift. A door that was hard to open would have been a problem for anybody who was in a hurry to escape a impending tornado. Not as bad as a locked door, but bad enough.

Rhodes let the door drop open on the ground with a solid thump and looked down into the cellar. Concrete steps led into the dark below, and he couldn't make out anything in the murk. He'd have to go back to the Tahoe for his flashlight.

"I guess it's a good thing I came back out here for the dog food," a voice behind Rhodes said.

Rhodes turned around. "I'd have been glad to bring it back to town for you if Joyce or Ellen had asked me to."

"Well," Will Smalls said, "they didn't think of it, and neither did I. I could've gone to Walmart and picked some up, but I figured, why buy it when there's a bag of it already open? So here I am."

Smalls stood facing Rhodes, the sun glinting off his rimless glasses, his hand on the butt of his pistol. Rhodes thought about the little Kel-Tec in his ankle holster. A man who has a pistol in an ankle holster isn't in a good position for a fast draw.

"See, I never thought you'd look in the storm cellar," Will said. "That's why I told Joyce it'd be okay for you to come on out here and poke around. I can see now that was a mistake. I wanted you to look around in the house and decide there was nothing to find, but now you've gone and messed things up. That's a real shame."

"That's not the only mistake you made," Rhodes said. "Getting involved in theft and then killing your brother-in-law, that wasn't too smart, either."

"You don't know what you're talking about," Will said.

He drew the pistol, racked the slide, and pointed the gun at Rhodes. It was a Glock 17, and Rhodes wondered how good a shot Will was with it. Probably good enough, considering that he was only fifteen or so yards away. Just about anybody could hit a man at that distance if he fired enough shots, and at the moment Will looked like the type who'd keep pulling the trigger as long as he had to.

"Gimme your gun," Will said.

Rhodes raised his arms. "Do you see a gun?"

"Turn around," Will said, and Rhodes did.

"Okay," Will said. "I guess you don't have a gun. You wanted to see what was in the cellar, so get on down in there."

Rhodes didn't think going into the cellar would be a good idea, but he couldn't think of another alternative, not with the Glock pointed at him. He looked into the cellar again.

"Go ahead," Will said. "It's not so bad."

"I heard there were spiders and snakes down there," Rhodes said, thinking of an old song. "I don't like spiders and snakes."

"Those are gonna be the least of your problems," Will said.

"I figured as much."

Rhodes bent over and started into the cellar. He heard movement behind him, but before he could straighten up and turn, Will had kicked him in the rear and sent him stumbling down the steps.

Rhodes wasn't quite able to maintain his balance, but he didn't fall, either. He landed at the bottom on his feet and dropped to his hands and knees in two or three inches of water. He stood up as quickly as he could, but when he turned the door slammed down, leaving him in almost complete darkness.

His only chance of getting out was to shove the door open before Will could get the hasp screwed back into place. He felt his way up a couple of steps. Bending, he positioned himself and shoved as hard as he could against the door. It bounced up maybe an inch, but that was all. Will must have been sitting on it to put the screws in the hasp. Will wasn't big, but he was big enough to hold the door down.

Rhodes shoved again with the same lack of success.

"Won't do you any good, Sheriff," Will said. "You might's well make yourself comfortable."

Rhodes didn't think there was any chance of getting comfortable in nearly total darkness in a dank cellar with several inches of water on the floor, not to mention an untold number of spiders and snakes hiding out in the various nooks and crannies, so he sat down on one of the steps to think things out. The boards of the door were too heavy for his pistol to shoot through, so that wasn't an option. He couldn't think of any others, either.

He wondered how long it would take a man to go blind in total darkness. Probably longer than it would take him to starve, unless there was some food in the cellar. Some people did put tin cans with a little food in cellars, just in case. He wouldn't have to worry about water. There was plenty of that.

He might not have to worry about going blind, either. A little bit of light came in through the vent, not much, but enough to keep the place from being completely inky. There might be a flashlight somewhere, too, unless Melvin counted on bringing one from the house in case of storms.

Rhodes wasn't really worried about all those things, however. The Tahoe was parked in the front of the house in plain sight, and he'd told Hack where he was going. He might be trapped in the cellar for a while, which would be uncomfortable, and it would be embarrassing to have to be rescued, but he'd survive if the spiders and snakes didn't get him.

"Sheriff, I got a little problem," Will said.

"I hope you're not expecting any sympathy from me," Rhodes said, "because you're not going to get any."

Will ignored the remark. "See, the thing is, I forgot about moving your vehicle. I was gonna put it in the barn, but I can't do that."

"Because you don't have the keys," Rhodes said.

"That's right. I forgot to get them from you."

Rhodes laughed. He was glad he wasn't the only one who had those little forgetful moments. Will wasn't a very professional criminal, and Rhodes was glad of that, too.

"Here's what I'm gonna do," Will said. "I'm gonna take the hasp off again and open the door an inch or two. You can throw the keys out to me."

Rhodes laughed again. "That'll be the day."

Will was quiet for a few seconds. Then he said, "I guess I'll have to take 'em, then."

It occurred to Rhodes that while the ankle holster was a disadvantage at times, it had one thing going for it. Will didn't realize that Rhodes was armed.

"I guess you will," Rhodes said.

Will was quiet again, but Rhodes heard him working on the screws. While he was doing that, Rhodes got his Kel-Tec from the ankle holster and got ready.

"I'm gonna open the door now," Will said. "I don't want to shoot you, but I will if I have to. You can give me the keys or get shot. It's your choice. You know what I mean?"

"I know what you mean," Rhodes said.

" 'Cause it doesn't make any difference to me now," Will said. "I'm already in about as much trouble as I can get in. Shooting you won't make much difference to me. It will to you, though."

Rhodes didn't think that Will was stupid. He'd open the door, all right, but he'd do it fast. He'd also do it from the side that wouldn't leave him visible until the door was fully open, and by then he'd have the pistol out. Rhodes had a little plan that covered the situation, however. He got himself set and ready.

The door started to open.

Chapter 21

▼

Rhodes sprang up and put his shoulder into the door, straightening his legs and shoving upward, hard.

Will was caught off balance and fell backward, landing on his back. The door fell onto his feet, and he fired his pistol into the air. He tried to bring the weapon to bear on Rhodes, who had popped out of the cellar, but Rhodes had his own pistol out and shot before Will had a second chance to pull the trigger.

The bullet hit Will in the wrist of the hand that held the pistol. Will screamed and dropped the pistol. Rhodes had to admit even to himself that it was a shot worthy of Sage Barton, or it would have been if Rhodes had actually been trying to make it. Sage Barton was an incredibly accurate shot, but Rhodes had been shooting only to scare Will or at least get his attention. The fact that he'd hit him was nothing more than an accident. Of course, if he'd hit him in the head, that would've been an accident, too, but not a happy one.

Will twisted his body and reached for the pistol with his uninjured hand. Rhodes stepped over and kicked the pistol aside.

Will lay back. "You've killed me, Sheriff. I'll bleed out right here."

Rhodes looked down at Will's wrist. Will was small, but he had wide wrists, and by another happy accident the bullet had taken only a little chunk out of the edge of his wrist. It hadn't hit bone or an artery. Will wasn't in any danger. He probably wasn't even in much pain.

"You'll be fine," Rhodes told him. "The handcuffs might hurt a little bit."

"Handcuffs? You'd handcuff a dying man?"

"You're not in any danger of dying," Rhodes said, "but the county doesn't like for prisoners to complain about their care. I'll call for the EMS crew to come get you, just to be sure you're well taken care of. You better clamp a hand on that wrist to stop the bleeding. I was just joking about the handcuffs."

Will didn't laugh about the joke, which was no surprise, but he did clamp down on his wrist.

"While we're waiting," Rhodes said, "you can tell me what you stole and why you killed Riley and Melvin."

"I'm not telling you squat," Will said.

Rhodes went over to where Will's pistol lay. He picked it up and stuck it in his belt. Two-Gun Dan Rhodes. Then he walked back to Will.

"I'm arresting you for assault on an officer. That's going to be the least of your troubles, though. There'll be more charges later after I make up a list, so I'd better tell you what your rights are."

Rhodes recited the Miranda rights and asked Will if he understood them.

"I've seen this stuff on TV," Will said. "I know what it is."

"And they say TV isn't educational."

"I never said that," Will said.

"That was a joke," Rhodes told him. "Stand up."

"I don't know if I can. The damn door's on my feet, and my ankles are broke, or maybe my feet. Something's broke. I'm in a bad way."

Rhodes doubted that. "Give it a try. You can do it. I'll help you."

Rhodes bent and lifted the door with his left hand while keeping his pistol aimed in Will's general direction. He couldn't lift the door very high like that, but it was enough for Will to wiggle his feet free.

"Now you can get up," Rhodes said.

Will struggled to stand, still holding his wrist, which was hardly bleeding now, and complaining about how his feet were broken. He managed to get upright and stay that way, although he looked a little wobbly.

"I can't walk," he said. "It's bone on bone down there."

"I don't think so," Rhodes said. He didn't believe Will was hurt nearly as badly as he pretended to be. "Let's walk on back to the front of the house. You first, hands behind your head. I'm not calling the EMS until we get there, so don't dawdle."

"I'm gonna sue the county," Will said, "and you, too. You can't shoot a man and break his ankles. It's police brutality."

"What would you call shoving somebody down into a cellar to starve?"

"That was an accident. I slipped."

"Tell that to your lawyer."

"I don't have a lawyer."

"Then you'd better get one. The lawyer might even believe you. It's going to be hard to convince anybody that sitting on the door and screwing that hasp back on was an accident, though."

Will didn't say anything. He just stood there looking like he'd rather be somewhere else, anywhere else. Rhodes didn't blame him.

"Start walking," Rhodes said.

Will started walking, or limping, toward the front of the house, still gripping his wrist, although the bleeding had just about stopped. Rhodes stayed a few feet behind him, keeping his pistol ready in case Will was faking.

Which he was. His pickup was parked not far from the Tahoe, and they had to walk past it to get there. As they passed the pickup, Will made his move. He jumped to the side, fell to the ground, and rolled under the pickup.

Rhodes could have shot him, but he didn't want to hit a vital spot and wind up in the news for having shot a man who was rolling on the ground. So instead of shooting, Rhodes lowered the tailgate of the truck and climbed into the bed. He stood in the middle so that he could see the ground on either side with just a glance and waited for Will to roll out.

It was quiet under the truck, and when Will didn't appear, Rhodes said, "You don't have a weapon hidden under there, do you, Will?"

Will didn't answer.

"You're just adding to your misery, Will. Resisting arrest, unlawful flight, bad stuff. It's not going to look good at your trial."

Will kept quiet, and Rhodes wondered what it would take to get him out. Maybe there was something Will cared about enough to come out if Rhodes coaxed him. Or threatened him.

"I'm not going to shoot you, Will," Rhodes said. "The old 'prisoner killed while trying to escape' would get me off if I did, but I don't want the hassle it would cause me. What I'm going to do is shoot your truck. I'm going to shoot a hole in the back window to start with. The bullet will go through the windshield, too. Then I'm going to shoot your dashboard. After that I'll put a few holes in the doors and sides."

"You can't do that," Will said. "It's destruction of private property."

"I'm not too worried about that, for some reason," Rhodes said. "I'll give you ten seconds to slide out from under the pickup, and if you don't, I'll start shooting. I'll start counting now so you'll know how much time you have. A thousand and one, a thousand and two, a thousand and three—"

"Okay, okay, I'm coming out," Will said, and he slipped out on the driver's side. While he was lying on the ground, he adjusted his glasses, which had slipped sideways on his face.

"Just lie right there," Rhodes said, "while I get down."

Rhodes took a couple of steps to the rear, stood on the tailgate, and jumped down. He wasn't as agile as he'd once been, but he could still jump down a few feet without collapsing and keep his pistol steady while he did it.

"You can stand up now," Rhodes said.

Will stood up and said, "I think I hurt my wrist again."

"For some reason I don't believe that," Rhodes said. "I'm not going to bother to call the EMS. I'll give you some first aid before I take you into town and put you in jail. If you need any treatment after we get there, we'll call somebody for you after you're booked."

"What about my ankles?" Will asked. "They're broke."

"I don't think so," Rhodes said. "You seem to get around pretty well when you want to. Don't start about the wrist again, either, when I handcuff you."

"You said you were joking about the handcuffs."

"That was then," Rhodes said. "This is now. I have a first aid kit in the Tahoe. I'll get you handcuffed, and then I'll take a look at that wrist."

Will didn't bother to thank him.

After Will was booked into the jail and put into a cell, he refused to talk to Rhodes without a lawyer in the room. He made a call to Randy Lawless, the best in the county, but Lawless was in court and couldn't be reached.

"I'm not talking to you," Will told Rhodes. "I'll wait until I can get my lawyer here."

Rhodes couldn't do anything about that, so he let Will relax in the cell, as much as relaxing was possible, at any rate. He tagged Will's gun and put it in the evidence room. It had been nice to be Two-Gun Dan for a while, but it wasn't a name Rhodes wanted to keep. The pistol worried Rhodes because it wasn't a .32. It hadn't been used to kill Riley or Melvin. That didn't mean that Will didn't own another pistol, but it didn't help Rhodes's case in the least.

After dealing with the pistol, Rhodes had to tell Hack and Lawton all about the capture, which he did without going into all the details. He didn't want the story turning up on the Internet, although he wasn't sure Hack and Lawton wouldn't just fill in some details from their imaginations if Jennifer Loam asked about what had happened.

When he'd finished the story to their satisfaction, Rhodes asked what he'd missed out on while he'd been gone.

"Major crimes only?" Hack asked.

"Whatever," Rhodes said. "And no stories. Just give me a listing."

Hack looked hurt, but he complied. "We got a guy walking

along a county road without a shirt. Had some warrant out on him, so Buddy brought him in. He's locked up now. Got him a nice orange jumpsuit, so he don't need a shirt. Was a fight out at the trailer park, but it broke up before we could get anybody out there. Got a call about somebody looking in windows, but nothing came of that, either."

Lawton interrupted the recitation. "Tell him about Ms. Fortson."

"I was gettin' to that," Hack said.

"I just wanted to be sure you didn't forget," Lawton said.

"You sayin' there's somethin' wrong with my mem'ry?"

"I just said I didn't want you to forget. Bein' helpful, is all."

Rhodes sighed. He'd asked that there be no stories, but he knew he was about to get one, whether he wanted it or not.

"What about Ms. Fortson?" he asked to stop the argument that was developing and delaying the inevitable.

"She gets the newspaper," Hack said.

Rhodes got the newspaper, too, and while it was a mere shadow of its former self, while it had been sold to some publishing group from outside the county, while it had laid off everybody except one or two people, and while it was no longer published daily, it was still a newspaper. Rhodes had nothing against Jennifer Loam's Web site, and it was certainly more up-to-date than the newspaper, but now and then he liked to unfold a real paper and look over the articles, no matter how out of date they might be. If he got a little ink on his fingers, well, it was worth it.

"What's wrong with getting the newspaper?" Rhodes asked.

"She's not payin' for it," Hack said.

Rhodes didn't see anything wrong with that, either. He paid for his own newspaper, but it would be a much better deal to get it free, which was about what it was worth these days. He knew there was more to the story, though, and he knew Hack was waiting for him to ask the logical question, so he did.

"What's so bad about getting a free newspaper?"

"That's what I wanted to know," Lawton said.

"Don't butt in," Hack said.

"Well, that's what I wanted to know, ain't it?"

"Never mind that," Rhodes said. "Just tell me what the problem with getting a free paper is."

"Gettin' it ain't the problem," Hack said.

He waited. Lawton wisely said nothing. Rhodes finally cracked.

"Then what *is* the problem?"

"Free ain't always free," Hack said, and gave Rhodes an expectant look.

"I'm dense," Rhodes said. "Explain what that means."

"It means she thinks it's a scam," Hack said. "She's a widow-lady, and she thinks the newspaper's trying to take advantage of her."

"Not the newspaper," Lawton said. "A newspaper can't take advantage of anybody. The people who run the newspaper can, though."

"We know that," Hack told him. "It's just a way of puttin' things."

"Well, you made it sound like the newspaper was the thing doin' it."

Rhodes broke in before they got to the "did not," "did so" stage. "How could anybody take advantage of her by giving her free papers?"

"Easy," Hack said. "Sure, they're free now, but what if the paper decides that she's been spongin' off them, gettin' newspapers without payin' for 'em? What if they come at her and try to collect? Maybe go back a year or so and say she ain't been makin' the payments? Maybe charge her some big bill she can't pay? What happens then?"

"Has she called them to stop the deliveries?"

"Says she has, but they didn't stop. She quit pickin' 'em up for while, but they just kept on comin' and lay there on the end of her driveway, pilin' up and ruinin' the whole look of her place, so she gathered 'em up and called again. That didn't work, either."

"It's just some kind of mistake," Rhodes said.

"Prob'ly is, but you can't tell Ms. Fortson that, not and make her believe it. Well, maybe you can. I sure as heck can't."

"Okay. You don't have to make her believe it. Just call the newspaper and tell them to stop delivering the paper. Tell them if they don't, we'll arrest them for harassment."

"Can we do that?"

"That was a joke," Rhodes said. "Just tell them to stop. I'm sure you can convince them it would be a good idea."

Hack didn't look so sure. "I wouldn't bet on it."

"I would, but I'm not a betting man. I'd do it myself, but I have more work to do on this Will Smalls problem."

"What kinda work?"

"I have to find out for sure that he's guilty."

"He's guilty, all right," Lawton said. "Got the wound to prove it."

"It's not much of a wound," Rhodes said.

"Shot the gun right outta his hand."

"That's not what happened," Rhodes said.

"Close enough," Lawton said. "Wrist, hand, it's all the same thing. Mighty good shootin', I'd call it. I'd like to see the Lone Ranger do any better."

"Or Sage Barton," Hack said.

"That's enough," Rhodes said. He didn't want them to get started on Sage Barton. "I have work to do."

"I thought we just decided Will was guilty," Hack said.

"There's a problem with that," Rhodes told him.

"What problem?"

"Proof," Rhodes said. "I don't have any proof."

Chapter 22

▼

Rhodes had missed lunch yet again, and he was tempted to stop at the Dairy Queen for a Jalitos Ranch Burger. And maybe a Blizzard to top it off. However, it was Bean Day. Rhodes was as big a fan of pinto beans and cornbread as anybody, especially if the beans were spiced up with some black pepper, salt, bacon grease, and a little bit of jalapeño pepper. He also liked a bit of jalapeño pepper in cornbread.

The problem was that a lot of other people in Clearview were fans of Bean Day, and the place would be all too crowded. Rhodes figured it would be better just to get something at the drive-up window, but there was a line there, too. He could either wait or go through one more day without lunch. He supposed he could stand to miss another meal. In fact, he was getting used to it, so he drove on to the Smallses' house.

He glanced at the backyard when he got out of the Tahoe and saw that there was a separate storehouse located there. He had a feeling that if he looked inside, he might find some of the proof he was looking for. Maybe Ellen Smalls would let him take a peek.

He went to the front door, knocked, and waited. Ellen opened the door after he knocked a second time.

"Back again, Sheriff?"

"I have to talk to you and Joyce," Rhodes said.

Ellen took a sharp breath. "Is it about Will? Is he all right?"

"It depends on what you mean by 'all right.' Can I come in?"

Ellen stepped back from the door and let Rhodes into the den. He noticed that the Smallses, like Riley and the Hunts, had a big-screen TV, but it wasn't new. It was a good bit thicker than the current models.

"I'll get Joyce," Ellen said, and she disappeared through a door.

In few seconds she was back with her sister, and both women stood there looking at Rhodes.

"We might feel better if we sat down," he said, and the women sat on a worn sofa, leaving Rhodes to sit in a pink upholstered pedestal rocker.

"We need to talk about Will and Melvin," Rhodes said when he was seated.

The rocker was a precarious perch. It could be turned in either direction all too easily. Rhodes would have preferred something a little more stable. He felt that he might tip over to the side or go spinning around at any second.

"What about Will and Melvin?" Joyce asked. "Where's Will?"

"That's what I came to tell you," Rhodes said. "Will's in jail."

General consternation ensued. Rhodes waited for it to die down.

"What for?" Ellen asked after she got control of herself. "What's he done?"

"That's what I was hoping you could tell me. It looks as if he and Melvin and their friend Riley Farmer were involved in the thefts down in Melvin's area."

More consternation, along with protests and denials. Once again Rhodes sat in the wobbly rocker and waited them out.

"I don't see how you can say that about Melvin," Joyce said. She was calm but indignant.

"Or about Will," Ellen said. "Those two are as honest as the day is long."

Maybe a December day, Rhodes thought, but not a summer day. He had to admit, however, that Joyce and Ellen's confusion and concern seemed real. If they'd known about their husbands' criminal activities, they were concealing the knowledge well. He'd thought they might know something, but he now thought he'd been wrong about that.

"I suspected Melvin from the start," Rhodes said. "How could anybody get past Gus-Gus and Jackie to steal the welding rig? The way they acted when they saw me made it pretty clear that a prowler wouldn't stand a chance. Melvin tried to make you think it was Gene Gunnison who stole the rig, Joyce, but it wasn't. It was Melvin. He even stopped drinking when the stealing started. He had something to keep his mind off his troubles, and he had the insurance money, too."

"I still don't believe he did it," Joyce said.

"I don't, either," Ellen said, "especially about Will."

"It looks as if Will might have killed Melvin," Rhodes said.

This time the consternation, protests, and denials were accompanied by tears and shouting. Rhodes had to wait longer this time, but eventually there was just sniffling. Ellen left the room and came back with a box of tissues. She and Joyce dried their eyes, blew their noses, and started in on Rhodes.

"You must be crazy," Ellen said. "Will would never do anything like that."

"And Melvin would never steal," Joyce said. "Ellen's right. You're crazy."

"Maybe," Rhodes said, "but let me tell you what happened a couple of hours ago before you decide for sure."

He told them about Will pulling his gun on him and shoving him into the cellar. "He planned to leave me there. I don't know for how long, but I got the feeling that I might wind up just a skeleton in a few inches of water if I didn't drink it all before I starved to death."

Ellen was stunned into silence by the story. Joyce didn't have anything to say, either.

"I'll be going back out there later," Rhodes said. "I have a feeling I'm going to find stolen goods in the cellar, things Melvin hadn't been able to sell or was planning to keep. I expect there might be some stuff around here, too. Maybe in that storehouse in the backyard."

"I can't believe it," Ellen said. "I just can't."

"We could have a look," Rhodes said.

"I'm not sure Will would want me to let you do that."

"Will's in jail. If he's innocent, then there's nothing in the storeroom that can hurt him. If there's nothing there, it might help him."

"He *was* kind of secretive about that storeroom," Joyce said.

"All right," Ellen said. "We can go look."

Gus-Gus and Jackie were happy to see them when they came into the yard. They greeted Rhodes as if he were an old friend. They must have enjoyed their romp in the woods with him.

After the dogs calmed down, Rhodes discovered that the storehouse was locked with a hasp and padlock. Ellen said she didn't know where the key was.

"I never come out here," she said. "I didn't even know it was locked. I don't think it used to be."

The key was probably on the key ring that Will had turned in with the rest of his property at the jail, Rhodes figured, but everybody kept a spare key around somewhere. He looked above the door and didn't find one. The storehouse was up on cinder blocks, so he felt along under the bottom edge. Sure enough there was a key on a nail, and the key opened the door.

Just inside the storehouse, Rhodes saw a can of diesel fuel, which was out of place since Will didn't own a diesel engine as far as Rhodes knew. The can probably had once belonged to Billy Barton. The whole storehouse was stuffed with tools that Rhodes was sure would have been headed for a flea market as soon as Will got a chance to take them.

"I don't know where all of those things came from," Ellen said. "I know Will put things in here now and then, but I didn't know they were stolen."

"We still don't know that," Joyce said. "Maybe these are all Will's tools."

Rhodes saw a hammer with a wooden handle. He picked it up and showed it to the two women. The B-Bar-B brand was burned into the wood.

"That's Billy Bacon's brand," Rhodes said.

"Maybe Will borrowed the hammer," Ellen said.

"How likely is it that he'd borrow a hammer from someone's barn way on the other side of the county and bring it here?" Rhodes asked. "I see a few other hammers, too. How many hammers did he borrow?"

"I don't know," Ellen said.

"Look over there," Rhodes said, pointing with the hammer. "See that saddle stand? Will doesn't have a horse. He's never had a horse."

"No," Ellen said. "He's never had a horse."

"That's Billy Bacon's saddle stand," Rhodes said. "Will must have stolen it and sold the saddle."

Ellen was shaking her head, but Rhodes could tell she was convinced that her husband was mixed up in something he shouldn't have been.

"Have you asked Will about any of this?" she asked.

"I have," Rhodes said. "He won't talk to me without his lawyer, and his lawyer's in court."

"He'll talk to me," Ellen said, her voice firm. "Come on, Joyce. We'll go to the jail."

"I'll make you a deal," Rhodes said. "You can talk to him if I can listen. Would Will agree to that?"

"He'd better," Ellen said.

The little interview room was crowded with three people in it, and it would be even more crowded with four, but it wasn't meant to be a comfortable place. The old table and the metal folding chairs seemed to look shabbier than usual to Rhodes, but that might have been because of the reactions of the two women. They looked at their surroundings as if they'd been tossed into a dungeon right out of the Middle Ages.

Lawton brought Will into the room and left. Rhodes got everybody seated at the table, Ellen and Will on one side and Joyce with Rhodes on the other.

"I'm ashamed of you, Will Smalls," Ellen said. "I can't believe you're in jail."

Will looked a bit sheepish, as well he should have, but he didn't say anything or even look at his wife. Rhodes thought Joyce might have something to say, but she just gave Will a look that made Rhodes glad she didn't have a weapon.

Then Ellen saw Will's wrist. She took his hand and asked what had happened.

"The sheriff shot me," Will said.

Ellen gave Rhodes a look that should've turned him to stone.

"It was my fault," Will said. "I shot first."

"Will Smalls! You tried to kill the sheriff?"

"It was just an accident. He threw a door on me."

"A door?"

"You tell her, Sheriff," Will said.

Rhodes explained what had happened and how Will had come to fire his pistol, though Rhodes was pretty sure he'd have fired it anyway if he'd had a chance.

"He broke my ankles, too," Will said.

"He did what?" Ellen asked.

"The door fell on his feet," Rhodes told her. "He's not hurt. He was walking just fine."

"I can't believe you're in this mess, Will," Ellen said, ignoring Rhodes. "I never knew you had a bad side to you."

"I'm not bad," Will said. "It wasn't my fault. Well, not all of it, anyway."

Rhodes thought he'd better interrupt and set the ground rules for the conversation.

"Will, you do understand that you've waived your right to have an attorney present, don't you?"

Will nodded.

"Better say it aloud," Rhodes told him.

"I understand," Will said.

"Good. Then let's get started with some questions. I know you've been involved with Riley Farmer and Melvin Hunt in stealing farm equipment, tools, and household goods—"

"That's not right," Will said. "You've got it all wrong."

Rhodes wasn't surprised that Will was protesting, but he was surprised he'd protested so soon.

"You want to tell me about it?" Rhodes asked.

Will looked at Ellen. She nodded, but he still didn't say anything. She gave him a poke in the side with her elbow.

"All right," Will said, "but if I tell you, will you go easy on me?"

"I'm not the one who'll decide what happens to you," Rhodes told him. "That will depend on the charges that are filed, and after that it will depend on the jury. If you clear things up, I'll tell the DA that you cooperated. That's the best deal you can get."

"He'll take it," Ellen said. "Isn't that right, Will?"

"I guess so," Will said. "I never meant to get into this mess in the first place. It was all Melvin's fault."

Joyce spoke up. "Don't you dare try to blame this on Melvin."

Will had a good strategy, Rhodes thought. Blame it on the dead man. Melvin wasn't going to be able to testify on his own behalf, so maybe Will could pull it off.

"Melvin's the one got me into it," Will said. "I don't want to hurt your feelings, Joyce, but that's the truth of it. It started when he stole his own welding rig."

"He never did that," Joyce said, her face getting red.

"He sure enough did," Will said. "He'd taken a few things

before, but this was his first big score. One day when you were in town visiting Ellen, he called Riley Farmer. Riley went out to your place, hooked up the unit to his pickup, and hauled it down to Houston. He sold it and gave Melvin some of the money, maybe most of it. They never told me that part of it. Whatever they got, it wasn't a bad deal, since Melvin collected the insurance on it, too. He got more out of it than it was worth in the end. You got a new TV, too, and got hooked up to the satellite. He told me about it 'cause he knew I wouldn't blame him for doing it. He was hard up and needed the money bad."

"That's a lie," Joyce said. "We needed the money, all right, but somebody stole the welding rig. Melvin didn't have a thing to do with it."

"I'm not lying about it," Will said. "I know it's hard for you to think of Melvin as a thief, but that's what he was."

"So are you," Joyce said.

"I never stole anything in my life," Will said. He paused. "Not since I was a kid, at least."

"What about all that stuff in our storehouse?" Ellen asked.

"I didn't steal that. I was just keeping it there for Melvin and Riley, doing a favor for some friends. Riley didn't have any place to put it, and Melvin couldn't keep it all at his place. See, what happened was that Melvin found out how easy it was to steal from himself and make some money. He hadn't really thought about how easy it was before, but now he was sure of it. He could take whatever he wanted to. People around here don't always lock their doors, and some people even just leave stuff lying around in plain sight, like Billy Bacon. Melvin didn't like Billy one bit, so he thought he'd relieve him of some of his property. Besides, if the people Melvin took stuff from had insurance, they could get their money back, same as Melvin did. If you look at it from his point of view, he wasn't hurting anybody but the insurance companies, and they have plenty of money."

"If you weren't involved," Rhodes said, "why keep me out of Melvin's house? Why lock me in the storm cellar?"

"That was just to protect Joyce," Will said.

"You better not try to put what you did on me," Joyce said, her face getting even redder.

"She's right, Will," Ellen said. "Trying to blame somebody else is nearly as bad as stealing."

"It's the truth," Will said. "I hoped nobody would find out that Melvin was stealing. He was dead, and that was bad enough. I wanted to be sure nothing was left in the house. I couldn't do anything about the storm cellar. There was more than I wanted to haul off, and I didn't think anybody would look in the cellar anyway. The things Melvin kept in there were mostly things he wasn't going to sell. He was just going to bring something out now and then and play like he bought it. When I got out to the house and found you snooping in the cellar, Sheriff, I didn't know what to do. You were going to find out about Melvin, and I thought you might rope me into it, even if I was innocent and all, which I was. I wasn't thinking straight when I kicked you down those steps, and I'm sure sorry about it. I'd have let you out of that cellar after I came to my senses."

The apology wasn't going to do Will any good because Rhodes didn't believe a word of it. He was sure Will was more involved than he was admitting, although his story might be good enough to get him a fairly short jail term, especially if he could make the jury believe he hadn't really intended Rhodes any harm.

"What about killing Melvin?" Rhodes asked. "Why did you do that?"

Will looked surprised at the question. "I didn't kill Melvin."

"Then who did?"

Will looked down at the table. He didn't want to answer. Ellen gave him the elbow again.

Will jumped. "All I know is, I didn't do it."

"You don't have any ideas about who might have done it?" Rhodes asked.

Will looked at Joyce. "To tell you the truth, I thought she did it."

Chapter 23

▼

Joyce jumped to her feet and kicked back her chair. It scraped across the floor and hit the wall with a clank. For a second Rhodes thought she might jump across the table and throttle Will, but she just stood there staring at him, breathing hard through her nose. Her face was so red that Rhodes was afraid her head might explode.

"I can't believe you'd say a thing like that about Joyce, Will," Ellen said. "You know better than that."

"I've seen a lot of TV shows about stuff like this," Will said. "It's always the wife."

He and Ivy would be in agreement, Rhodes thought, at least on that point.

"It's not the wife this time, Will Smalls," Joyce said, her voice tight.

Rhodes thought it was time to see if he could get another reaction from any of them.

"There's something we need to remember," he said. "Melvin's not the only one who's been killed."

"What?" Joyce said. "Who?"

"Riley Farmer's dead," Rhodes said. "Shot, just like Melvin."

"Riley? Who'd kill Riley?"

"I had Will in mind," Rhodes said.

Joyce walked over to her chair and pulled it back to the table. She sat down and said, "I think you're right, Sheriff. Will did it. Or maybe he wants to blame that on me, too. Are you going to accuse me of killing Riley, Will?"

"I didn't accuse you of anything. I just said—"

"Never mind what you said," Ellen told him. "Sheriff, you'd better tell us what's going on."

"That's what I'm trying to find out," Rhodes said.

He'd watched the two women carefully when he'd told them about Riley's death. Will had known already, so he hadn't been surprised. Both Ellen and Joyce seemed genuinely shocked.

"I didn't kill Riley any more than I killed Melvin," Will said. "I never killed anybody. I didn't steal anything, and I didn't kill anybody. I was wrong to try to lock you in that cellar, Sheriff, like I've been saying. I did do that, and I know it was wrong. If I had it to do over, I'd just let you look in there. Anyway, I don't have it to do over, and I did lock you in. That's all I did, though."

It wasn't all he'd done, not by a long shot, but Rhodes didn't want to enumerate all the rest of it in front of Ellen and Joyce. They were upset enough as it was.

"My ankles hurt," Will said. He gave Ellen a pitiful look, but she didn't show any sympathy. "I think you did break them, Sheriff, or at least sprained them. I don't plan to sue or anything, though."

"That's mighty nice of you, Will," Rhodes said, "but it's not going to help your case. There are two dead men and a lot of stolen goods that you're partially responsible for. If there's anything else you know, you need to tell me now."

"You hear him, Will?" Ellen asked. "You tell him whatever else you know."

"I don't know another thing," Will said. "Not one single thing."

Rhodes tried a few more questions to draw him out, but Will was through talking. He'd already said a lot more than Randy Lawless would have allowed him to say if he'd been there, but Rhodes didn't believe most of it. There was one thing that struck Rhodes, however, and reminded him of something that he wanted to think over.

He ended the interview and walked with Ellen and Joyce back into the main office of the jail. Ellen was more upset than she had been during the interview with Will, but Joyce had recovered her composure and was comforting her.

Buddy was at his desk, writing a report while regaling Hack and Lawton with his latest adventure, which involved someone trying to steal a window air conditioner from a deserted house. Rhodes interrupted the story and told Buddy to take Joyce and Ellen home.

"I'm going to the courthouse," Rhodes told Hack when they'd left. "I'll be in touch."

"You gonna go over there and do some thinkin'?" Hack asked.

"That's right."

"You could just think in here," Hack said.

"There's too much going on in here," Rhodes said.

"Nothin's goin' on here. You just want a Dr Pepper in a glass bottle."

"I'll resist the temptation," Rhodes said.

. . .

A Dr Pepper in a glass bottle was harder to resist than Rhodes had made it sound to Hack, and there was an old machine in the courthouse basement that still dispensed them. However, Rhodes steeled himself and walked right past the machine without giving in. He'd reward himself for his strength of character later if he could talk Ivy into going out to dinner for a third night in a row.

It was late in the afternoon, and the courthouse was quiet. Rhodes seldom used his office there, going over only when he wanted to avoid people, and this was a perfect time of the day for privacy. He got to his office without seeing anyone at all.

The office was much nicer than his space at the jail. The desk was newer, and its top was bare of paperwork. There were no annoying dispatchers and jailers trying to drive him crazy. Somehow, however, Rhodes never felt really at home there.

He sat in the desk chair, which was more comfortable than the one at the jail, tilted back, and put his feet up on the desk, something he never did in the jail. It was feet that had started him thinking about, or rethinking, the whole case.

It was obvious that Will Smalls's feet weren't seriously injured. They might be bruised, and his ankles might even be strained, but not sprained or broken. He was trying for sympathy from Rhodes at first and then from his wife. He'd had better luck with his wife, but not by much.

It had occurred to Rhodes that Will wasn't the only one who could fake an ankle injury. Take that injury away, and everything changed. The puzzle pieces all started to fall into place. Not all of them, but enough, considering what Rhodes had decided earlier in his little trip down the creek with Buddy. The picture was just about complete. It still had a couple of pieces missing right in the middle, but he hoped to find those later.

Could he prove that what he was thinking was the truth? Maybe not. He might need a little bit more evidence, but he thought he had an idea where that could be found. He'd have to get it, and that might not be easy. He'd need a search warrant, but while he still wasn't sure about everything, he had enough evidence to convince the county judge to issue one.

Rhodes swung his feet to the floor, picked up the receiver of the old black telephone on the desk, and called the judge, hoping that he hadn't left for the day. He hadn't, and when Rhodes explained what he wanted, the judge said to give his administrative assistant the information, and he'd have the warrant ready by the time Rhodes could get to the office.

"I'm in the building," Rhodes said.

"Then give us fifteen minutes," the judge said, and transferred Rhodes back to his administrative assistant, whose name was Becky Carr.

Rhodes gave her the information, hung up, and thought things over one more time. The missing pieces bothered him. A couple of things just weren't right, but he decided not to worry about them. Maybe one of his earlier suspicions had been correct. If so, that would solve the problem. For the moment he was going to go with what he was almost sure was right and work out the rest of it later.

He went down the hall to the county judge's office. The building was almost deserted now, and in a few minutes everyone would be gone. Rhodes had called just in time.

Becky Carr stood up at her desk when Rhodes walked in and handed him the warrant.

"Thanks," he said.

"Good luck finding what you're looking for," she said.

"It's not about luck," Rhodes told her. "It's about good police work."

It wasn't entirely good police work this time, though. Some of what Rhodes was relying on was guesswork. The guesswork was *based* on good police work, however, so Rhodes thought he was on safe ground to say so.

"Right," Becky said. "I know that. You and Sage Barton know the drill. He kills a lot more people than you do, though."

"I plan to keep it that way," Rhodes said.

"Probably a good idea," she said.

Rhodes thanked her again and went back to his office, where he called Hack.

"Is Buddy still there?" Rhodes asked when Hack came on the line.

"Nope. He's back out on patrol."

"I'm about to leave for Gene Gunnison's place," Rhodes said. "Call Buddy and tell him to meet me there."

"You gonna tell me what for?"

"I'll put you in the loop when we get back," Rhodes said.

"Yeah, right. But that's okay. If you don't, Buddy will."

"It's always good to have a backup source," Rhodes said.

" 'Specially with you bein' the primary one," Hack said, "and not very forthcomin'."

"Just get Buddy on the way out to Gunnison's."

"I will if you'll hang up."

Rhodes hung up and got on the way himself.

Rhodes parked the Tahoe at the end of the road leading up to Gunnison's house and waited for Buddy to arrive. He showed up about five minutes later and parked beside Rhodes, who put down the window and motioned for him to get out of the car.

Buddy got out of the county car and came over to the Tahoe. "What's going on, Sheriff?"

"I think Gene Gunnison killed Riley Farmer and Melvin Hunt," Rhodes said. "You and I are going to confront him about it. If he denies everything, I have a search warrant, so we can search his property. We should find the evidence we need to arrest him."

"You mean it wasn't Melvin's wife that killed him?"

"Why would you think that?"

"It's always the wife," Buddy said. "On those TV shows, anyway. You ever watch those?"

Rhodes thought, not for the first time, that the world might be better off without TV.

"Ivy watches them," Rhodes said. "I don't. Anyway, it wasn't the wife this time. At least that's not the way the evidence points."

Buddy didn't argue the point. "Okay." He patted the grip of his big revolver. "I've heard Gunnison's a rough customer."

"We shouldn't have to shoot him," Rhodes said, "but we'll be ready, just in case."

"We?" Buddy asked with a skeptical look.

Rhodes turned sideways as well as he could and drew up his knee far enough to reach the ankle holster. He removed the Kel-Tec pistol and showed it to Buddy.

"We," Rhodes said.

"All right," Buddy said. "You want me to follow you up there?"

"Good idea," Rhodes said.

He put the pistol on the seat and waited for Buddy to get in his car. Then he started the Tahoe, put it in gear, and headed up the road.

Chapter 24

▼

Gunnison was sitting in his usual spot on the porch with his foot up on the bucket when Rhodes and Buddy drove up. Rhodes got out of the Tahoe and stuck his pistol in his belt while he was concealed by the door. Buddy got out of his county car and walked to the front of it. Rhodes stood in front of the Tahoe. It wouldn't be a good idea for the two of them to be standing close together.

"You must have heard us coming," Rhodes said.

"Yeah," Gunnison said. "That's what I like about having a long road up to the house. You might remember that I told you before I'm not very social. Now I got two visitors. I don't much like it."

"We're not here for a visit," Rhodes said.

"I can't think of any other reason why you'd be here. If you're not visiting, what do you want?"

"I want to talk to you about marijuana. To start with."

Gunnison brushed a gnat away from his face. "We talked about that already. I told you I don't know anything about it, so why don't you and Peewee there go on back to town and leave me alone?"

Rhodes noticed that Buddy stiffened, but the deputy was a professional, and his fingers didn't drift toward the Magnum on his hip.

"Well," Rhodes said, "I don't think you told the truth about the marijuana. I think you're growing it in four different places in the county and maybe more. You have a boat and access to the creek. It would be easy for you to establish some crops in out-of-the-way places along the bank."

Gunnison shrugged. "So could anybody else."

"It wasn't anybody else who was nosing around Melvin Hunt's house the other day. I chased you through the woods, remember?"

"Wasn't me."

"It was you, all right. You were there to kill Joyce Hunt."

Gunnison's left cheek twitched, but that was his only reaction. "Why would I do that?"

"For the same reason you killed Melvin. He knew about your marijuana. I think that one day he must have walked along the creek to Billy Bacon's place to do some stealing or to look things over, and he caught you in the field. Maybe he asked you for a little money to keep from talking about it. You thought it over after he left, then followed him up to the barn and shot him and left him there in Bacon's barn. After you got to thinking about it later, you wondered if Melvin had come that way on purpose, if maybe he'd been that way before when you weren't around, and you wondered how much he'd told his wife and Riley Farmer, since Farmer was his best friend. So you decided to get rid of them, too. You got Riley, but I showed up at Melvin's house before you could get to Joyce. You took off, and the dogs and I followed you."

"I said it wasn't me."

Rhodes ignored that. "Joyce told me that her dogs liked you because you brought them treats. You had some with you at the house, and you tossed them on the ground to distract the dogs when you were running. I thought it was funny that they ran over and ate something on the ground. Now I know it was those treats."

"You got any remains of the treats to prove it?"

"No, but I know that's what it was."

"There's a little problem with all your guessing, Sheriff," Gunnison said with what he might have thought was an affable smile. He took his cane and touched his ankle boot. "I can't do any running."

"Anybody can put one of those things on," Rhodes said. "You might have had a bad ankle once and kept the boot. You put it on in case I showed up, which I did. It was a good alibi and I even believed your story. I tend to be a little gullible sometimes. Then I saw your tracks down by the creek at those marijuana patches."

That wasn't the whole truth. What Rhodes had seen was cow tracks, or something that looked like cow tracks. It took him a while, but he remembered that Gunnison's family had been bootleggers back in the old days, and using wooden hoofs strapped to their shoes was an old bootlegger's trick. Rhodes was pretty sure that's what Gunnison had done. Probably had the family heirlooms to use for the purpose.

Gunnison seemed sure that Rhodes couldn't prove it. He touched his boot again. "Any tracks you found aren't mine."

"I think they are. Here's the thing. Nobody with a badly sprained ankle can get a jon boat out of the back of his pickup and store it away somewhere, and yours has been moved. Took me and Buddy both to load one in my pickup this morning."

Gunnison shrugged again. "I'm a strong guy." He looked at Buddy. "I can see why Peewee would need some help."

"My name's Buddy," Buddy said, his voice flat.

"Good to know," Gunnison said.

"You storing that boat away got me to thinking," Rhodes said, ignoring the byplay. "Melvin's dogs were sure interested in it the other day. I think I know why."

"And I guess you're gonna tell me."

"I am. It's because after you brought Riley Farmer out here and killed him, you took him off in the boat to dispose of him. You hadn't cleaned his blood out of it when I showed up. You might've tried to get the blood out while you were still at the creek, but you couldn't have gotten it all. When I have it checked, we're sure to find some traces."

"You're not going to look at my boat."

"Yes, I am," Rhodes said, tapping his shirt pocket. "I have a search warrant right here. Buddy and I are going to take a look around."

"No, I don't think so," Gunnison said.

"You don't want to argue with the sheriff," Buddy said.

"Well, maybe you're right, Peewee," Gunnison said. "I make it a point never to argue with the law. Let me get up, and I'll show you around."

Gunnison appeared to have given up his antagonism. That should have been a warning, but instead Rhodes relaxed a fraction as the big man leaned forward to move the bucket from under his foot. When it was out of the way, he lowered his foot carefully to the porch.

What happened next was almost too fast for Rhodes to follow. Gunnison whipped off the ankle boot and came up with a pistol that he'd had hidden in it.

Buddy and Rhodes both went for their guns, but Gunnison fired twice before they could get them.

Gunnison's first shot ripped through Buddy's hat, which flew off onto the hood of the county car. The bullet went straight on and punctured the windshield.

Buddy and Rhodes dived to the side, and the second shot ripped into the hood of the car.

Rhodes lay on the ground, but he had his pistol out and managed to get off a wild shot that hit the galvanized bucket and made it ring like a tin bell. Buddy fired, too, and his shot blew out the window on the right side of the front door.

Gunnsion left the porch fast, going through the front door and slamming it shut. Buddy and Rhodes jumped up and went after him.

"Watch the door," Rhodes said. "Don't go inside. I'll check the back."

When Rhodes got to the back of the house, he saw Gunnison running toward the creek. Rhodes called for Buddy and went after Gunnison, who had a pretty good head start. Rhodes wondered if Gunnison had put the boat in the creek earlier and would try to get away on the water.

Gunnison had such a good lead that he was able to stop, step behind a tree, and fire off a couple of shots at Rhodes. Or maybe he was shooting at Buddy, who wasn't far behind. In any case, he missed, so it didn't matter.

Rhodes and Buddy didn't stop running. Rhodes knew there was no use to return fire. A man running down a slight hill had about as much chance of hitting his target as he did of flying to the moon, so there was no point wasting ammunition.

Gunnison took off again. When he got to the creek, Rhodes was only about fifty yards behind, and Buddy was right at his shoulder.

Gunnison splashed into the creek. Rhodes had no idea how

deep it was that near the bank, but it couldn't have been more than a few feet. The bottom was muddy, and it would be slow going. Gunnison didn't seem to think so. He'd said he was strong, and he didn't let a little thing like mud and water slow him down much.

Rhodes noticed that Buddy had stopped. He looked over his shoulder and saw that Buddy had his .357 in a two-handed grip and was ready to pull the trigger.

"Stop!" Buddy called. "Stop or I'll shoot!"

Gunnison stopped, but not to surrender. He raised his pistol to shoot first.

Before Buddy could react, Gunnison went under the water as if jerked by a wire. He yelled and thrashed in the water, then disappeared from sight. The water roiled where he'd gone down, and Gunnison's head popped up. He might have been about to yell for help, or to scream, but he didn't get a chance to do anything before his head went under the water again.

"What's going on?" Buddy asked, walking up to Rhodes.

Rhodes handed Buddy his pistol.

"Must be the alligator," he said, and ran to the creek.

"Don't go in there," Buddy said.

Gunnison's upper body came out of the water. He gasped for breath and barely had time to take in any air before he went back down.

Rhodes plunged into the creek. His feet immediately sank several inches down into the mud. The warm, muddy water was up to his knees. He wasn't as strong as Gunnison, but he pulled his feet out of the mud and took another step. The creek deepened quickly. The water now came to his waist. That was when he felt the gator's tail hit him in the shins.

If his feet hadn't been anchored in the mud, he would have

fallen. As it was, he swayed and nearly went down. He kept his balance and took one more step before going under the water and grabbing at the gator's tail. He got hold of it somehow, but he doubted that the gator noticed. The tail whipped back and forth, with Rhodes holding on and pulling himself along.

Rhodes didn't know where the gator had grabbed Gunnison, but probably by the leg. It wasn't going to let go any more than the snapping turtle would have. Even if Rhodes could help him, Gunnison was going to be torn up. Rhodes was up to the gator's back now, and he got his arms around a front leg.

The gator made an attempt to roll, but with Rhodes hanging on to him and Gunnison fighting him, the attempt failed. Rhodes inched forward and found himself near the gator's head. The animal's skin wasn't nearly as rough as Rhodes had thought it would be, but it was knobby and tough and not a pleasure to be in contact with.

Twisting itself mightily, the gator tried hard to throw Rhodes off its back. They broke the surface of the creek, and Rhodes was able to catch a breath. He thought he heard Buddy yell, "Ride 'em, cowboy!" but that was probably just his imagination.

Rhodes remembered having read or heard or thought that a gator's eyes were sensitive to pain, whereas the rest of it pretty much wasn't. Rhodes had no idea if this was true, never having had an occasion to try it out, but it seemed like his best bet, so he started to feel around for something that might be an eye. He moved a hand to the general vicinity of where an eye should be and found one, or what he thought was one. He didn't hesitate. He jabbed it as hard as he could with his stiffened thumb.

The gator went wild. Its former thrashing was nothing compared to what it did now. Rhodes had to cling with his legs and free hand to hold on. His lungs were burning, and he need air badly, but he didn't let go. Since the first jab seemed to have worked well, he gave the eye another one.

The gator rose out of the water like a bucking horse. Rhodes was tossed off the animal's back and dropped to the side, gasping for breath as his feet sought the mud of the creek bottom. He saw Gunnison float to the top, and he heard Buddy splashing toward him.

"Watch out for the gator," Rhodes said.

"He's swimming the other way, fast as he can," Buddy said. "I don't know what you did to him, but you put the fear into him."

Rhodes didn't care about the gator as long as it was moving in the other direction.

"Help me get Gunnison out of here," he said, noticing for the first time that there was blood in the water all around them.

Rhodes grabbed Gunnison's belt, and Buddy grabbed an arm. They pulled him to the creek bank and out onto the bank. Gunnison's left thigh was badly mangled, and he was unconscious. Rhodes didn't know how much blood he must have lost.

"We can't carry him out of here," Buddy said.

"Try your cell phone," Rhodes said. "Call the EMS. Tell them to hurry."

"They always hurry," Buddy said.

He took his cell phone from his shirt pocket. It wasn't too wet, and while he was making the call, Rhodes took off Gunnison's belt and tied it above the wound.

Buddy ended the call. "They're on the way. I hope they get here in time."

"They can make it in fifteen minutes," Rhodes said. "If they drive fast."

"You sure do look a mess," Buddy said.

Rhodes figured he looked like eight pounds of mud in a five-pound bag. He felt like it, too.

"It's not the first time," he said.

"You know what?" Buddy said.

"I probably don't."

"I don't think Sage Barton has ever fought a crocodile."

"Alligator," Rhodes said.

"He hasn't fought one of those, either. It's not everybody who can fight a crocodile."

"Tarzan," Rhodes said, "but this was an alligator."

"What's the difference?"

"I don't know."

"Well, there you are. You think Gunnison's going to live?"

"I hope so," Rhodes said.

"I wish he hadn't called me Peewee," Buddy said. "It's made me kind of indifferent about what happens to him."

"He needs to recover," Rhodes said. "I have some questions for him."

"I still don't much care about him, but getting his leg nearly bitten off by a gator is bad enough punishment for him, I guess. Well, that and the fact that if he killed Melvin and Riley, he's likely to get the needle one of these days."

"He killed them, all right," Rhodes said.

"A whole lot worse than calling me Peewee."

"You got that right," Rhodes said, "but we have another problem."

"What?"

"We need the pistol. It's evidence."

"You want to flip to see who goes for it?"

"I'm the sheriff," Rhodes said. "You're the deputy."

"Dang," Buddy said, but he got up and handed Rhodes his cell phone and his revolver. He took off his duty belt and started for the creek.

"Watch out for the alligator," Rhodes said.

"I'll let you do that for me," Buddy said. "If you see him coming, jump in and do whatever it is you did for Gunnison."

"I jabbed it in the eye. You might want to remember that."

"I'd rather you do it."

"I will if I can get there in time," Rhodes said.

He didn't think the alligator would be back, but he didn't know much about alligators.

"You're a real comfort," Buddy said.

"People tell me that all the time," Rhodes said.

Chapter 25

▼

Buddy got lucky and found the pistol on his second dive. He brought it out and put it on the ground beside Gunnison.

"You can enter it into evidence at the jail," Rhodes said, looking at the pistol. It was a .32, which was what he'd expected. "Better do it before you clean up."

"We both look a sight," Buddy said.

"I've looked worse," Rhodes told him.

Getting Gunnison to the ambulance after it arrived wasn't easy, but the EMTs managed it with Rhodes and Buddy helping. The EMTs said that Gunnison had lost a lot of blood and was in shock. They didn't know any more than that, but it was certain that Rhodes wasn't going to be able to question him until at least the next day, if then.

Rhodes told Buddy that they didn't need to do any searching at the moment. They could come back and get the jon boat, but for the moment what they needed to do was to go back to town and clean up.

"You can put Hack and Lawton in the loop when you go by the jail," Rhodes said.

"They like to know what's going on," Buddy said. "I try to keep them up-to-date."

"I guess somebody has to," Rhodes said. "They couldn't stand it otherwise."

He and Buddy left together, with Rhodes following the county car. However, by the time he was halfway back to Clearview, Rhodes had decided he wasn't going to clean up. He was still muddy and damp, and maybe some of the dampness was Gunnison's blood instead of water, but that was all right. He thought maybe his appearance would work in his favor.

Before he got to town, he called Seepy Benton on his cell phone. The Tahoe had a Bluetooth hookup that allowed him to make hands-free calls.

When Seepy came on the line it sounded like he was outside, and he was a bit out of breath.

"Are you okay?" Rhodes asked.

"Yes. I'm out working the yard. You've seen my Golden Rectangle, and now I'm adding two more cabalistic yard sculptures. One is a Semiotic Tree of Life, and the other one's a labyrinth created from the ten Hebrew letters that name the ten Sephiroth."

Rhodes had no idea what Seepy was talking about, and he was afraid to ask. So he said, "I'm sure they're wonderful, but what I need is some marijuana information."

"You have the right man on the line," Seepy said. "What do you want to know?"

Rhodes told him.

. . .

Nadine Bacon answered the door and gaped at Rhodes. He probably looked like the Creature from the Black Lagoon's first cousin.

"What on earth happened to you, Sheriff?" she asked.

"I got into a little tussle in a creek," he said. "Is Billy here?"

"He just got in from work, and he's having some iced tea. Do you need to talk to him?"

"Yes, I do."

Nadine gave Rhodes a dubious look. "Why don't you go on around the house to the patio. We have a table and chairs back there, and it's a good place to talk."

"Good idea," Rhodes said. Nadine and Billy weren't going to be happy with what he had to say, and he didn't want to add ruining their indoor furniture into the bargain. "I'll meet you two back there."

"You want to talk to me, too?"

"Yes, both of you."

"All right. You go on back, and I'll get Billy. Would you like some tea?"

"No thanks," Rhodes said, and started around the house.

The lawn looked so good that Rhodes almost hated to walk on it, but he did. The concrete patio was covered with a metal roof, and a glass-topped table sat in the middle of it. Four white metal chairs with a lot of scrollwork stood at the table. Rhodes pulled one back. It was heavier than he'd expected. He sat down and waited.

In a minute or so, the sliding glass door from the house opened, and Billy and Nadine came out. Billy was holding his glass of tea in one hand. The glass was beaded with moisture.

"You look like you've had a bad day, Sheriff," Billy said.

"You should see the other guy," Rhodes said.

Billy set his tea on the table and held a chair for Nadine. When she was seated, Billy sat down, too. "Nadine says you wanted to talk to me."

"That's right," Rhodes said. "Both of you. First thing, I want to tell you that we have Gene Gunnison in custody. I believe he killed Melvin Hunt and Riley Farmer."

Billy had been about to pick up his glass of tea. Instead, he nearly knocked it over. He grabbed it with both hands to steady it and looked at Rhodes.

"Gene Gunnison?"

"That's right. The man who was growing marijuana on your place."

"Really? And a killer, too? It's a good thing you caught up with him."

"It is," Rhodes said, "but that's not the end of the story."

"It's not?" Billy said.

He reached for his tea and picked up the glass, but his hand was still shaky enough to rattle the ice cubes against the side.

"No, it's not the end," Rhodes said. "I think you knew all along that Gunnison was growing the marijuana. You claimed you never went down to the creek, but you'd worn a path down there with your truck. I noticed that there were no weeds growing in the tracks you made. Now, I don't know if you allowed Gunnison to grow his crop there or if you asked him to do it, but you knew about it."

"I don't know why you think that," Billy said, "because it's not true."

"Oh, it's true, all right. I'm not saying I blame you. I understand that Nadine's been doing a little better lately. Right, Nadine?"

Nadine looked at Billy, who looked away.

"I'm doing better, I guess," she said.

"Breaking away from the benzos isn't easy," Rhodes said. "Some people say that cannabis can be a help."

"I . . . don't know."

"I do." Rhodes looked at Billy. "I have a good source of information. Cannabis can help a man who's under a lot of stress, too. More than iced tea can, and it might even relieve the pain from an old football injury for a little while."

"Did Gunnison tell you I knew about the marijuana?" Billy asked.

"He's not in any condition to talk," Rhodes said. "He was the other guy."

"I see." Billy set his tea back on the table. "Is he dead?"

"No, not dead. Just a little torn up from his run-in with the alligator that he had guarding your cannabis patch."

"It's not mine," Billy said.

"It was yours and Gunnison's. Gunnison shot two men to keep it quiet. He would've shot you by now if you weren't involved already."

Billy relaxed a bit and leaned back in his chair. "It sounds to me as if you don't have any proof of anything you're saying."

"That's true," Rhodes said, "but when Gunnison's able to talk, he's going to implicate you. I just wanted to warn you."

That wasn't true. Rhodes had hoped he might goad Billy into a confession, but Billy wasn't having any of it.

"I thought from the start that you might have been the one who cut the lock on your gate," Rhodes said. "Nobody had come there that day in a vehicle, but you didn't want me to know that, so you had to do something to make it look like someone had. You hoped that would keep me from checking down in the bottom."

"That's not true," Billy said.

"Don't think I'm not sympathetic to your situation," Rhodes said, ignoring him. "I am, but growing marijuana is still illegal in this state. Even worse is failure to report a crime. The good news is that you didn't try to conceal it. Did Gunnison call you to let you know what he'd done, or did he just leave Melvin's body there for you to find?"

"I'm not going to talk about this anymore," Billy said. He stood up. "Come on, Nadine. We don't have to talk to the sheriff if we don't want to unless we're under arrest."

"Are we under arrest?" Nadine asked, looking first at Rhodes and then at her husband.

"No," Rhodes said. "You're not."

"Then we're going inside," Billy said. "You're welcome to sit out here and enjoy the evening if you want to, though, Sheriff."

Rhodes stood up. "No, thanks. I think I'll just go on home."

Rhodes didn't care that Billy hadn't confessed. It had been a long shot, but it had been worth a try. Even if Gunnison didn't implicate him, Billy was on notice. Rhodes was sure that all the puzzle pieces were in place now and that the picture was complete, or as nearly complete as it was likely to be. Gunnison might fill in some of the blanks. Will Smalls might fill in some of the others after he talked to his lawyer. Maybe even Billy would after he'd had time to think things over, but that was all in the future. For now Rhodes was satisfied.

When he got home he went in through the back door. Yancey ran to greet him but backed off almost immediately.

"What's the matter?" Rhodes said. "You never saw a creek monster before?"

Yancey came up to sniff at the cuffs of Rhodes's pants. While he was doing that, Ivy came into the kitchen.

"Oh, my," she said. "It's the Legend of Boggy Creek."

"I saw that movie on TV," Rhodes said. "The legend's about a monster, not a sheriff."

"I should've said the Legend of Crockett's Creek," Ivy said. "The sheriff is the legend this time, but beating the monster. You're about the biggest thing on the Internet since Kim Kardashian."

"Who?"

"Don't try to kid me," Ivy said. "You know who she is."

"Barely," Rhodes said.

"Doesn't matter. You're a true hero in the Tarzan style, fighting a crocodile barehanded and saving a man's life."

"It was an alligator," Rhodes said, knowing for sure that Buddy had given Jennifer Loam the story.

"That doesn't matter, either. The headline is 'The Crocodile Fighter of Crockett's Creek.' I like the alliteration."

"Clickbait," Rhodes said.

"See? You know more about the Internet than you pretend."

Rhodes decided not to mention that he'd never heard the word until yesterday.

"I wish those stories would stop," Rhodes said. Yancey started to growl and bite at one of his pants legs. "Stop that, Yancey."

Yancey stopped and went to sit under the table, looking sad-eyed.

"If you want the stories to stop," Ivy said, "you'll have to stop being so heroic."

"I don't feel heroic," Rhodes said. "I feel like I fought an alligator."

"At least you won."

"I don't feel like I won."

"I know what you need," Ivy said. "You need a day off."

Rhodes thought about his most recent attempt to take some time off and all that had happened. He laughed out loud.

"You know what I think?" he said.

"No. What?" Ivy asked.

"A day off is the last thing I need," Rhodes said.

PROBABILITY AND PROBABILITY DISTRIBUTIONS[†]